PENGUIN BOOKS
STORM IN CHANDIGARH

Nayantara Sahgal is a novelist and political journalist who has published two volumes of autobiography and seven novels, of which *Rich Like Us* won the Sinclair Prize for Fiction in 1985. She lives in Dehra Dun, India, and her chief involvement outside writing is with the civil liberties movement launched during the Emergency.

D1057424

NAYANTARA SAHGAL
STORM IN CHANDIGARH

PENGUIN BOOKS

Penguin Books (India) Ltd. 72-B Himalaya House, 23 Kasturba Gandhi Marg,
New Delhi-110 001, India
Penguin Books Ltd. Harmondsworth, Middlesex, England
Viking Penguin Inc. 40 West 23rd Street, New York, New York 10010, U.S.A.
Penguin Books Australia Ltd, Ringwood, Victoria, Australia
Penguin Books Canada Ltd. 2801 John Street, Markham, Ontario, Canada L3R 1B4
Penguin Books (N.Z.) Ltd. 182-190 Wairau Road, Auckland 10, New Zealand

First published by W.W. Norton & Company Inc. 1969
Published in Penguin Books 1988
Copyright © Nayantara Sahgal 1969, 1988

Made and Printed in India by Ananda Offset Private Ltd. Calcutta.

To Nirmal

Chapter 1

"Violence lies very close to the surface in the Punjab."

The man who spoke was not a Punjabi himself. Small, slight, and dhoti-clad, he had been born in a village outside Banaras, spent his adult years working in a newspaper office before he joined the national movement, and now, in the evening of his life, found himself Home Minister of the Government of India. It was a task that, with its immense territory and seething complex of problems, seemed too great a burden for his frail old figure. Vishal Dubey had come to see him, tucking away his objections to the job offered, because it had intrigued him to know why he and not some other civil servant had been thought of for this assignment.

"I mean, of course, that whole region, Punjab and Hariyana. It was all the Punjab till recently," the Minister went on. "It may have something to do with their ownership of land. They have a long, unbroken tradition of it, unlike other parts of India. We forget that area was under the British only ninety years and agriculture did not undergo any major change. Bengal, on the other hand, had two hundred years of the British and a complete upheaval of its land system. I think the northerner, the man from this Punjab-Hariyana region, gets his confidence from his pride of possession. The belief in the strong right arm is apt to flourish in that kind of atmosphere."

Dubey thought for the second time that morning of the incongruity of the slight figure facing him talking of violence and the strong right arm, though these were subjects he had to deal with every day in the keeping of law and order. Outbursts of brutal, calculated violence had become a feature of the cities. There were too many in the congestion and chaos who had nothing to lose by violence, too many others who sat inert and indifferent, their sap sucked dry, watching it mount and ebb like some great tidal wave, waiting for it to engulf them. Passively waiting, as they waited for the rains, for the harvest, for the births of unwanted children, for death. Violence had become routine and expected. It was given different names, indiscipline, unrest, disorder. It was dealt with each time—and forgotten. The Minister was concerned this morning with another brand.

"I have never had much experience of violence in my own life," he continued, as if apologizing for his limitations, "except for the teacher's cane when we did not know our work, but we expected that and the teacher did not cane us out of anger."

Dubey pictured a row of small boys seated cross-legged in the dust of a village school, or packed into an ill-ventilated mud-walled room, droning the day's lesson, the teacher alert to a missing word or sentence and quick to rectify the omission with his cane.

"In this ministry one becomes a student of the subject. In a situation like we have now between Punjab and Hariyana, we are faced with a violence of attitude. And that may, and often does, lead to the other kind. But at the moment there is this attitude that brooks no compromise and rejects all but one solution. These are people who have no feel for the periphery of a problem, for light and shade and the nuances in between. That is the source of their energy and, in a queer way, their integrity. It is useful to realize this before one tries to produce a solution."

The Home Minister was known to be strictly a light and shade man himself with a reservoir of patience that explored the furthest reaches of every problem. His admirers found this his finest, and his critics his most infuriating quality. As far as the Minister himself was concerned there was no other way. He was the last surviving figure of the Gandhian era left in public life, years older than his colleagues in the Cabinet, and he felt almost fatherly towards the young man who would soon be completing his first term as Prime Minister. He referred to himself humorously as a relic, but he had no intention of relinquishing his portfolio for a less taxing one, which the Prime Minister had urged him to do.

"I may be feeble," he had told the harassed young man bluntly, "but since when has muscle been required in this ministry? There's the police force for that."

He said now to Dubey, "Still, the restraining voice has great value at a time like this. The approach makes so much difference, the way one tackles a thing, even the tone of voice one uses."

Dubey looked down at his own hands crossed over the knees of a well-cut suit now in its fourteenth winter of good wear. He had had the suit made a few years after he had left Oxford. He wished he could light a cigarette, but it was something no one did in the old man's presence.

"Well, when will you go?" enquired the Minister.

"This may be irrelevant," said Dubey, "but I wonder why you want me for the job, sir. I hardly know that area."

The Minister spoke thoughtfully. "Somewhere in that taut situation there must be an opening that will let in a little air, and once a breathing spell is established it will not explode. It will hold—maybe only for a short while—but in that interval there might arise some chance of saving it. We do, in this country, place a value on persuasion."

Dubey's query still hung in the air.

"Much of life is like that, Mr. Dubey. Taking just one step ahead. Holding on. Waiting."

That incredible, insidious, double-edged word again. Waiting. When did it cease to be a philosophy and become a disease? An ennobling exercise for the spirit as long as it was not translated into the ugly reality of empty cooking pots. Dubey concentrated hard on the stripe of his suit to avoid thinking about the packet of cigarettes in his pocket.

"You ask why I want you to go," the Minister went on. "I think you have the capacity to counsel patience."

The report Dubey had seen from his last Chief had also said he had the gift for tackling a problem at the human level, but the Minister did not mention this. Waiting on a volcano had its excitement, but Dubey wondered whether he wanted that kind of excitement enough to land himself in a crisis that might end disastrously.

"We would be in touch," the Minister added by way of reassurance.

Dubey was not reassured. He did not believe he would take the job. He would ask for a few hours to think it over and give his answer that evening.

"How soon can you leave for Chandigarh?" The Minister seemed to have taken his acceptance for granted, and to his surprise Dubey heard himself say "Tomorrow."

It was the Minister's turn to be surprised. "You have no family? You don't need more time for leave-taking? They would, of course, follow later."

"My wife died six years ago. I have no children."

Back in his office in the Secretariat Dubey lit a cigarette and smoked half of it before dialling Gauri's number to give her the news that he would be leaving for Chandigarh the next day.

"Oh." She sounded taken aback. "Just a minute, Vishal."

"Are your nails wet?"

"Yes, how did you know?"

"What's this one called?"

"Nude Pearl. There, it's all right now. Have you got time to talk?"

"No," he admitted, "I'm in a rush. I have to go through the files connected with the job, then go home and pack. I'll drop in this evening if you're not going out."

"Come and have dinner with us. Nikhil is leaving for Calcutta tonight so we'll have to dine early. Can you come at half-past seven?"

He said he would.

"Vishal, how awful. Are you glad you're going? Never mind, I know you're busy. We'll talk about it later."

He collected his thoughts. He was more than glad now to be going. He was almost impelled by the need. He felt stale. He had been in Delhi too long. There was nothing in his day's routine that stretched his faculties or kindled a spark in him. The small talk and small ideas of a confined society had begun to suffocate him. The days had died behind him one after another in monotonous procession, leaving little imprint. Dubey decided wryly that he must be in a minority of one. Delhi was the top drawer and once there, no official budged if he could remain, unless it was to become a state governor or an ambassador, or become the recipient of a generous international grant for work abroad. The handful of senior names, the highest in official-dom, were those of the men who circulated at the confer-ences and cocktail parties, and lined up for the big jobs ahead. No one ever went back to the smaller canvas and the comparative obscurity of state administration. Dubey felt he was not only stale, he was curdled. He did not need just a change of scene. He needed a shot of aspiration, the feel-ing that the next five or ten years were leading somewhere, that the structure of the administration in which he had spent his working life was a living one, that it was dealing with the earth, not with the kingdom of heaven. At eleven o'clock this November morning at the age of forty-five, he needed that assurance badly if he were not to slip into the rut of seniority, promotion, and spiritual vacuum. But it was hard for a man who had begun to doubt his basic credentials to find assurance.

What, for example, did his Brahmin inheritance have to contribute to the age in which he lived? What use was he in a setup that had forged no confident working alliance between government and civil servant? In the past several years the answers had steadily receded and only a husk of conviction remained in him. He had thought of getting away from the routine and putting his ideas on paper, and had even applied for an American grant for his work.

"What did you have in mind?" asked the visiting pro-fessor from the New England university to which he had written.

The topics the university sponsored were political, ad-ministrative, or economic.

"The role of Brahminism in our culture," said Dubey.

"Boston would be the place for that all right," smiled

Professor Aldrich. "But you mean Hinduism."

"Only as background," said Dubey. "What I'm interested in exploring is the role of Brahminism specifically and whether it has a constructive role to play today, or whether the whole notion of aristocracy, that is, the quality a people evolves for itself, is outdated. Personally I don't think it is, but it has become ineffective. We seem to be in the grip of impotence, stuck for answers, because the most effective part of our inheritance isn't brought into play and made to provide the answers in ways that would best suit our temperament."

"The most effective part of your inheritance being Brahminism?"

"It is what we have considered 'quality,' " said Dubey, "and that is a product of the ages, of slow, profound development. It's the only thing that can't be copied or borrowed or mass-produced."

"I'd agree with you there," said the professor. "There are governments called people's governments that are really built on the destruction of a people's whole foundation. Not only have they overthrown a tyranny but a religion and a philosophy as well, and tossed away an accumulation of racial experience. Revolutions have to take place when living conditions become unbearable, but even a revolution should not destroy a people's framework. It should stop short of that. Tear that down and you have a bewildered society, people who've lost their moorings and don't know where they're going."

"If we're going to avoid that here," said Dubey, "tradition has to be upheld and *used* in a big, enlightened way. But it hasn't so far. We've got this superb intellectual heritage supporting feeble issues like the preservation of cows, and we don't seem to be able to climb out of the stagnation onto the high road where the fresh air blows. We have the unholy trappings of tradition going on and on and on while the reality of it isn't there at all. I want to explore the reality of it in this paper."

The professor had liked Dubey's ideas and had said he would write to him on his return. Dubey now took his letter —an avenue of escape from Delhi—from his briefcase and replied to it:

Dear Professor Aldrich:

I am sorry I have been so long replying to your letter. I want to thank you for your offer of a year's residence at the university to write my paper on the topic we discussed when you were here. I had been waiting for this and it is a great opportunity, and I am greatly tempted to accept it at once.

But now without warning I have been asked to go to Chandigarh, the joint capital of Punjab and Hariyana, in the capacity of a liaison officer between the Centre (Delhi) and the two state governments, and I have accepted the assignment. It has an immediacy and urgency that made it difficult for me to refuse. I do not know how long I will be there, but this will, in any case, make it impossible for me to take advantage of your invitation for the coming academic year.

I deeply regret this and can only hope I will have another opportunity later. I want to thank you for your interest and help.

He did not believe he would have another opportunity. There were too many eager applicants for the benefits of American dollars and a year or more was a long time ahead to plan. He gave his peon the letter to post and for the rest of the day worked methodically on the papers connected with his new assignment, trying to unravel the complexity of it.

The map of India, once a uniform piece of territory to administer, was now a welter of separate, sensitive indentities, resurrected after independence. Psychology seemed to play as important a part in understanding them as did history, geography, and economics. Much more than facts and figures were required in coping with political rivalries that had now ceased even to make bargains. As long as a bargain could be made, work could go on. When that capacity wore out, only a collision was possible. In the new states, Punjab and Hariyana, just carved out of the former Punjab, the quarrel over boundaries, water, and electric power continued, intensified by the presence of both new state governments in a common capital, Chandigarh, which each claimed exclusively as its own. And now Gyan Singh, Punjab's Chief Minister, threatened to demonstrate the strength of his demands by launching a crippling strike that would cover both regions. Dubey had the uneasy feeling that it was too late to consider persuasion. The man now thinking in terms of a showdown had committed too much of his reputation to it. In all these years there had been no open conflict between state governments though there had been disagreements. No one had yet had the will or the organization to risk an open threat. It was not surprising that the threat, when it came, had come out of robustness and prosperity.

Dubey went over the information before him. The production of coal, iron, and timber had given industrial importance to India's richest agricultural region. A concentration of some three thousand factories in the main industrial belt employed, he calculated, about a hundred thousand workers. Not a great many in terms of numbers, thought Dubey, even if a big strike were launched. He had seen demonstrations nearly that size when Parliament was in session in Delhi, protesting against everything from teachers' salaries to cow slaughter. It was not the numbers that mattered but that incalculable factor, their behaviour.

He turned the pages giving production and export figures to a study of the two states' common irrigation and power system. It was highly centralized. Fed by three rivers, its control points were two huge reservoirs at Bhakra and Pong. These supplied power to areas as widespread as Delhi, Himachal, and Rajasthan and as far north as Kashmir, besides Punjab and Hariyana. The whole power scheme came under the Centre's control, and Gyan Singh now claimed control of it for his state. With his reputation as a labour leader, he could not have chosen a more apt setting for a showdown. What was the other Chief Minister, Harpal Singh, doing, Dubey wondered—waiting? Yet how else did one cope with a threat of this kind? His own role of liaison between the Centre and the two states would not make him popular. He would probably not gain the confidence of either. The Home Minister had said, terminating the interview, "There are, of course, two sides to every question, Mr. Dubey, but both are not always right."

There was one question Dubey had not asked the Home Minister. It was why, in the first place, the Centre had allowed the Punjab to be redivided twenty years after the gruelling Partition of 1947. Why had this new mess been created? It was the kind of question civil servants did not ask politicians.

When Dubey left his office the Home Minister collected his impressions of the interview. Dubey had fulfilled his expectations by taking the job. There were other more senior officers, one or two who might have been willing to leave their desks in Delhi to go to the uncertainties of a state crisis. The Minister had considered and rejected them. The post he had created called for a spirit that had been dwindling since independence. Perhaps dedication was not too strong a word for it. In his youth they had used words like that freely and they had not had a hollow ring about them. Dedication, sacrifice, austerity. Each one now clanked tinnily with empty repetition. He never used them in his speeches any more. But he took them out, like valuable old coins no longer in use, and looked at them when he was alone. He was satisfied that they existed and had worth.

Casting about for a man to send to Chandigarh, his mind had gone back to 1947, a long time, he supposed, though it seemed to him like yesterday. He had been touring the border districts between Uttar Pradesh and Punjab with their heavy concentration of bedraggled refugees. All normal transport had been disrupted and communication with the field had been by overworked wireless. The problem had been to feed the thousands on the march, and those locked within their own neighbourhoods unable to move for terror of attack. He had worried particularly over a Muslim neighbourhood surrounded by Hindu residents and had been relieved to hear that grain was reaching it. There was a young rationing officer called Dubey, he was told, who had continued to get supplies to it against formidable opposition. He had a small organization of men who had worked sturdily against the hostility of the surrounding Hindu population. How had it happened, the Minister had enquired. The men liked Dubey, he was told. They took risks because they were fond of him. For a brief while in the madness the Home Minister had felt the breath of hope. He had come across Dubey again quite recently and had heard that he had been in Delhi for nearly five years. "I doubt if he will want to leave," his informant had told him. The Minister had rather thought he would.

Chapter 2

Dusk gathered early that November evening, enveloping trees and houses in smudged, soft outline. Gauri's drawing room was alive with warm colour, bowls of chrysanthemums, and an air of quiet, unassuming wealth. There were not many Bengali residents of long standing in Delhi. It was Nikhil Ray's father who had bought land and set up the mills that were the source of his family's income outside the growing capital. Dubey never entered this house without wondering how long the world of gracious and privileged living it represented would remain secure in India.

He and Nikhil helped themselves to drinks. Gauri sat placid and velvet-eyed, listening to their talk, hardly saying a word herself, neither drinking nor smoking. Dubey realized he had never even seen a book in those hands. Whenever she did her reading, and he wondered how much of it she did, it had never, in all these years, been in his presence. She merely sat, the picture of composure, and hurry and harassment dissolved into her world of exquisite calcula-

tion. He had started coming to this house during the confused remorseful year after Leela's death because there was
no sign of strain in it.

"The Home Minister was saying today that he thought
violence lay very close to the surface in the Punjab," said
Dubey.

"That's the kind of absurd generalization the Government gets caught out on in all its enterprises and pays for in
lakhs of the taxpayers' money," said Nikhil. "Everything
we do is based on some generalization or somebody's pet
theory or crusade. You can't make sweeping statements
like that, or run this country on theories. It's too vast and
varied a country for that. You have to forget the theories
and get down to brass tacks. A ministry for brass tacks is
what we need."

Nikhil got up to pour himself a drink and went on talking. "Violence lies close to the surface everywhere. What
makes the Home Minister think the Punjab has a monopoly
of it? I'd say there's an ugly temper in the country generally. I deal with it at the mills. When the men are roused
they don't just want a bonus or an adjustment of pay
scales, they want your blood if they can have it." He added
irritably, "Why don't they get their terms straight? How
can they expect a bonus unless the company makes a
profit? But profit or no profit it's a bonus they want. The
trade unions should dream up another name for their next
demand."

"There's a very fine dividing line between calm and agitation," said Dubey. "I think what the Minister meant was
that it's even finer in a certain type of personality. I might
tell you something that changes the look on your face. A
joke does that. Or a shock—one that might go deep—and
change more than your facial expression. It depends what
the arrow touches and where it stings, and at what temper-

ature the blood boils. Beyond a certain level we are all
primitive. What matters to the rest of the world is how we
express ourselves when we are stung. Some turn inward
and brood, or commit suicide. Others like your workers
wreck property."

"This man Gyan Singh must be a megalomaniac," said
Nikhil.

"There's an element of that in most politicians. This one
is going further than most."

"I don't know why it should surprise us," said Nikhil.
"It's been coming for years. First the labour legislation
making a monster out of labour. Then the Congress crack-
ing up. And now this combination of the two. We've ignored all the signposts of trouble for the last twenty years.
What actually is the issue between these two men?"

"God knows," said Dubey. "One likes coffee, the other
likes tea. Or one gave the other a black eye at school. Or
some private feud about something. There doesn't seem to
be any real difference. It's a clash of personalities, but that's
what politics has degenerated to. There are no issues left,
only squabbles. The Home Minister seems to have an immense weariness with it all."

"Well, keep the transport moving," said Nikhil, "from
the bullock carts to the buses. That's the most basic need. If
that goes on, the politicians can argue their heads off, at
least the people won't panic." He turned to his wife.
"Gauri, better ring up Chandigarh later and let Saroj and
Inder know Vishal is coming. Saroj is my cousin," he told
Dubey, "and Inder runs our mill there."

After dinner they drove with Nikhil to the airport and
then back to the house. During the four years since Dubey
had known her, the urgency between him and Gauri had
evaporated and they had settled into a friendly familiarity.

But he had not been able to bring to an end the affair so mindlessly begun. As she undressed in the half light of her bedroom and came, warm and pliant, into his arms, he realized he could have done without making love to her for some time now and enjoyed just the sight of her. Why could one not tell a woman that? Why, between men and women, did passion so quickly find acceptance, while affection and friendship were so little cultivated—even between him and Gauri who, he was sure, would have been content to spend an evening in quiet conversation, had it ever occurred to her that such a thing was possible between the sexes. Yet the demand for something more had continued to hang in the air, not her demand or his, but as if this was the exercise expected of them, and in obedience to which they both responded. He wished he had not taken that direction with Gauri at all. He knew he was the kind of person who should not touch anything or anyone not deeply significant to him.

"I wish you weren't going," said Gauri.

She lay within the circle of his arm, her voice muffled against him. She made no emotional demands on him partly, Dubey guessed, because she was happy with her husband. She was lazy too, with a catlike talent for making herself comfortable and no desire to venture beyond what she recognized as dependable ground. He felt that the grace and favour she accorded him, and perhaps others of whom she was fond, were the overflow of a generous spirit. Giving came easily to her and he had strayed accidentally into that region of her natural, luxuriously feminine bounty. He could leave her with ease and come back to her with the certainty of a welcome. Everything about her was lovely and languid and opulent, from her body to the embroidered coverlet on her bed. She housed a deep inner contentment he had neither disturbed nor added to, and she had left a hard, critical core within him untouched. She knew this and referred to it as his no-man's-land.

"Has any woman ever made a lasting impression on you?" she asked.

There was no coquetry in the remark. Her lack of it was one of her charms.

"I had a teacher once who did—"

"Not a teacher, Vishal. I'm talking of a woman. Someone you've held in your arms and made love to."

She left the tumbled bed, switched on the light, and sat down at her dressing table, exquisitely reflected above jars of imported perfume and enamel-topped bottles, brushing her hair. He feasted on the curve of her back and the upward sweep of her naked arm. He wanted to tell her she had made a lasting impression of beauty on him, only that was not what she wanted to know. She looked at him in the mirror.

"I said I wish you weren't going," she repeated.

"I need to get away from Delhi."

"How like you," she said softly. "No comforting flattery."

He came up behind her. "This woman needs no flattery. She is beautiful and generous and honest. *And* I am glad to be going."

Gauri laid down her brush. "Vishal, does it ever strike you that a woman doesn't want the truth all the time? Tell me a lie. Say you don't want to go."

"Tomorrow," he said, "when I'm on the road, you'll be so busy with your activities, you won't realize I'm not here."

"You're a fool."

She put on a dressing gown of some soft bright material and turned to face him.

"But you've been happy here, haven't you?" she insisted.

Happy. Gauri could use words like that guilelessly, as a child did, like the correct supervised letters her daughter wrote to her and Nikhil from boarding school in Simla: "Dear Mummy and Daddy. I am well and happy. How are you?" His own stay in Delhi had carried him through the tortures of remorse with which his abruptly ended relationship with Leela had left him, into the quieter meadows where living had assumed a steady if not deeply significant rhythm. Happiness had not at any stage entered the picture.

He sat down at the end of her bed. "What do you call happiness?"

"A cup of tea first thing in the morning. Love. A massage from Jenny Souza."

"Love and a cup of tea. As simple as that?"

"You left out the massage," she reminded him. "No, of course it's not as simple as that. But it should be. One tries to simplify it. You make things too complicated."

Yet love had never been simple for him or even entirely possible. That was why he had found release in compassion, the disinterested equivalent of love, the equal attachment to all. In spite of the universal commandment, you could not love your neighbour. You could only interest yourself in him, make him your concern, make almost a job of him, and thus keep alive the spark in yourself that died or flickered so feebly in so many. You could also thus spare yourself the real encounter, the intensely personal confrontation. You could be attached to all humanity, yet go your way alone. Attachment to a single individual bound you.

In the more impersonal context he was an inveterate sharer of all that happened to him. It was what had first attracted Gauri to him. In a crowded cocktail party where the conversation had been in broken sentences and attention hard to hold, she had casually asked him how the talks on the setting up of the new division in his ministry were going. He had told her about them in detail, plucking the conversation out of generalities and pinning it into vivid focus for her. She had listened absorbed. When pleasantries were all that one expected of a social encounter, it was both bracing and bewildering to receive more. It was some time before she noticed that he never talked of his feelings.

"Vishal, are you listening to me? What's wrong with wanting to stay in Delhi? Ambition is a good thing. It's natural. There's something spineless about a man who doesn't want to get ahead."

It was not how he understood the richness of ambition. The road to Delhi and the fat jobs was its opposite. It seemed a lack of zest that kept men riveted there till they retired. It needed an insensitivity to all the possibilities of living to be able to do that. Ambition had more compelling faces.

"You could get almost any job you want here," she went on. She had always been a little awed by his reputation, which continued to thrust him ahead in spite of his irreverence for the Establisment.

"Or become an ambassador," he suggested.

"Yes," she said vehemently. "Why not?"

"Because it would be too complicated to work out what I was representing—a famine or a strike or just sheer inertia."

"There are other ambassadors—"

"They probably know what they are representing, and feel they can make a good job of it."

"You're so difficult. Can't you leave the arguments alone and just live?"

"Without a mind?"

"Without such a demon of a mind."

When he got up to go and touched her cheek, she raised

his hand to her lips in an uncharacteristic gesture of humility that disturbed him. Normally he would have thought
about it on his way home, but other thoughts crowded his
mind.

The luminous dial of the clock in his car showed it was
nearly midnight as he drove through dim empty streets.
Parking his car in the garage, he sat in it for a moment. He
had planned to make an early start, but he was packed and
felt free for the first time since morning. Tomorrow a new
chapter would begin. He had not spoken to Gauri about it
in emotional terms. He had learned not to share his feelings
during a marriage that had turned out to be a vanishing
search for communication. When had he given up that
search, he wondered. On some day or night indistinguish-
able from any other, without knowing it, possibly in his
sleep. And when it happened, it had condemned him to an
isolation not of his choosing. Marriage after that had taken
on a baffling quality. He had stood looking quietly at it as if
it had been an entity outside himself, rather like a piece of
clay that had yielded to no mould and after a number of
years still lay shapeless in his hand—a thing he did not
know how to cope with. He never came to terms with the
fact that two people could live in intimacy all their adult
lives and still remain strangers to each other. It took a long
time for him to admit to himself that this was what was
meant by torture.

Chapter 3

The road, the smoothest stretch of concrete in North India, flowed away swiftly under Dubey's car. On either side fields of sugar cane ready for harvesting streamed past and red chillies lay drying under the sun beside half-built, abandoned brick structures once intended as factories. The late Chief Minister of the Punjab had wanted to industrialize these miles between Delhi and Sonepat, plans that had been shelved by his successors after his brutal assassination on this very road. So much in India had been slowed down because tumultuous passions had carried the day. Dubey thought of the Colt lying in his glove compartment. He had been asked to carry it for his own protection and he wondered ironically what use it would be against an armed gang such as had murdered Kairon, even if he had been adept at using it.

The truck traffic was not heavy at this hour but occasionally he had to slow down as he passed one carrying supplies between Chandigarh and Delhi. Sometimes the man standing behind the driver waved or whistled cheerfully, exhilarated by the fine crisp winter day. In the evening the road would become an artery of goods traffic which would fan out all over India.

There were evidences of poverty along the road but the sight of it did not make Dubey uneasy as driving through parts of his own impoverished Uttar Pradesh always did. These people were in business. Here right along the highway they were running restaurants and repair shops. He caught sight of a bicycle lying on its side, the morning sun glinting on its polished metal while its owner pumped air into its tyres, and, further on, a saw at work on a slab of wood outside a furniture shop, scattering peeled shavings into the morning haze. There was not a beggar to be seen near the small cafe where he stopped for a cup of coffee served in thick white local pottery. The boys who clustered round his car did not have the dull, incurious stare of those who have long since withdrawn themselves from their environment, nor the incomprehension of people gazing at a rare sight. These children were familiar with machinery and its manufacture. They looked at the car as if they were measuring its capacity and performance, comparing it with others they had seen, and even anticipating ownership of such a car one day. Eagerness, attentiveness, and greed lighted their faces, all emotions living men experienced unless hunger contorted their vision or hopelessness destroyed it. If there were any people in India worth giving loans and assistance to, and who had repaid them with hard, productive work, thought Dubey, it was these—and yet they were the ones who least needed help, who would always, of instinct and vitality, help themselves.

Most people were the result of their landscape. Apparently not these. Concentrating only partially on the clear thoroughfare, Dubey thought of the paradox of people

being uncompromising when they lived amid so much
bounty and dispensed it, he knew, so freely in their daily
lives. He associated a different geography with the inflex-
ible approach. Men like that would inhabit the stark regions of the globe, the wastelands, the deserts, and the
steppes where they would have to toil incessantly and have
little time for the tranquil pursuits; where bare hills, slate
skies, and a leaden austerity would rule stretches of stony
soil. Hardship would produce strongly delineated character, making issues black or white, right or wrong, good or
evil, either-or. That would be the climate and the geography to sustain old feuds and kindle vendettas. But what
had all of that to do with this sleek natural abundance?

It was noon when he arrived in Chandigarh. Huge tree-
less spaces fell away on either side of the road. The line of
flowering trees down the middle of the wide dual carriage-
way looked decorative and fragile, struggling to make an
impression against the sprawling emptiness. There seemed
nothing in the way of public transport serving a city so
spread out. He passed no vehicle on the road. He slowed
down as he came onto the lake boulevard, beyond which a
double row of hills rose in the sunshine. On the plain below
them lay the complex of buildings he could identify from
illustrations as the High Court, the Secretariat, and the
Legislature. He wished these had been erected on the hill-
side itself to command a dramatic view of the lake and the
plain. Instead, the hills formed a backdrop to the city. He
turned right on the boulevard and drove to the state guest
house where he was to stay. His suitcases were taken to his
room and he stood for a long time on the verandah upstairs
watching the sun light the hilltops and glimmer on the lake.
Chandigarh, built on field and pasture land, had been more
than a new capital. It had symbolized the journey to re-
covery. It was industry made to thrive and abundance to

flow again, and a people made whole after the terrors and uprooting of the Partition. Now it reflected the uneasy truce between the two states whose joint capital it was. Dubey was to meet one of the two Chief Ministers, Harpal Singh, after lunch.

Hariyana, said Harpal Singh to himself. The word touched no chord in him. It had not existed until a month ago. Even now it had a preposterous sound, though it was a state, some forty-four thousand square miles of it, over seven million people in it—yet another subdivision on the map of India of what had once been the Punjab. Through all the agitation for it, the fevered discussions and proposals, one certainty had flashed fire within him. He did not want Hariyana to exist. He had faced Gyan Singh across the conference table in a fever of desperation. After the decision had been taken he had driven back from Delhi repeating dully to himself that he was driving through Hariyana. The Punjab did not border Delhi any longer as it always had. It now began miles from Delhi, after Ambala. This was Hariyana. Twenty years of effort are in splinters this day, he had thought. It was given to few men in their lifetime to see the fulfilment of their dreams. But what had he done to deserve the criminal destruction of his?

He knew the road well. He had driven along it to conferences in Delhi and on tours of the state. The land he was passing, the fairest in India, the earth most blessed, had a throbbing reality for him. Born and bred on it, he belonged to it. But it was more than his home. It was in part his achievement. He had worked for its reconstruction, put heart into the refugees who had settled on it after the Partition, and welcomed those who had straggled back to it once the massacres were over. And he had loved it. Above all he had loved it. But the divisionists had shown no mercy. They had carried out their butchery, taken the body of the Punjab and resolutely carved it up again, ostensibly in the interests of the Punjabi language. Yet there was something sinister at the root of the Partition mentality and those who upheld it. Mankind's journey was towards integration, not the breaking up of what already existed. Punjabi would have flourished without partitioning the state further. What possessed men to stamp their name, their brand, their ego on every bit of God-given soil that came their way?

"There's a knot of people up the road, *janab*," his driver had said as they had approached Ambala. "Shall I stop the car?"

"Yes, stop."

It was a jubilant crowd gathered with garlands and banners to welcome him, the first Chief Minister of the new state. He could not find fault with their exuberance. Carve up the land into six more pieces to suit six smaller loyalties and parcel them out, and those loyalties would rejoice. He had nothing against little loyalties as long as the larger vision united them all, but there was no big vision any more. He got out and accepted their greetings. A young reporter called out, "Any comments, sir, on the formation of Hariyana?" The crowd cheered lustily at the word, then fell silent to hear what the new Chief had to say. Harpal bent and picked up a sod of damp dark earth. It felt strangely comforting in his hand, the one substantial reality in this passing show of ambition. He said, looking at it, "Let us dedicate ourselves to this earth and its flowering, by whatever name it may be called."

"Sir," said the young reporter again in the hush that followed, "would you tell us how you, a Sikh, have accepted chief ministership of this new Hindi-speaking state? Your own language is Punjabi."

Harpal Singh clothed his anger in deliberate irony. "I did not know when I accepted this post that the public would require me to cut my hair and shave my beard. Is that what I am to do?"

There was a delighted chuckle of denial and they cheered him on his way.

As he drove on his mind went back to the day that had unwittingly started him on his political career.

Harpal's father had owned a provision store in Jhelum. In the summer of 1947 when uncertainty about the Partition of India had filled the air, he had wondered whether to close down his business and move it to a safer place. He did not want to do so. He had lived there all his life and everyone knew him. The success of his small enterprise and the exceptional ability of his young son had enabled him to send the boy to college on a scholarship, an opportunity he himself had been denied. He had a reputation for kindliness and honest dealing, a man with no axe to grind whose influence counted in his small community. People looked upon him as a leader. When he made the decision to remain, his colleagues in the neighbourhood agreed to do so too. They talked it over collected round the radio in his shop one evening soon after the formal announcement of the Partition. The last British Viceroy had guaranteed the safety of all citizens. Local political leaders were urging people to remain in their homes and carry on business as usual. It was advice that appealed to his own calm, practical instincts. Harpal's father and his friends had stayed. Two months after their decision bedlam broke loose in the town when gangs armed with knives and pitchforks looted the shops and killed those who stood in their way.

Harpal, who was employed as a clerk in a cement factory in a nearby town, had come home anxious about the rumours of trouble he had been hearing. He wanted to

reassure himself his parents were all right. He had arrived
to find the locality where they lived in flames. He had paid
two rupees for his bus trip home. He paid two hundred
rupees, the entire contents of his purse, to leave on the last
vehicle remaining in town.

Twenty years had blurred but never wiped out the anguish of that day. He could never think of it as a communal
riot. It had nothing to do with religion. He had lived
among these people all his life and religion had been no part
of their dealings with one another. It was more like the
clock turned back to a primitive century. Men had always
wanted power over each other's minds and religion had
been only one weapon in their hands.

In retrospect the day had begun to seem unreal, as all
great evil seems impossible and strangely puzzling afterwards. Could it actually have happened? Had he, Harpal, a
college graduate, a man with a steady job and the prospect
of promotion, dressed in his best, with his savings in his
pocket, come upon his home burning down before his
eyes? Of all the debris of the shop flung far out into the
street, his eyes picked out a carton of toothpaste. Long
flames devoured the carton and the stench of burning,
blackening metal filled his nostrils as the tubes hissed and
spit. The sight had started a long screaming protest in him.
He did not know if the scream left his lips and became part
of the chaos in the street, or if it stayed and burst inside him
in an intolerable explosion of raw grief and pain. He knew
that he ran wildly in the direction others were running, his
only thought to escape the full impact of what had happened to his father and mother. He pushed his way hysteri-
cally through the dense crowd at the bus depot, empty, he
could see, except for a single vehicle. Panic filled him that
he would be left behind, never get away from the funeral
pyre that had once been his home. He found himself pant-

ing and sobbing in a clearing in the crowd and was brought
to a dead stop by more than the knowledge that the man
facing him was in charge of the bus.

The man, about his own age, and massively built, looked
immeasureably older in the uncanny contrast he presented
the men and women beseeching his help. There was
nothing in his appearance and manner to suggest that the
town behind him was a death trap and the people surrounding him fleeing for their lives. He might have been
about to conduct a sightseeing excursion. He did not seem
to hear the pleas or see the frantic, fumbling fingers unty-
ing coins from corners of grimy saris and dupattas, the
creased rupee notes held out in worn hands. He was
briskly selecting the better customers, the merchants who
had been able to rescue their money boxes from the wreck-
age of their homes, and relieving them of their savings as he
admitted them to the bus.

"Are you the driver of this bus?" Harpal had heard his
own choking voice ask.

The man had said levelly, "I am driving the bus." And
Harpal had not noticed the distinction till later. The man
had measured him coolly against the clamouring, bedraggled crowd, asked for his purse, noted its contents, put
them into his pocket, and said, "All right, get in."

In another few minutes the bus, packed to capacity, was
moving with a groan and a blast of petrol fumes into the
fading evening light, away from the cries and outstretched
hands. It had not occurred to Harpal till then to ask where
it was going. Rammed into his seat, his left arm caught
painfully between the arm of his seat and his neighbour's, he
asked him where they were going.

"To Delhi," said his neighbour.

"Why?" Harpal wanted to know.

The man had given him a curious look that changed to

quick concern and said, "I am going because my family is there. I thank God my wife and children were there visiting her parents when the rioting broke out. If you are alone, come with me."

Harpal did not answer. He tried not to think of the men and women abandoned to a lawless mob. He looked at the driver's broad back, at the black hair growing low on the nape of the neck below the turban and springing on the broad wrist he could see on the wheel. The driver's eyes met his in the mirror and Harpal looked away. Devil-driven bus. The phrase leapt to his mind and a fit of trembling took hold of him.

"Are you all right, young man?" his neighbour asked. "Here, share my blanket."

"I'm all right."

But he was not all right. He had been half crazed with sorrow and stunned by his loss. Now he was afraid of something he could not define. Evil carried him along the darkening road to Delhi. Cramped and chilled, his head throbbing, Harpal fell asleep, waking with a start to find the driver staring down at him.

"You can get down here. I'm making a short stop."

The bus was empty. A street lamp, its orange glow diffused by fog, hung framed like a detached eye in one window. Harpal shook his head, possessed by the nameless dread again. Two hours later they were in Delhi and the driver emptied his passenger load like vomit into a street corner in the old city where refugees sat immobile as pockmarks on the pavement. And then he vanished into the night. Harpal met him again five years later, an interval he thought of as his dim years, when he had groped to make a niche for himself and to struggle out of the lonely anonymity into which the Partition had cast him. His work for the Congress Party had been fanatical in its devotion. He had had nowhere else to expend himself and his earnestness had impressed his elders. They believed he would go far and took a gamble when they chose him, a young unknown, to stand for the Punjab state legislature from a constituency where the last candidate had made a poor showing. But long before that he would not have known what to do if the stranger beside him in the bus had not taken charge of him at Delhi.

Harpal had not asked for help. The stranger had taken him home without a word, kept him for days—or had it been weeks—until he had recovered enough to locate his mother's cousin in the city. It was not, Harpal discovered later, an isolated act of kindness, but part of a harvest of solicitude and kinship that great disasters seemed to produce. Men killed each other but apparently they could not stamp out their own decency. That survived and flourished in the heart of destruction. He was nearly whole again when he and the bus driver met again, and Gyan Singh did not remember him.

Harpal, repeating the unlikely word Hariyana, thought, it's no good expecting restraint from him now. It's too late. And I helped to make him what he is.

When Dubey entered the Hariyana Chief Minister's office in the Secretariat he was struck by the tall, slim, grey-bearded figure at the desk in the centre of the room who stood up courteously to greet him. Maturity had added sternness to the features whose clean modelling showed the young man he had been. Dubey was immediately aware both of his age and his youthfulness, and the shadow of some conflict between the two that had not been resolved. Harpal came to the point at once. The problem, he told Dubey, was one of keeping the peace.

"I hope you are prepared to spend a few nights without

sleep," he said. "We have a great deal of work ahead of us."

He wanted Dubey to study a note stating his state's attitude towards Gyan Singh's strike threat and to prepare one making an appeal to all industrial establishments to keep their machinery working. The Hariyana Government intended to keep its own concerns going.

"Next month there is the cattle fair at Rohtak. We want to hold it on schedule. It's a big event and it should be the occasion for a celebration once all this is over."

Harpal was in a hurry. He was going to an anniversary meeting of the government machine-tool factory at Pinjore, fifteen miles from Chandigarh. Dubey accompanied him to his car at the entrance to the Secretariat and waited till the driver started it before walking to his own parked a few yards away. He waited for the Chief Minister's car to precede his. He heard the whine of the engine followed by a stutter, then silence. After a repetition of this Harpal got down, glancing impatiently at his watch. Dubey drove forward to the entrance.

"You should have had the carburetor checked," Harpal was telling his driver irritably.

"It is not the carburetor, *jenab*," the driver spoke in an injured tone. "It's the piston ring that needs changing. I've been making do with the old one. Now it won't work any longer. I put in an application for a new one a month ago."

Dubey swung open his door and the Chief Minister got in beside him.

"The assembly plant is on a go-slow strike. It's part of this general upset. They take orders but they don't deliver them on schedule. There's no knowing any more how long it will take an order to be completed and arrive. I am sorry to inconvenience you, but it might be a good thing if you came to this function. You need not sit through it. I'll get a car there to bring me back."

They drove in silence till Harpal said worriedly, "It's rather important, this meeting. This factory has been manufacturing steel tubes and cast-iron pipes and fittings that are finding a market all over the Middle East, and in Africa, Canada, and the United States. It will be a bad thing if the men put down their tools."

"Is that inevitable? Is there no hope that Sardar Gyan Singh's attitude will change?"

Harpal, looking straight ahead of him, said with the first gleam of lightness he had shown, "That, Mr. Dubey, is what you are going to tell me as soon as you are able."

At Pinjore an audience of workers heard the Chief Minister in silence. But something was wrong. This was not an atmosphere of attentive interest. It was a slack indifference. Dubey left before the meeting was over. When he arrived at the guest house it was growing dark and he felt he had been driving a long time. Already he was removed from a world where things went according to schedule to the beginnings of an unnatural pall, the only kind of situation impossible to handle. The Home Minister had been wrong. This was not a taut situation. One could come to grips with a stir, an agitation of some kind—and there had been plenty of those—but what could one do with paralysis? He was reminded incongruously of the long brooding silences during his marriage, the hours when he had felt trapped in helplessness and had wanted desperately to cry out, "*Talk* to me." A hundred times during those silences he had stood accused, sentenced, and hanged for crimes he did not know he had committed, a guilt he could not acknowledge or understand.

When he rang up Gyan Singh's residence he was told the Punjab Chief Minister was out of town.

Going home from the Pinjore meeting Harpal remembered that he had come face to face with Gyan for the second time in his life outside the dingy office of the district Congress Committee during his election campaign. It was Harpal's first visit to the office. A group of workers squatted in a corner of the verandah with cups of tea. In the yard a boy was whistling as he fitted a loudspeaker to the handle bar of his bicycle. He looked up at Harpal.

"Here, would you talk through this thing? I'll hold the bicycle."

Harpal cleared his throat and said tentatively, "Vote for Harpal Singh."

"Very nice," said the boy. "Those fellows at the corner heard you."

He took a dirty rag from his pocket and wiped the mudguard of his cycle carefully.

"Think I can take this along now. I wonder when this Harpal Singh is turning up. He wasn't on the morning train. A bunch of us went to the station. Missed school to go."

Since his initial astonishment at having been chosen to stand for election to the Punjab legislature, Harpal had been through a series of ups and downs. Alternately jubilation and nervousness assailed him. But he had never felt as stripped of confidence as he did at that moment. He cursed himself for missing his scheduled train and arriving unaccompanied at the Congress office.

"Hey, haven't you gone yet?" a resonant voice from the office demanded.

"Going, Gyan."

Gyan Singh came to the door and Harpal recognized him at once. He gave an impression of overwhelming physical strength. It had preceded him in the powerful voice. It rippled now in his muscular forearm when the sleeve of his kurta fell back as he gestured. It flashed in his eyes and his black-bearded face. Next to him Harpal felt colourless,

stern, and puritanical. Some men seemed to shed the years
like ·skins they had outgrown and move onto every new
stage without a scar. Gyan hardly showed his years except
in an accumulation of confidence. The Partition had not so
much as grazed him. Harpal resented this immunity when
he thought of all that the experience had cost him in health
and emotional damage.

"D'you think you're going for a joy ride?" Gyan blasted
the boy. "Stop flicking that *jharan* around and get on with
the announcement of the meeting."

"Going, going," chanted the youngster peaceably, folding the dirty rag with care and putting it into his pocket.
He mounted his cycle and waved.

Gyan turned to Harpal. "That's what comes of having
no jeeps, no transport of any kind, not even a wretched
motorcycle so far. Have to get workers who own bicycles,
and kids like that one, for the jobs of announcement and
distribution. That kind has just bought his bicycle. Guards it
as if it were the national treasure."

"I'm Harpal Singh," Harpal found it necessary to say.

Gyan looked hard at him. "I should have known you.
They've sent enough pamphlets with your picture."

He took Harpal into the one-room office and pointed a
blunt finger at the posters and pamphlets piled high in a
corner. "They," the high command, made decisions and
appointments, chose candidates, weeded out some, and
brought in others. It was nothing to do with him, Gyan's
tone implied. His business was to get them elected, whoever they were, with or without the funds and transport.
He was tired of telling "Them" this would be a more and
more important area. It was not the back of beyond. Luck-
ily, he told Harpal, it was an industrial area and the
workers' transport could be borrowed. Harpal listened,
dreariness settling into him like the dust in every crevice of

the room. The thrill of his candidature had fled as he
stepped into the dirty office whose chief had not even
known who he was. He had thought of this election in
terms of a very personal endeavour where he would meet
people, acquaint himself with their problems, and establish
a living communication with them. But instead he was a
"candidate," a minor cog in a huge machine, and his fate
rested on transport and funds, not on his sincerity of purpose. The ones who paid for their own campaigns could
afford sincerity. The unknown and obscure were safer doing as they were told.

"Your meeting is at five o'clock when the factories close.
The last candidate was all right but he talked above the
people's heads," said Gyan.

From what Harpal had heard in Delhi the last candidate
had disappeared into the vast anonymity that was the fate
of the unsuccessful in politics. Elections were lost by many,
but only the big could afford to lose them. For the others
there was no second chance. A mediocre barrister or doctor could go on making a living, but a failure in politics was
a zero. Harpal was acutely conscious that the Congress
organization was all that stood between him and a blank
future. He had no background, no family, no profession,
and no identity except through it. What if he should fail?
He sat down on one of the two ancient chairs and listened
while Gyan explained the problems of the constituency to
him, and what he should highlight at the meeting.

"You can say what you like once you're in," said Gyan.

Harpal caught at the security of the sentence and basked
in the flood of warm feeling it released in him. The man
opposite him had been in this business longer than he had.
Gyan knew these workers. He had fed and nursed them
through their strikes and during the last trouble had organized a boycott in the town of the wholesale dealers they

represented. He knew what they wanted. On the train, thinking of what he would say at his meeting, Harpal had divined that what was needed was the disarming impact of a man on the crowd he faced, the impact that would clearly say, "This is *me*. We don't know each other. I'm a stranger to you. But from now on it's going to be you and me together." Something like that. During his work in the refugee camps near Delhi he had been able to establish personal contacts, even convey an assurance he had at times been far from feeling. But those had been people like himself, victims of a holocaust, and he had spoken their language. He abandoned his ideas as he listened to Gyan.

Outside the enclosure where the public meeting was to be held a loudspeaker blared national songs. The meeting was packed, but Gyan kept looking worriedly at the entrance.

"Where has that kid and his crowd got to? They should have been here by now."

The boys had taken out posters earlier in the evening. He nodded, satisfied, as he saw a group of boys straggle in and stand pressed against a rope barrier at the back of the enclosure. It was seven-thirty when the meeting ended and Harpal and Gyan came out into the smoky darkness.

"I don't see that kid," he persisted. He called one of the boys.

"He was with us, Gyan, when we were pasting the posters at the station, and then a gang that was trailing us kept tearing them off and we got into a fight and ran away from there."

"Wasn't he with you when you ran?"

"I don't know. We just ran." In the yellow light from the dais the boy's face looked pallid.

"All right, what did you do with the posters?"

"We dumped them outside the station. That's where we

were when the fight started. Sorry Gyan—"

"All right," grumbled Gyan, "but what could have happened to the one who announced the meeting?"

The boys looked round. "I thought he'd come away with us," said one.

Gyan turned to Harpal. "I'm going to see if I can find him. It's not like him not to show up. There's a gang that has been after our posters."

It was Harpal's constituency. "I'm coming with you," he said.

Gyan gave him an odd look but said nothing.

At the station they found one poster, ripped down the centre, stuck fast to the outer wall. Others lay in shreds below it. A stack, still neatly tied, lay in the road. There was a double row of hutments near the station. They had come up at the time of the Partition and in these five years had taken root. Rusty corrugated iron sheeting had replaced the original flimsy hardboard in the makeshift permanence of shattered human beings. At this time fires were lit behind every one of them and the smoke and smell of cooking rose above the huddle. Gyan rattled the sheeting at the far end of the row, demanding entry. Voices argued inside, making up their minds, till a woman came to the entrance, her dupatta covering half her face.

"Where's the boy?" Gyan said.

"There's no boy here."

Gyan pushed her aside and went in. There was a pile of bedding in a corner, a clutter of cooking utensils, and a man on the floor eating his evening meal.

"Your gang tore off my posters," Gyan said, looking down at him.

In the shadowy room he looked immense, his arms hanging loosely by his sides, his body rigid. The man went on eating. Gyan kicked away the brass plate. The man leapt to his feet. In the second before they locked in a fierce struggle Harpal thought it uncanny that the woman did not scream. She crouched in her corner, a hand clamped across her mouth over the cloth of her dupatta, and only her eyes showed panic. She began to moan only when she saw them down on the floor, Gyan astride the man, his hands in his hair, pounding his head again and again on the ground in a repetition of carnal savagery. He stopped suddenly, as if emptied of the last drop of lust and grunted, replacing the turban that had fallen off his head. He lifted himself off the body and said to the woman, "Where's the boy?" She pointed to the strip of cloth hung over a length of string that served as a curtain. Gyan went behind it and found the boy lying in a crumpled heap. He picked him up, hung him over his shoulder, and went out. The woman's screams broke loose and there was pandemonium as the hutment dwellers came to life.

The boy was unconscious but breathing. Back at the station Gyan examined him for broken bones, made sure he was intact, and took him home. Then he remembered Harpal was with him. They had not exchanged a word since leaving the meeting. Gyan said, "Tomorrow morning we'll cover the rest of the constituency."

Harpal found his voice. "That man—"

"He won't make trouble again."

"Is he—he must be—dead. We'll have to make a report to the police."

"Leave all that to me," said Gyan evenly.

That, too, was a part of the election campaign Harpal had left to Gyan.

Harpal straightened and rolled down the window glass as the car turned into his house. There were people waiting at the gate, even at this time of night. There was no respite from work at any hour of the day. Harpal wanted it this

way. For years he had received visitors and complainants
without appointment when he returned home from office.
A good man, they called him, one who worked tirelessly
for the people, one who cared. His car passing through the
gate was the sign for the sentry on duty to allow the
waiting callers in. Harpal greeted them before going indoors to wash.

There was a conversation he had carried round with him
for years, ever since the murder in the hutment. It began:
"What happened to that man? Was anything done about
him? And what became of the woman?" It had never been
put into words. It had been transcribed instead to another
medium, converted to a mode of living. His speeches in the
Assembly had reflected it. His concern for causes had become well known. He had been one of those who had
agitated for the clearance of the hutment area, for housing
and employment for displaced persons. He, an unknown
on the political scene, had soon come to represent the revival of aspiration among the dispossessed. As much as any
man could be who belonged to a party, he had been his
own man. He went out to the verandah where people
waited to see him, and turned to the old woman nearest
him.

"Yes, mother, what is your problem?"

She launched into her recital and he listened patiently.
He could not remember a time when he had wanted power.
What he had passionately wanted was recognition as a
champion of the underdog. And he had earned that. The
old woman relating her woes was proof of it. There were
so many evidences, if evidence were needed. No one
needed it but him and none of it blotted out the memory of
the woman he had not championed because he had wanted
to be elected.

Chapter 4

The week was nearly over before Dubey had time to call on Saroj and Inder Mehra. It was not far to the sector where they lived in a row of well-spaced houses set in small gardens. There was light through the curtains and sounds of liveliness reached him before he got to the front door. It flew open almost as he touched the bell. A tired, surprised face stared at him until its possessor, recovering herself, said foolishly, "Oh, I thought it was Inder." The young woman stood holding the door open, forgetting to invite him in. The lower edge of her sari hung wet and heavy as if she had stepped through a puddle, and the sleeves of her brown woollen cardigan were pushed up to her elbows. Her hair was tied back, her face unmade-up, all its character concentrated in its delicate moulding, all its vulnerability in a soft, childlike mouth.

"I'm Vishal Dubey," he said. "The Rays were going to let you know I was in Chandigarh."

"Oh yes, Gauri phoned. Please come in." She spoke as if

preoccupied, leaving the door ajar behind him. She looked down apologetically at herself. "I'm sorry I'm in such a state. I've been giving the children their baths and then we're supposed to dine out, only my husband isn't back yet."

She paused in the middle of the room and pulled the ribbon off her hair, shaking it free. It fell straight and sudden below her shoulders. The children, of whom he counted two small boys, seemed a great many more in the confusion of toys and picture books spread all over the floor. He noticed as she bent awkwardly to retrieve her hair ribbon that she was pregnant.

"I won't keep you if you are dining out," he said. "You must have a lot to attend to before that."

"It's worse than usual these days," she admitted. "My ayah left last week and I'm looking for another, and meanwhile everything is in a muddle. I do have to get ready but that won't take long. Please sit down. My husband should be here any moment."

The solitude and concentration of the past week, the return from work to his empty room at the guest house, decided Dubey. He sat down in a corner of the faded sofa, glad he had come. One of the small boys on the floor fixed him with a solemn unblinking stare, then went back to his jigsaw puzzle. A servant laid the table in the dining alcove, brought the children's supper to it, and called them. Neither child paid attention to the summons. It was rather like the situation the Centre faced here, thought Dubey, its appeal falling on deaf ears. The Home Minister had been as good as his word. His ministry had kept in touch and twice that week Dubey had phoned Delhi. The servant repeated his summons, then came into the drawing room, hoisted one child up by the arms, and propelled him to the table. He came back for the other who protested vigorously as part of his jigsaw scattered.

"It's simpler than argument," said Dubey.

"They take it from Sham," said Saroj. "They wouldn't from me."

"Why not?"

"They *expect* argument from me."

"Maybe our politicians expect to be hoisted out of their positions without argument, and that's what we should do," said Dubey.

"How?"

He liked the direct question, oddly at variance with her look of reserve. He thought she was very unlike Gauri until he remembered she was Nikhil's relation.

"No one seems to know," he admitted.

"I'm afraid," said Saroj.

Her level voice carried the word home to him in a way no slight inflection would have done. Fear was a feeling he had been avoiding, trying to believe the days ahead were not bedevilled, each one not dissolving towards a mounting anxiety.

"What are you afraid of? There's no reason to panic. Everything will be under control."

"Oh, I'm not worried about any great disaster. I'm afraid of *usual* things going wrong, like milk not being delivered and my tins and packets running short, and the iron not working and not being able to get it repaired," she trailed off. "D'you know what I mean? It's when ordinary things go off the rails that life becomes unbelievable."

The word struck him as apt.

"You know, an atmosphere you can't put your finger on. If the children fell ill I'd know what to do about it. But if they woke up dead silent tomorrow morning and didn't say a word till lunchtime I'd be terrified." She stopped. "I'm so bad at expressing myself."

"I don't think you are."

She glanced towards the children, who were eating docilely.

"I'd better get ready," she said.

Upstairs in her bedroom she stood in front of the full-length mirror studying her reflection pensively. Her petti-coat was stretched over the slight protuberance of her stomach. The bulge at five months showed much more when she had all her clothes on. She stood still, not sure if she had imagined the flutter within her, and here it came again, the sensation of a butterfly held in cupped hands, the first unmistakable stir of life. She felt exultant. You won, she told the nameless tenacity that had survived her efforts to destroy it. She had not wanted to. It had had something to do with Inder's face when she had told him two months earlier about the baby, the flash of painful incredulity that was replaced not soon enough by annoyance and then resignation. A brief argument had flared between them over her ineptitude. She had never been able to use anything effectively.

"Hundreds of women use the damned thing success-fully," he had said irritably. "It's madness to have three children nowadays."

Saroj had wilted, the seed within her adding itself to the great, unused burden of longing she had carried for so long. She had wanted suddenly to be rid of both. But now the seed had stirred and she wanted to laugh and sing and celebrate. There was nothing to do with life but affirm it. Even if you had not planned it, not wanted it, the mere fact of it took charge. She hugged her joy close.

When she came down fifteen minutes later Dubey noticed there was not much difference in her appearance. She had washed her face but she still wore no makeup. In place of the brown cardigan she had draped a white stole over her shoulders. The long straight hair had been brushed and left loose. She sat down carefully on the edge of a chair. They heard a car on the gravel and the sound of rain through the door she had forgotten to shut and a man came in, walking with a confident, muscular grace, radiating energy. The children left the table to rush at him and he shepherded them back to their places.

"Sorry I'm late," he said, as Saroj introduced him; then, with a touch of impatience, "Saroj, give Mr. Dubey a drink. I'll be down in five minutes."

He picked his way over the scattered jigsaw and started up the stairs.

"There isn't any," said Saroj.

"Any what?"

"Whiskey. You were going to stop for a bottle on your way home."

"Oh damn." He said to Dubey, "This isn't a very organized household as you can see. I won't be long."

"We're dining out," she reminded him.

Inder called down, "You must come with us, Mr. Dubey. Yes you must. These are good friends of ours."

"I've got some Coca-Cola," said Saroj.

"I don't want anything," Dubey told her, "and I'm not sure I should come to this party. It may not be convenient for your friends."

"It'll be perfectly all right. This is Chandigarh."

She seemed to consider that explanation enough and he accepted it immediately, though Inder's invitation had left him in doubt. They left the house in a thin drizzle and were glad of the log fire in the Sahnis' drawing room. A tall slender young woman in orange slacks came to greet them. Dubey found himself in a deep black-upholstered chair, a white rug at his feet, a glass of whiskey at his elbow. The walls were a stark white, the ceiling black. It would have been a luxurious room but for the austerity of its decor.

"It's our own whiskey," his hostess said.

Dubey looked at her enquiringly.

"Jit's firm makes it," she explained. "If you don't like it we have another brand, plain old Scotch, but he's very keen on everyone trying this one this evening."

Dubey tasted it. "It's good," he told her.

"Don't be polite. If it's ghastly, this is the time to tell Jit. Don't you think most Indian brands are ghastly?"

"Well they're not Scotch," he admitted, "but I like this."

There was a great deal more noise in the room than the number of people warranted and none of the atmosphere of ordinary social intercourse. These were obviously people who knew each other well and whose arguments were picked up where they had been left off. A stranger, Saroj had been right, made no difference to the gathering. He was simply ignored. Dubey had been given a drink and left to fend for himself. The talk near him was political. The man who had come to sit beside him listened quietly to the discussion.

"It's strange," he remarked to Dubey, "when Mara and I decided to settle in Chandigarh we thought it would be the one place in India that would be immune from this sort of thing." He waved the stem of his pipe in the direction of the heated argument. "If there was any noise here it was the architects who made it. The decrees had nothing to do with government either. They were about vegetable barrows being painted bright colours, about cows not being allowed within the city limits, about no building going up haphazardly. Well, all of that's still there. The vegetable barrows still look gay and there are no cows or erratic building—at least not so far—but people have moved in."

He sounded perplexed and Dubey smiled.

His informant went on, "In the early days when our

house was being built and other houses were coming up, there was a complete absorption with building—just the solid fact of it, something going up where nothing had ever been, shape and form being given to plans and dreams. It was a remarkably untainted atmosphere. We used to walk along the lake every evening, Mara and I, and look across to the High Court and tell each other that the whole conception was too big, too true to be a setting for petty people. I don't like a lot of the buildings here but there's something fearless about the whole idea. Only the people haven't measured up. Are you a Punjabi yourself?"

"No," said Dubey.

"Then it may be difficult for you to imagine what Chandigarh meant to those of us who were thrown out of Lahore. It was a second chance, a starting from scratch. And now this place rings with the same cant as any other place. The architects couldn't find the right breed of human beings to inhabit their perfect blueprints."

He gestured again with his pipe. "Those people talking about leadership mean strength. And there's only one kind of strength that's understood here. Force. Authority. The other kinds are for the books." There was a trace of bitterness in his voice.

"Force makes an immediate impact," said Dubey, "but in the long run that impact doesn't always last."

"What do you call the long run? Do you mean that after the deed is done, wisdom prevails? But by then the deed is done. It's one reason why Gyan Singh has a following. People feel he means business, gets things done, while Harpal Singh doesn't make any impression and gets put in the shade every time. As far as the civilized instincts are concerned human beings haven't come very far. The crude basic instincts still rule us, hunger, sex, power. They are what decide our actions, and I suppose always will. I sometimes wonder about people like myself. Will we just get exterminated eventually by the brutes?"

He did not wait for a reply. "By the way we were not introduced. I'm Jit Sahni—"

Dubey said, "I didn't realize—" and introduced himself.

"How do you like the whiskey, Mr. Dubey? The world's newest brand. Everyone else advertises the age of his product, I advertise the newness of mine. I released this only last week. I couldn't import peat from Scotland as I believe the Japanese do, but I think it's good. Ever since its release there's been this labour trouble threatening. If I could only get it going properly I'd find a market all the way to the United States."

He took away Dubey's glass to refill.

Dubey sat back in his chair listening to the people around him. They were talking with their bodies, gesturing, arguing, interrupting one another. Saroj, coming towards him, was oddly unexpected and contained in that gathering. He half rose to offer her his chair but she took Jit's high-backed one.

"I don't feel comfortable on that kind any more," she said.

It struck him that the cheerful extroverts, the back-slappers among men were also the most difficult to know. There were times when joking even seemed a poor substitute for human contact. In the roomful of strangers she seemed a friend. The thought surprised him. Friend was not a word he used easily. Nor was wife. Soon after his marriage to Leela he had stopped thinking of her as his wife. He looked at his watch. He had known Saroj just under two hours.

"Are you hungry?" her eyes followed his glance. "Dinner is usually late in this house."

"I was thinking I've known you only two hours. It seems

longer than that."

"How much longer?" she asked.

"I don't know," he admitted, "but a good long time."

Inder stood at the drinks table with his hostess after the others had gone into the dining room. His relationship with her grew and receded according to its own laws. Mara never knew what to expect of him.

"Were you very late?" she asked him.

"Yes, and I forgot to stop for whiskey on the way home."

"You could have taken a bottle from here. Why didn't I think of it?"

"It's not the brand we keep," he pointed out. "Not that Saroj would have noticed."

Mara drew a slender forefinger along the surface of the glass-topped table, making a trail of moisture left by frosty glasses.

"I didn't know Saroj was expecting a baby. I never noticed before. How many months is it?"

"It's usual for people to have children. We live in the same house, in the same room. For heaven's sake, Mara."

His loss of poise amused her.

"I live in the same house with Jit. I can't see what that has to do with it. Saroj has a queer kind of hold on you."

"She hasn't got any kind of hold at all. She doesn't care what she looks like from morning till night. The house is in a mess. There's going to be one child too many, and she's all wrapped up in God knows what."

It was such a rare outburst for Inder that she stared at him.

"What on earth did she want another child for?"

"She didn't."

With a lightheartedness she did not feel Mara said, "I

think you need to get away from it all more often."

He closed up again. "I shouldn't drop in as I do. People will talk."

"About what?" she demanded.

"About my dropping in," he said shortly. "There doesn't have to be anything much for people to talk about."

Her eyes, clear and candid, nearly level with his own, searched his face. "What bothers you more, someone finding out you drop in occasionally or you finding out you like coming?"

The look on his face warned her to stop. She sensed he was a man capable of deep passionate intensity, as long as it were given no name. He would never admit his need. She would have to discover it and then pretend with him that it was not there. She thought suddenly of the wooden crates, any number of them, when she and Jit had moved to Chandigarh, each securely nailed with iron bands. One of them had split open during the journey and its contents had been splayed out into the truck, but the iron bands had stayed in place, rigid and intact, incongruously protecting nothing.

"Stop looking like doom and have a drink." She took his hand but he withdrew it quickly. "All right, we'll pretend we don't know each other."

"Don't you worry at all what Jit might say?"

She thought it over. "No," she said.

She left him to go into the dining room to look after her guests. Inder saw her slip an arm casually through her husband's and looked away.

Saroj lay in bed, luxuriating in her loose nightie and in the freedom from the tight construction of the sari round her waist. No matter how comfortable it was when she tied it, by the end of the evening it was tight. She crossed her hands under her head and her relaxation was so complete, so much what she wanted that she brought them to her sides again. She looked forward to playing the game of relaxation by inches. The sound of the tap in the bathroom was turned off and Inder got into the bed beside hers.

"I felt it move today," she said. "Want to feel?"

She reached for his hand and pressed it over her stomach. He discerned a slight hardness, but no movement. He felt squeamish about the processes of her pregnancy and it embarrassed him to keep his hand there. Sex with her came easily and satisfactorily to him. It was an act with a beginning and an end, a need never put into words, neatly enacted and dispensed with in darkness. There were no traces of it to account for in the morning. This, the touch without sexual significance, the caress of affection, was different. It cost him an effort to make it. It exacted more from him than the performance of an act. It called for his lingering attention and demanded that he give her part of himself for a while for no specific reason. That kind of companionship had always been difficult for him, just as to take a walk with her became a meaningless expenditure of time, when a restlessness took hold of him to get back to whatever work he had to do. His hand felt leaden on her stomach.

"What does it feel like to you?" she wanted to know.

"I can't feel a thing."

"You will in a minute," she held her breath. "There! It moved!" She rotated his hand gently over her abdomen.

Why couldn't she have a baby like other women did, without putting every stage of it into words? A wife was one half of an enterprise, the complaint partner who presided over home and children and furthered her husband's career. Saroj had no interest in any of it, and not because she was gifted with any accomplishment that took her time. It was her preoccupation with herself that unnerved him.

That, and the curious concentration of her spirit upon whatever came her way. Now, replete with her commonplace miracle, she fell asleep under his hand, while he lay awake staring into the darkness, the tension in him unabated.

He thought of the tapering white candles in their branched silver candelabra on Mara's dining table, and their long bright flame when she had put the overhead light out. They were like Mara. Slenderly feminine, she yet reminded him of a man, of qualities he associated with men, strength and resolution. Knighthood in flower was the phrase that came unbidden, read somewhere and stored in memory long ago. He never used such phrases. But that was what she was, a gallant, oddly fearless creature.

When the last of their guests had gone and Jit had supervised the locking of doors and windows, he went upstairs to find Mara still fully dressed, smoking in her favourite chair in a panel of moonlight. He took his pipe out of his pocket, sat down, and lit it. She came and sat at his feet, her back against his legs. With his free hand he massaged the nape of her neck and shoulder blades under her silk shirt. She slumped forward over her knees, enjoying it.

"My back's not aching, Jit," she mumbled sleepily.

"Then what is, love? Any place I can reach?"

His tone both humbled and annoyed her. She sat up.

"Jit, be angry."

"About what?"

"About something. There's so much to be angry about. The country's going to pot. The world is in a hideous snare."

"My world isn't. It's very orderly."

"How can you say that? You've got this strike threat hanging over your head and a hundred and one problems with your new whiskey."

"Those aren't my world."

She turned to face him in exasperation.

"I suppose it wouldn't matter if it all blew up tomorrow."

"Of course it would matter. But it's not my sanity. If it blew up, I'd still be whole."

She got up, put on the light and started moving nervously around the room, undressing haphazardly. He could be so blindly serene. One had to be blind to be serene. That would never be her lot. She wanted all the worlds she could lay hands on and the best of each—the softness of Jit and the hardness of Inder. Was it wrong to want the best of everything, so long as one took only the best, and nothing spurious or unclean? Was it wrong to fulfil and integrate oneself through fragments of other natures? What other way was there to live but through the life and the people around one? Yet that more-than-one life was an ache and a strain to live, a perpetual seeking beyond her own safe domestic frontiers. Why couldn't all of her be happy in this house, planned with devotion, built with such care? She had everything a woman could want, except children, and in place of her own she had the school. She got into bed, part of her mind occupied with the schedule she had planned for the following day. Jit was at the window, puffing tranquilly at his pipe.

"There's a full moon tonight," he said. "It's a beauty. Come and look at it."

"I've looked."

"Not properly," he said. "Not happily. You mustn't go to sleep without seeing it."

She got up, grumbling, and stood, his arm lightly about her shoulders, looking at the lunar landscape, its peace filling her, stirring the buried gratitude in her that she would never allow fully to come into its own.

"Now you can go to sleep," said Jit.

She was thinking by then of how she had first met Inder.

Her school had blossomed quickly from a small beginning and Mara was having trouble keeping the numbers
down. She had bought a shed and converted it into an
attractive three-room schoolhouse. There was enough
ground with it for a garden. She had set up a jungle gym, a
swing and a seesaw on one side and on the other a vegetable
patch which the children watered and weeded and where
they planted quick-growing mustard and cress and rad-
ishes. It looked like any other nursery school but it took
the community no time to discover it was different. No
ayahs were allowed on the premises. No one called Mara
"Aunty." She was gravely adult with the children, a new,
rare element in their lives. So was the strong soap and disin-
fectant with which they washed their hands before eating
the midmorning snack they brought with them, and the
fact that they cleaned and tidied the rooms and toys themselves, which few of them did at home. She did not know
what happened when they went home but here for three
hours every day they lived in the heaven of the expected,
the comforting world of disciplined, responsible citizen-
ship, where they could not do just as they liked. She had no
problems with the children, only with their parents. Mara
first met Inder the day he brought his children to the
school. She was having a cigarette in the small anteroom
she used as an office, her slippers kicked off, her legs up on
the table when he walked in. She got up, smoothing her
shirt over her slacks.

"I don't see parents at this time, but do come in now
you're here."

Inder, who had come to have the children admitted, had
not anticipated an interview. She offered him a cigarette

and the only other chair in the room and noticed that her informality had the effect of making him ill at ease. He sat down, looking rather tense. The trim business suit and the air of authority about him made it obvious he was used to the executive side of the desk. And he was looking at her as if she were a trade union.

She said comfortably, "I think I should explain what I do here."

Inder looked surprised that an explanation of nursery school activity should be necessary.

"You mean children do something besides play at this age?"

"They learn," she said pointedly. "I teach them their alphabet and numbers in the first year. And in the second year they learn to read and do sums. And of course they paint and do some clay modelling and sing, all the activities through which they can express themselves."

"I see."

"And the third year is really the most interesting—"

He had a fixed look on his face. She guessed he had never spent that many minutes on a matter concerning his children. Through the open door of her office he could see the big bright adjoining room with easels lining one wall. She wondered if the equipment would interest him more.

"I had those made here by a local carpenter. Come and have a look around. I'll show you the books I use."

"I'm in a bit of a hurry, actually."

He looked impatient to settle the admission and be gone and she had an obstinate desire to detain him, to crack through the stiffness and challenge the determined formality. And she had no intention of abandoning the initiative on her own domain nor of allowing him just to dump his children and go.

"I don't want to delay you," she said with elaborate

concern. "Would you like to come back another day, then, about the admission?"

"No, I may as well see to it now." He was not very good at concealing his annoyance.

"You're the first father who has come," she said.

"My wife isn't well or she would have come herself."

"Oh? I took it as a sign of your own interest. Child-rearing seems rather one-sided here."

"It's a woman's job," he said flatly.

"That's just what it isn't, you know."

For the first time he looked closely at her. So very light-skinned and in those slacks, perhaps she was not Indian. He asked her if she was. She was used to the scrutiny and the question, one that waited for and never got the relieving response that she was not one of them.

"Good Lord yes," she replied. "Oh, you mean this out-fit. It's easier to run around in."

She knew he did not mean the outfit. There was an air of independence and forthrightness about her, as if she were used to speaking for herself. She led him through the room, determinedly showing him samples of the children's work, a new batch of oil colours she had been able to get from a friend abroad, blunt coloured plastic scissors with which they could start cutting.

"I tried to have parents' meeting once a month," she said, "but I had to stop. The fathers never came and very few of the mothers attended regularly. How do you ex-plain that?"

He had no explanation to offer. She took him back to her office and took an admission form out of the desk drawer. Inder glanced down the printed page. Child's name. Date of birth. Address. Telephone number. Father's business. None of *her* damned business, he thought. He had wasted enough of the morning on this ridiculous mission. Anyone would think this was a university instead of a place for four- to six-year-olds to spend the morning so that they would not make nuisances of themselves at home.

"It's not just a place where children spend their mornings, you see," Mara said uncannily. "It becomes a second home for them, a focus. And it's useful for me to know a little about their backgrounds. That's why I wanted the parents' meetings."

He was scowling at the next line on the form: Any comments the parent would care to make concerning the child's personality and interests.

"I'm afraid this is beyond me. My wife can supply this later."

He took his pen from his pocket and filled in two forms. It gave him a grim satisfaction to sign them illegibly at the bottom. He paid the admission fee, then looked out of the window for his boys.

"I suggest you leave them here, though half the morning is over," she said. "They seem happy."

"All right then, I'll slip out." He looked relieved.

"No, don't do that. Tell them you're going."

He stopped in his tracks, irritated with her. Why didn't she mind her own business? Then it struck him that that was what she was doing. He went with her into the garden. It was alive with small boys and girls. Bunny and Muff were on the jungle gym. Bunny saw him and climbed down. Inder said good-bye and walked rapidly away. As he got into his car he saw Mara bending over Bunny, showing him something in the hollow of her hand.

On Saturdays Inder came to fetch the children and one Saturday she asked him to give her a lift home. He had been surprised to discover that she lived in the unusual house so different from the others in the row. He had often noticed it, driving past. She introduced the man with the

boyish smile who came out to greet them and to open the
door of the car for her as her husband. Inder could not take
his eyes off her as she stood, her skin very milky in the
sunshine, her arm linked through her husband's. He had the
strange sensation of having trespassed.

"Come in and have a drink," she offered, remembering
her guest.

"Yes do," the man said. "I've begun to think the school is
a figment of Mara's imagination, or at least that the parents
are invisible. You're the first one I've met in the flesh."

Inder looked at Bunny and Muff squirming on the back
seat.

"They'll have a drink too," said Jit, "and they'll like the
bear rug in the hall."

Outside the drawing room there was a small courtyard, a
trolley with bottles and glasses glinting in the sun and
wrought-iron furniture grouped beside a pond. "Mara's
pebble pond," Jit called it.

"What do you think of a woman who prefers pebbles to
lilies or goldfish?" he asked.

Inder looked down at the smooth pebbles, large and
small, of all shapes, shining under the water. He didn't reply
to Jit's question.

Jit made gin and lime, took it to his wife, and lit her
cigarette, surrounding her in those few gestures with a
charming attentiveness.

"How was the morning, love?"

"Hectic," she said. "Priya fell off the swing and was hurt
quite badly. I had to take her home."

Jit gave Inder his drink. "You wouldn't think anyone
would spend so much time doing what they don't really
enjoy doing."

"Don't you enjoy the school?" Inder looked surprised.

"I love the kids, but I'm not really *in* it," she said.

He was unfamiliar with the distinction she made.

They urged him to come again and to bring Saroj. They began to see each other often. Inder did not know when he began dropping in on Mara in the evenings on his way home from the office. Without a word spoken she had made him aware he was isolated, that the distance between him and any other person was an infinity he might never span without help. It seemed to him brazen and improper to visit her in a seclusion that was alive with possibilities, in an attraction she made no attempt to hide, in surroundings that were home to a relationship of subtle understanding and affection. Yet he continued to do so and he found himself talking to her of his work. He had told her this evening of what had happened at the office.

It had happened just as he was thinking of leaving for home. He had been feeling rather pleased that there had been no trouble at the mill so far. In fact, business had never been better. The venture into nylon had progressed by leaps and bounds. Inder had never cared for Saroj's family but he had to admit Nikhil Ray had good judgment. He had introduced nylon to the Punjab at the right time. People had money to spend. And women were beginning to earn and spend their own money, a new development since independence. They were the ones who needed saris that would not crease or need ironing. Inder had argued against it. Other mills in the country were struggling to keep going. There was too big a gap, he said, between production costs and the consumers' purchasing capacity.

"Not in the Punjab," Nikhil had assured him, "and nylon isn't for the masses."

Nylon had its drawbacks. It could not be worn in the kitchen. There had been the case a year ago of a woman whose sari had caught fire while she was cooking and one whole side of her had been burned and scarred. She had barely survived the shock and the firm had had to face some ugliness over the incident but the fabric was here to stay. Inder had before him the booklet of new designs sent by the head office, mostly floral patterns, roses, fleurs-de-lis, leaves and buds entwined into sprays in imitation of the coveted French chiffons that were beyond the means of most women. The working woman's chiffon, Nikhil had called his nylons, and women had certainly taken to them. Inder heard the commotion outside as he put away the booklet. A group of men were furiously jostling and gesturing outside his window. He could not hear what they were saying.

"There's a batch of men here from the mill," said his stenographer, coming in. "They want to speak to you."

"Ask their spokesman to come in."

The stenographer looked apprehensive. "The others will not be left outside."

Inder decided to see them all outside. The numbers seemed to expand before his eyes. No one greeted him. The men—he knew them all—fell sullen and a thrill of fear shot through him, settling at the pit of his stomach.

"You wanted to see me?"

One of them stepped forward.

"We are not satisfied with the canteen arrangements."

"What's wrong with them, Nahar Singh?" Inder spoke easily, pleasantly, but no one responded to his cue.

A murmur went through the crowd.

"What do you get?" he asked, though he knew perfectly well what they got.

"There are stones in the wheat flour," said Nahar Singh.

"Yes," he agreed, "the wheat has not been of good quality lately."

"We are told this rubbishy wheat is shipped from America. It is the waste which is fed to the pigs over there," said Nahar Singh.

An angry rustle swept the men behind him.

"We grow good enough wheat right here. Why are we fed pigs' food?" someone shouted.

They were all talking and shouting at once. What in God's name had gone wrong? Inder had got this mill going. These men had been with him then, and nothing between him and them had changed.

"I am glad," he said, "that your complaint isn't about the work. These other difficulties—"

"We will not work if we are not fed."

In the babble Inder no longer knew who was doing the talking. Nahar Singh had stepped back among the men and Inder was facing a solid wall of hostile faces. He wanted to look squarely at them but there were too many of them, reminding him of an intelligent, menacing animal straining at a leash that might snap at any moment.

"Your complaint will be looked into," he said.

A voice, anonymous, unidentifiable, shot out derisively from the crowd.

"Where will you look? In the government *godowns* where the rubbish is stored till it rots and the rats get at it before it reaches us? Into the *baniyas*' storehouses where it is stacked while people starve? We are not working till we are fed."

The spuriousness of the complaint alerted Inder. The message hammering at the back of his mind suddenly came through. He became sharply aware of the small building behind him that housed his office, newly painted and furnished, and near it the mill with its new machinery churning out the new cloth. These were the men who turned it out. Now, somehow, it would have to be protected from them.

Inder realized before he fell asleep that he had not told Saroj about the incident.

Chapter 5

Prasad, Chief Secretary to the Hariyana Government, came into the office. Talking to him a few days earlier, Dubey had found him cordial, helpful, and attractive, with the keen mind and impressive memory of the practised administrator. He had asked him to come in for a talk in the office before he left the state. Prasad had been posted in Delhi for ten years before coming here and had now asked for and been given a transfer back to the Centre. Dubey sat with the zonal map of the city spread out on his desk, marked with police posts and stations.

"I see you're at it," said Prasad.

"I wish you weren't leaving us," said Dubey fervently, wondering who he meant by us—Hariyana, Punjab, or himself in his anomalous position between the two. "Why doesn't Gyan Singh call off this strike threat like a sensible chap and let everybody settle down to work?"

"That's a very old-fashioned idea," said Prasad, "and it would seem rather odd if some factory weren't going slow or closing shop for a day or two."

"Harpal Singh's car wouldn't start the other day," said Dubey.

"I'm having trouble with my own."

Dubey had been consulting the file on the law-and-order situation. There was a complaint in it against a police officer for wanton killing and extraction of money. The earliest notation about it was dated a year earlier.

"I wanted to ask you about this policeman," he said to Prasad.

"It's an old story," said Prasad. "You remember the firing at the Agricultural Institute here last year? This was the man who gave the order. He's a junior officer but he was the one at the *thana* when the trouble began. I don't think he had any alternative but to warn the demonstrators to disperse and then open fire. In a case like that it's a matter of discretion and that can always be interpreted in different ways. Six people were killed and some fifteen injured. Two policemen were killed too and a number hurt, but the public never takes any notice of that. It just gets emotional about a firing, keeps raising the question of whether it was justified or not. In this case it was. The police were at the mercy of a stone-throwing mob. Part of the building was damaged too."

Instructions, Dubey knew, were to use the minimum force. But it was anybody's guess what that was. Did you start firing when the mob was twenty feet away or ten feet away—or just wait for it to reduce everything to rubble?

"Is anything being done about it?" Dubey asked, referring to the case.

"There isn't much to be done," said Prasad. "The facts were published long ago. It's always the same pattern. There's a demonstration of some kind. Violence comes into the picture, stone-throwing or burning whatever is at hand.

The police have to be called in and if they can't scatter the crowd or quieten it they have to use force. Then they get called names, the Government's image suffers and an enquiry commission is appointed. Everybody knows exactly what happened, so why legal preliminaries have to put it into more elaborate language I don't know. But they do. And for some reason a sop has to be provided for the ones who started the trouble in the first place. It never does to condemn anyone outright, apparently. A scapegoat has to be found for bad behavior. Like your great-grandmother, dead these hundred years, being held responsible for your strangling your neighbour."

"I don't know much about the psychological angle," said Dubey, "but I think our great-grandmother does have a formidable influence on what we do. In a number of ways she's still alive. Sometimes I think it will need a tearing up by the roots to get her out of the way."

"What kind of tearing up?" Prasad demanded. "If you mean a dictatorship, we don't like dictators. We have such a horror of them that every man in the street becomes a little dictator, a regular hell-raiser, to make sure no one becomes a big dictator. I can't understand it when people talk of a revolution taking place in this country. Who would think of joining anyone else's revolution? Everyone's too busy with his own little upheaval. We're a nation of leaders, I tell you."

"I didn't mean dictators," said Dubey. "I meant fresh air."

"I wouldn't mind getting out of all this for a while," said Prasad.

It was the turn that conversation often took, thought Dubey, ending in a blank wall. No one was enthused about anything. People functioned without spirit. Yet somewhere in that cynical indifference there must be a spark, if only there were the concern—and the time—to ignite it.

"What about the accusation of money against this policeman?" Dubey asked.

"That's more complicated," Prasad admitted. "If one starts on that it's hard to know where to draw the line. There's money changing hands all down the line. Your peon makes his from the men waiting to see you. The upper crust responds to a different kind of bait. A man joins an American firm so that his son can be educated abroad and land a good job there afterwards. Who can blame him? Well, anything else? I'd better get back."

"It's a pity you are leaving," said Dubey. "It takes time to fill a gap like this."

Prasad shrugged. "I know, but there's no scope here. I want to get back to Delhi."

Dubey thought of this knowledge of the provinces, this experience and grasp from all over the country converging on Delhi and being dissipated at cocktail parties and official receptions. Prasad's undoubted ability would resolve itself into clever dinner conversation and later into the standard sophistication of a diplomatic assignment. It would never go back to the environment that needed it. And Dubey was still worried about the policeman, a man with charges against him, who would not be an asset if there were trouble in the city. He sent a message to Harpal asking to see him and was told to come in. There was a row of men waiting on the bench outside his own office. The one at the far end held his attention. Hair oiled flat, abnormally large liquid eyes, a dark face composed into an obsequious respectfulness, it was the kind of face one often saw in government offices. Dubey wondered what his normal expression was, deciding that he beat his wife, pampered his children, and made money without too many scruples. He was probably a pillar of local society and would die respected

by his community. He opened the door to the Chief Minister's office and found Harpal pushing his chair back, sig-
nifying dismissal to the P.A. who had been taking dictation.

"I'm sorry," he apologized to Dubey. "I hadn't noticed
the time when I asked you to come in. I'm already late for
an appointment. Is it important?"

"It's about a policeman against whom there is a complaint in the file."

"Yes. Prasad knows the case."

"I've just spoken to Prasad. He's inclined to let it alone
but I'm not sure we should."

"All right," said Harpal absently. "We'll look into it."

Dubey went back and stood at the window of his office.
People were leaving the Secretariat. He could see them
departing on bicycles, and felt an emptiness expanding
through the building. The evening was going to be rich
and plum-coloured. On the hill range to the left of the
Secretariat a streak of snow, known locally as silver
bangles, glistened on a conical peak. He looked at the
wealth of countryside spread out before him. His time had
been wasted. He had not begun to do the things he wanted
to do, not even walked around the lake.

There were files on his desk but none of them answered
the question in his mind. No one seemed to have taken note
of the real problem and it was there, glaring at them. The
newspapers had been asked not to build up an aura of crisis.
But build-up or not, the crisis was there, reflected in the
go-slow policies of the factories and the mood of labour.
He recalled the audience at Pinjore. That intangible—the
vibrations of a crowd—highlighted his uneasiness more
than any single fact. Of all the impressions he had gathered
it was the most vivid, and probably the only one that
would not go in the files, where only facts and figures
would be enumerated. The problem was not even that

there was a crisis, but that people now took it for granted.

He had spent most of the afternoon automatically coping with the business on his desk. He had lighted too many cigarettes and stubbed them out half smoked, drunk too much coffee, and written a wordy note that did not satisfy him. He looked at the ashtray and decided it was a long time since he had been so immoderate. But then deciding to marry in a fever of impatience was probably the only immoderate thing he had done.

He remembered Leela distinctly as she had looked the day he had met her, not what she wore, but the expression on her face. She had been standing in front of somebody's drawing-room fire, radiating health and vivacity, capturing and holding a mood of bubbling gaiety. Everyone in the room had been young, but all the sparkle and essence of youth seemed to be concentrated in her. He had wanted the woman and won her, and forever afterwards had tried to reach the person in her, the one to talk to when the day's work was done, the friend with whom one could be naked in spirit and to whom one could give the whole of oneself. The whole self was not heroic. Most of it was ordinary. It was soiled in part, maimed in part. It had lived, and all the signs and scars of living were upon it. But it was all one had to give. Leela had not been interested. She had selected what she wanted of him: the distinguished escort at parties, the successful civil servant with a promising future, the husband who could be relied upon to take pains with whatever problems she took to him. And she had ignored the rest. She had given herself selectively too, what she had considered it prudent and convenient to give, and left him empty of the reality of herself. Even her vitality had needed an audience. She scintillated in company. Time and again he heard her talk animatedly of what had happened a day or a week earlier, of an article she had read, an idea she had had, at a party. Alone with him she had little to share. Had their failure been their fault, or was there something at the very core of human dreams and longings that was fatal to fulfilment through marriage?

What she rejected of him grew to rebellious proportion, a life within a life, a citadel of thought and emotion with an energy of its own. She had grown to resent its invisible presence, for though it took nothing away from her, it did not belong to her. Through the growing gulf between them the one thing he had never considered was infidelity. He had made a mistake when he married her, but he had wronged her too. He knew he would not further injure her if he could help it. Forget it, Dubey told himself, it's over now. But he stood, restless and incomplete, near the window and he knew that nothing was over till one had understood it.

He picked up his phone and asked his P.A. to find out if the Punjab Chief Minister was back in town. The answer came back, "He's in town but not in his office today." It was becoming a problem to catch up with Gyan Singh, whom he had met once by chance in the corridors of the Secretariat but who had evaded him since. Now he was not in his office and not out of town. Dubey decided to go to his house without making an appointment. Enquiry at his house revealed he was at the cable plant. Dubey wondered what he was doing there at this hour. There was no car at the entrance as he drove up to it but there was a light on inside the building. He tried the front door. It was unlocked and he went in. The big man walking through an airy room that seemed to house more space than machinery did not look surprised at his entry. Dubey guessed not many situations took Gyan Singh unawares.

"What brings you here, Mr. Dubey?"

"I went to look for you at your house. They directed me

here."

"You are familiar with a cable-wire plant?"

"I can't say I am."

"I will take you round."

Gyan led the way. "I built this twelve years ago. I had an American firm as collaborator."

"This is your own factory," Dubey said in discovery.

"I was Industries Minister then. This is one of the few automated factories in the state. Fifty workers on three shifts. It is a model here."

"I can see that."

"You have seen some of the factories here?"

"No, but I can see there is pride and perfection here. People put up buildings for different reasons. You built this as a signature."

Gyan studied him thoughtfully and nodded.

"I am not a builder," he went on. "I wanted to put up only one building. For most men it would have been a house to live in. For me it was a factory. I released these plots in this area so that the work could get started. The industrial revival of this region was largely my doing."

It was not arrogance. It was the plain truth. He talked to Dubey about the problems of production and the factory's annual turnover of a *crore*. It wasn't much. And it was not indispensable to the economy. But it had been the first of its kind. The recital of these facts seemed in some way a statement of Gyan's life. He took a key from the pocket of his kurta as the tour ended and unlocked the door to a small office. It was warm, neat, and overfurnished.

"Where is your home?" he asked.

"Lucknow," said Dubey.

Gyan took a tin of Nescafé from a wall cabinet, milk, sugar, and china mugs, and plugged in an electric kettle. He sat down in the revolving leather chair behind the desk and motioned Dubey to the one opposite.

"You wanted to see me."

The invitation to talk was abrupt. Dubey discarded the half dozen openings he had planned and said, "I have been trying very hard to see you since I arrived, Sardar Sahib, but without much success."

"Yet no one would say I am hard to see."

Gyan indicated his extravagant size and rumbled into laughter at his own joke. Dubey found himself joining in the hilarity. It produced an instant amity, which he felt would be as instantly dispelled by a change of mood. For no apparent reason the word unreliable crossed his mind.

"I have been to Lucknow," said Gyan, sobering with an effort. "People do not laugh much there, not what we call laughter. We laugh from our stomachs and our guts. We do everything like that."

Dubey understood that Gyan had fully explained his stand.

"What did you want to see me about?" he asked once more, but as if it no longer mattered.

He got up to make the coffee and handed Dubey a cup. Dubey, marshalling his thoughts, was interrupted again.

"In Lucknow it takes as long to say '*adab*' as it takes us here to roll up our sleeves and build a factory."

Hugely enjoying his own joke, Gyan bellowed his laughter and again Dubey was carried along with it. He felt the crude, elemental attraction of the man, a human being uncomplicated in his functioning, one who would come to immediate grips with a situation and manipulate it to suit himself. He would not even recognize the power of a bargain. Not, Dubey thought, an unscrupulous man, for that would imply he saw scruples and ignored them. Gyan trod a path that involved no inner struggle. A careless Atlas carrying the world like a bundle that he would not think twice about dumping if he felt like it. Gyan subsided, wiping his eyes with the sleeve of his kurta.

"You do not mind my joking at your expense?"

"Not at all. It is interesting what makes people laugh. Some things always make a butt for jokes, like deafness, while blindness, on the other hand, is not a joke, but a tragedy."

"Who said so? Blindness is also a joke," said Gyan. "There was a woman who could hardly see an inch beyond her nose. But she wished to impress her lover with her eyesight. So one day she placed a needle in the grass about twenty yards from her, and when he came she said, 'Look at that needle lying there in the grass.' She ran to pick it up and on the way she stumbled over an ox."

Gyan's huge frame was convulsed with laughter again and Dubey bent double helplessly.

Gyan sighed and said, "Yes, Mr. Dubey. That is what happened. And now we should be going. But, what was it you wanted to see me about?"

Dubey picked up his coffee. "About that ox."

A smile played around Gyan's mobile mouth but it did not reach his eyes. The interview had begun.

"This threat of strike is an ox we should avoid stumbling over. Already the go-slow policies have cost two states dear," said Dubey.

"The strike is a lawful measure."

"Perhaps it is too late to talk of legalities, when there is so much at stake."

"You are right. It is too late to talk at all. It is time for action."

Gyan spread both huge hands on the table before him. What a country, thought Dubey. Either we sit paralyzed waiting for heaven to send us a sign, or we charge like bulls into the ring and call it action. He had so little respect for either attitude that he wondered at times what held him to this game. But it was, he knew, what held him to anything, a feeling stronger than loyalty for a concept larger than country. He supposed it could be called love for the very act of living.

"It will be a peaceful demonstration, after all, to back up a popular demand," Gyan was saying himself. Dubey was conscious of having said very little, yet of having measured the man before him. What Dubey or anyone else now said to him would not matter. Gyan had stepped onto the heights below which lay a kingdom. From that dazzling spectacle no one would be able to lure him. A sense of imminent peril gripped Dubey. It was Delhi, not Gyan, that needed warning if India were to stay whole.

Gyan had got up, no longer communicative, to put away the kettle. Dubey stood up, too, wondering how he was going to tell the Home Minister that the threatened strike might be in the nature of a colossal joke and nothing would deflect the man who had made up his mind to play it.

It was not only the tone of political life that had changed, thought Dubey on his way back. The ICS had changed too, imperceptibly, but it had changed. What it had little of now was men like Trivedi, to whom the Service had been principally, incredibly, a service. Those had been men whose resources had deepened and versatility widened in the solitude of district postings. Administrators had given birth all over the land to poets and painters, collectors of rare plants, and students of local history. If they had not been especially gifted they had still learned to cultivate and enjoy their leisure. Delhi had downgraded leisure. It was worse than unsought. It was not done. And retirement had become a nightmare. Few men wanted to face themselves stripped of office and rank. For too long these had substituted for their essential selves.

The old crop of the Civil Service, thrown into it for a variety of reasons—prestige, background, academic brilliance—had discovered their country through it. Learning to administer it they had walked in the hot sun, swallowed the dust and sand of miles of countryside, and come to grips with problems they would not have known existed. There was a conflict in the most sensitive of them, the deep roots of an overwhelming inheritance clashing with the job they did, administering their own soil for foreign masters. Trivedi had been an example of it, British-trained yet painfully involved with his own culture.

Dubey remembered him vividly. He had been Commissioner of the district at the time of Dubey's own first posting when, fresh from Oxford, he had arrived in the drought-stricken landscape of Uttar Pradesh's most impoverished corner. Trivedi's conflict ripened over a drink in the evenings after sundown, and unfolded over more drinking long after dinner as evening lengthened into night. Dubey recalled himself at the time, too lean for his height, hair easily dishevelled, and with an air of earnestness that never succeeded in shadowing his enthusiasm. He enjoyed the evenings at Trivedi's house. Not because there was hardly anywhere else to go, but because he respected his host and felt oddly gentle towards him. It may have had something to do with the fact that Trivedi's wife and daughters were uncommunicative at meals and left immediately after dinner to go to their rooms. There was no feeling of family in the house. Trivedi seemed to live alone.

"A drink for you, Dubey?"

Dubey, in his early twenties, groggy with sleep, yet unwilling to leave, did not notice that his chief had poured him one, ignoring his refusal.

"As I was saying, then, this heritage of ours is all up in

the air. The most ancient tradition known to man has been dependent these many thousand years on a sheeplike adherence to ritual. Dependent on pots and pans, if you like, on what we eat, when we fast and how often we bathe. And if it can be called worship at all, it is a worship of subtleties and abstractions. What actually are we commanded to *believe*?"

"Sort of like the British constitution—unwritten," murmured Dubey comfortably, not sure he would be heard. In a talkative mood Trivedi did not generally register what Dubey said. He became fascinated by his own theme, winding in and out of it, revealing glimpses of erudition, flashes of anger and suspicion, until at last he noticed the time and called the evening to a close. But this time he had heard.

"The British," he said heavily, grudgingly, "are the only people on earth who could sustain an unwritten constitution. Any other people would have served each other's entrails up for breakfast and dissolved into miserable confusion by this time."

He brooded on his love-hate for the British in silence before he spoke again.

"But this lack of definition doesn't suit us. Doesn't suit us at all."

He was apt to get repetitive as the evening wore on.

"I am not, understand me, Dubey, trying to circumscribe God."

"No sir."

"What I want is much simpler. I want to understand this 'dharma' of which I and my kind—you, too, Dubey—are the guardians. What is the meaning of Brahmin? Yes I know: priest, law-giver, adviser to sovereigns, custodian of the intellectual and spiritual heritage of the race. It's all there in the books. But how do you and I represent that image today? By joining the Civil Service? Where is the evidence *now* that those scriptures can inspire a people to *live*?"

A cluster of insects buzzed around the standard lamp and Trivedi studied his assistant sombrely.

"Why did you join the Service, sir?" Dubey asked.

"Because," he said, suddenly amiable, "my grandfather was a good friend of Sir Norman Trace. That's why most of us do things. Not because the light beckons. Why did you?"

"I tried for it because the family wanted me to, never thinking I'd get in. It was a fluke, I expect."

Trivedi gave the high-pitched chuckle that served him for a laugh. "As I was saying," he stopped to refill his glass and looked with regret at the level of the bottle as he held it up to the light, "you and I and our Brahmin ilk are the custodians of something we haven't a notion about. 'We worship not what we can but what we cannot understand.' I came across that in a book. Forget which book. It's all there in the books—the world's oldest. You are looking very sleepy, Dubey."

"No sir, I'm not," said Dubey stoutly.

He was struggling with the overpowering urge to let his drooping eyelids close, to lean back in the cane chair and sink into a few minutes' delicious unnoticed sleep. But he did not want to leave Trivedi. If the first ten minutes could be mastered he could stay awake and last another hour. He wanted to last for the sake of a man he liked and one whom he knew would face the defeat of an empty bedroom when he left. By day they tackled a desert of thirst and poverty. There was even a therapeutic quality to these nights they spent together. In the solitude of the district Trivedi had only him to turn to, while Dubey had the whole district, every bit of red dust in it. It had become his passport to a new kind of living. He had discovered to his astonishment that he would never be alone, that his home would be wherever he chose to make it. Trivedi was not like that and his loneliness was Dubey's responsibility, as his conversation and his keen, critical mind were Dubey's pleasure. And what he said was right. What use was this heritage to ordinary men? What did it create but quietude? Did it toughen fibre, give emotional satisfaction? Did it help the soldier to fight better, the businessman to do his job better? Did it hold any comfort for Trivedi in the night? Was it the thing you could cry out to, kneel to, surrender your spirit to? Was there some Intelligence to receive all that, or did the human cry fall unheard into a gaping void? Dubey sat up with an effort and took a cautious sip from the full glass before him.

"Of all the books, only the Gita tells us something specific, something besides ritual. Have you read the Gita, Dubey? And the fact that I have to ask that question goes a long way to illustrate what I have been talking about."

"Not cover to cover, sir, but passages."

"Well, do you know why Arjun fought and the Lord himself advised him to?"

"He did his duty," said Dubey.

"He fought because it would have been cowardly not to," said Trivedi, ignoring him. "Because you recoil from bloodshed is not sufficient reason not to fight. The pacifists after the First World War made the mistake of using that as an argument. They pointed out the horrors of war and said, 'Look what it does. Doesn't it revolt your soul?' And it did, but not enough to prevent people fighting another, as they had to, when it came upon them. The pacifists were appealing to cowardice, to revulsion from an ugly sight. It wasn't good enough. Men cannot commit themselves to any course of action based on cowardice. They have to act on some principle. They have to go forward. And that always has its dangers. Arjun had to go forward into battle."

The ice in Dubey's drink had melted. He fished out an insect with his finger and placed it carefully on the edge of the cane table. It staggered drunkenly, then shook its wings and flew away.

"But even the Gita does not *explain*," Trivedi went on. "It *assumes*. It assumes a caste system as the natural order of things. Even Arjun is not quite free to choose. When he faces his kinsfolk in war he is facing the total result of his past actions. But where the Gita triumphs, Dubey, is in its interpretation of the *nature* of action."

"I know those lines," said Dubey, and to his own surprise recited them flawlessly.

"Nonattachment," Trivedi summed up the Sanskrit verses, "duty unallied to reward. A job to be done. I suppose that's why I joined the Civil Service, apart from my grandfather and Sir Norman Trace."

It was one of the ways he explained it to Dubey, trying to understand his role in a political system his soul did not accept in the still of night, as he sat on a patch of exhausted earth in a tortured corner of his country. His blood tugged him earthwards while his mind looked for a solution that would contain all the contradictions. Dubey's affection for him was boundless.

"The Gita is occupied more with ethics than morality. I suppose that is what makes it so sensible." Trivedi, tired now, looked at his young companion, "What are your views, Dubey?"

"On ethics, sir, or morality?"

"Whichever you like." With a grand gesture Trivedi flung open the field to him in the middle of the night.

"I have very definite views about morality," Dubey said, wide awake now to the full throbbing impact of a favourite subject. "I don't accept what's commonly understood as morality."

"Indeed? You believe in free love and all that sort of thing."

Dubey laughed delightedly and took a great gulp of his drink.

"It's nothing to do with that at all. I don't—that is, I've decided not to accept the established ideas about morality, not to be bound hand and foot. I—for me—well, I've thought about it a bit, a good bit, and I've come to the conclusion there's a higher morality than all that. In fact, that's what I call it, the Higher Morality."

"The Higher Morality? So we have an original thinker among us. Well, what's this Higher Morality all about? The wail of conscience in new garb?"

"It's more than that." Dubey sat forward eagerly. "It's a search for value, and an attempt to choose the better value, the real value, in any situation, and not just do what's done or what is expected."

Trivedi sat silent, thinking it over.

"The search for value is a dangerous formula for living," he said dryly. "Well, well, Dubey. If you hadn't got into the ICS by fluke, as you put it, what might you not have been, the prophet of a new order?"

"Nothing of the sort, sir. I just like living and you have to live by some rules. Why should they be somebody else's?"

"Why indeed? History is full of those who didn't live by anybody else's rules—and of what happened to them. I suppose you do read history?"

"Oh yes," said Dubey.

"Then you have been forewarned."

Trivedi got out of his chair suddenly. "It's late. I never know the time when you're here. What do *you* get out of it, Dubey?" he asked abruptly.

Dubey gave the simple, obvious answer, "Your company."

Trivedi would have called it blatant hypocrisy if anyone else had said it, any bright-eyed youngster wanting to get on. But he knew it was true. He walked down the verandah steps to the gate with his guest.

"Well I'm sorry it's so late. But tomorrow is Sunday. Or do you get up early on Sundays too?"

There were half a dozen early-morning activities open to the elite even here, riding on an Army horse, a swim at the Club, or a game of tennis before the sun became too hot, or the time-honoured constitutional, all in the tradition of gentlemen.

"I'm having breakfast with my clerk tomorrow," said Dubey.

"You are doing what?"

"Breakfasting with Ramaswamy. He's from Madras, landed up here in a job hundreds of miles from his origins—and his wife, he tells me, makes the most marvellous *idlis*."

"You are addicted to *idlis*?"

"No," grinned Dubey, "but he's a nice chap. He has a lovely smile, perfect white teeth in his dark face. He's very articulate too, an M.A. in English."

In the dim wash of light from the verandah Trivedi, a small, dignified figure, stood studying his young assistant with the gravity he would accord a crisis.

"I am not concerned with snobbery, Dubey, but I am with the fitness of things."

"Or with an assumption of caste as the natural order of things," said Dubey wickedly.

Trivedi chuckled.

"Will it make any difference if I suggest you forgo the

idlis?"

"No sir."

"Well, goodnight then and enjoy yourself."

He need not have added that. The boy enjoyed every waking moment. Trivedi had watched other young men. This one had an elegance, if that word could apply to character and a pattern of living tailored to fine sensitivity.

Walking home, Dubey took a deep breath. The air was stale and tepid, like dense liquid that had stood still, unstirred, for too long. Tomorrow the fiery sun would rise on a countryside shimmering in heat, making the eyes clash painfully with every object they encountered. It would blaze over parched miles where not a drop of water had fallen for the many weeks of an overdue monsoon, where grain had withered on the stalk, and hope festered in the breast. Tomorrow the people would pant, swollen-tongued, looking for water, and he would continue investigating their agony and the reasons for it. He was wrapped up in it all as he worked on his report on the drought and the measures that must be taken to deal with it. What do *you* get out of it, Dubey? Trivedi had asked him. It—and everything else—might as well be left alone, the grain to wither, hope to die, unless you became part of the whole sorry mess and were driven to tackle it—not because it was your job and you were paid for it, but because it was yours, as everything you touched with tenderness became yours, even the maggots and sores and the shrunken dreams and anguished cries.

Chapter 6

Through the uncurtained window Saroj could see a single pale star glimmering above the dark cluster of trees, ineffably peaceful and remote from the wet steamy warmth of the bathroom and a child wailing because the hot water in the bucket was finished. She rubbed Bunny dry, dressed him in his night pajamas and dressing gown and sent him downstairs where Muff had started his dinner. The phone rang and she counted the rings as she went down herself, wondering if it would be Inder or Vishal. Vishal had called twice at this time to invite her for a walk, knowing she was usually alone in the evenings. It was Inder and he said he would be late. Saroj glanced across the room at her sons eating, rolled down the sleeves of her cardigan, and told Sham she was going for a walk. Outside she took a deep draught of air, filled with a sudden joy and recuperation at being part of the cold clean world again. What fragment of it should she make her own this evening? She wanted it all, the hazy purple hills, the violet light on the lake, the forest where nude branches etched a delicate tracery against the winter sky. But it was too late to walk alone in the woods and she went to the lake boulevard instead.

The geese had flown at sunset honking their lament. There were only a few late strollers left on the embankment. The hills beyond were lost in the gathering darkness and the massive shapes of the High Court and the Legislature were barely discernible. This evening the water, straddled by concrete wall and on its far side by the uneven curve of wood and field, resembled the rough grey granite of Chandigarh's public buildings. Saroj was familiar with its moods. At sundown it could recall illumined copper beaten into ripples and ridges, or reveal a satin glow in the later evening light. And on occasion it could return one to the secret fluid area within oneself. She could get lost then in her imaginings. But now it looked sullen and inscrutable under a rumbling, overcast sky. She lifted her face to a spatter of raindrops as Dubey came striding towards her up the embankment. He waved and called out, "You're getting wet. Come along to the guest house. I'll drive you home."

"But I like the rain," she protested.

He took her arm and piloted her towards the guest house.

"You're walking too fast for me."

He slowed his pace. "Sorry, I keep forgetting."

"Do you have any children, Vishal?"

"No. What is it like having one?"

"Just now it's a flutter and later it's a kick—and then it's a child," she finished in surprise.

They laughed into each other's faces and the rain stopped as suddenly as it had started.

"That was a warning. It's going to pour. All right, let's get to the guest house quickly."

"No, let's walk a bit first," she begged. "I've been in the house all day and it's such a relief to be out."

"Not tiring?"

"Sitting and standing are tiring. What I like best is being on all fours. That's lovely and relaxing. But Sham would wonder what had happened if I went around the house like that."

"Do all women like going around on all fours at this time? One doesn't hear of that sort of thing," Dubey admitted.

"All women don't know about it. They should. It would be so much more comfortable. I don't think it should be thought odd if all the expectant mothers at a party crawled around the room instead of standing around. Though of course it would make things awkward for the host, bending down to chat with them."

"Or one could hold the party at a lower level so to speak," suggested Dubey, "with the eats on the floor. Or if that didn't work out, then one could invite all the pregnant women one knew to the same gathering, and have the unpregnant ones another day."

Bands of phosphorescent light under their cement concrete shades glowed at spaced intervals along the grass. The wind blew a crumpled paper before them. Thunder hung in the air like an uneasy tremor, as if the sky vibrated above them, and narrow ribbons of lightning came and went.

"Saroj, you shouldn't come here by yourself so late in the evening. I'm not talking about the weather."

"I know. One hates to admit one doesn't feel safe along one's own streets in one's own town. It's so improbable. How has it happened?"

"I suppose one doesn't notice the things that happen gradually. We seem to have slipped into a kind of decay. One big upheaval might have had some meaning. But this noiseless chaos, like the ground dissolving as you walk on it, is uncanny. The funeral march of Hinduism."

"What does it have to do with Hinduism?"

"Most of us are Hindus. History will say, these were a people who couldn't survive modern times. The modern world was too much for them. They never came to terms with it. They just went to pieces. They could have lived if they had had the courage."

"The courage to do what?" asked Saroj.

"To change. To do what hasn't been done before. To hold up what we call sacred to the light and examine it, and to throw it away if necessary. There's something in us that won't face up to an issue. No other people are like that."

It was alarming in his view. Cultures met and blended, and gained or lost something in the process, emerging a little different all the time. But it hadn't happened here. A monolithic slab of antiquity had survived the ages. A way of life, wrongly called a religion, lay embedded in it. Against it the intellect foundered and the emotions were reduced to insignificance. And somewhere beneath it a great vitality lay untapped, waiting to be excavated by the living, if the living cared enough.

"There's another kind of courage," said Saroj. "Not throwing things away, but holding on. Grasping the next moment and the next. It's like clinging to a precipice, to all the dangerous places, by every hand and foothold, and never giving up. Maybe we have that kind."

She had given him, without meaning to, a glimpse into her life. He was strangely stirred by the striving of it. They walked to the end of the embankment where an iron crane rose like a symbol of revolution, marking the end of the concrete walk. The texture of the ground beneath their feet changed from smooth cement to rough pebbles.

"Is this where civilization ends and the woods begin?"

asked Dubey.

"Nothing so dark and dramatic as that," said Saroj, "only open fields and then the hills. This is smiling country. Even the woods on the other side of the lake are friendly."

A temple on a low invisible mound made a lone prick of light in the starless void.

"Have you been there? It's the Chandi Mandir this city was named for."

"No. Let's go one of these days," he said. "It must be years since I have been near a temple and I don't think I have ever worshipped in one."

"Nor have I," she said.

"What does that make us?"

"It makes us belong to the oldest religion on earth."

"But not very religious ourselves."

"But we are the most religious of all people," said Saroj.

"You and me?" he smiled into the darkness.

"All of us. This land. Everyone in it. There's sunlight and honey here for faith of any kind. Oh, we misuse it but it's there. And it's our strength."

He took her arm and turned her back the way they had come. She had everything in her to companion him. The things she said and the simple confidence with which she said them woke forgotten yearnings in him. He felt alive and growing again. Suddenly he became aware of the contour of her arm in his hand. He let it go and his hand hung empty and deprived at his side. But he knew that though he might not have the curve of her arm, here within his reach was the rest of her, the shine and shadow of an entire person—his, if he had the grace to understand her. Saroj sensed his change of mood and they slipped into an easy silence.

There were men whose job in life it was to deal with

paintings, with rare manuscripts or precious stones, whose eye and ear were trained to recognize the unmistakable quality of a work, the note of truth that set it apart from others of its kind. For Dubey excitement lay in human quality, in the search for the endless, delicate patterns between human beings—and beyond it to the buried dream, the persistence, however frail, that drove a person all his life, against all obstacles, towards fulfilment. He wanted more than anything now to understand Saroj. At the guest house when she told him she would go straight home, he said, "I'll drive you but come in for a few minutes first."

Without warning a sheet of rain fell from the sky and Saroj, smelling of wet wool, her hair pasted against her head, the ends dripping, her eyes shining, came in. There were logs in the grate. He put a match to them, made her comfortable near the fire, and went upstairs to fetch a bottle of whiskey. She had taken off her cardigan when he came down. The atmosphere about her was calm and she looked the eternal woman as she sat, serene and pregnant, in the firelight. But her intelligence, as she looked at him, was of this moment and not of all eternity. It was such a contrast from the masked faces of most women, those fugitives from thought and expression who pandered to the cult of the mysterious. For as long as he could remember he had rebelled against it. Enigmas did not fascinate him. Too often they were empty containers. Much that went wrong between men and women, between people, lay in what they withheld from one another. What fascinated him was the light, however harsh, and all that could thrive and grow in it. He sat down opposite her feeling receptive, wanting to know her better, but Saroj was quiet, her cheeks taking colour from the fire, both hands holding a glass of garish orange squash steady on the arm of her chair. He wondered if the walk had tired her after all, and if she wanted a cushion behind her. He felt vastly ignorant of the physical process in which she was so caught up and unwilling to be left out of it.

"I hope the walk hasn't tired you."

"It hasn't at all. I was just thinking there's no real rest except with someone of whom one isn't afraid."

He knew what she meant.

She went on, "Half the time one is afraid, you know—of saying the wrong thing or of being misunderstood—just of being oneself and being punished for it. So one spends such a lot of time acting, or at least hiding, and that's very tiring."

There was more than excitement in it now. There was a road he had to travel with her. Dubey considered how to say what he had to say without making it sound too personal or sudden.

"I hope you will never feel tired with me."

"I don't."

"But there's only one way to be sure of that," he said, "and that is to decide there will be no acting, or hiding, between us. Do you think you could bear that?"

"Bear it? What a funny way of putting it." She sipped her orange squash, then said, "It sounds like a formula."

Dubey made himself a drink. "Why shouldn't it? When a thing is manufactured, the makers have to use ingredients in various proportions. They don't just throw them together and hope for the best. I wonder why people think decent human relations just happen by luck or by chance."

"Well, how *do* they happen?"

"With care. With love, when possible, and otherwise with time and interest. And always with truth, or as much of it as the other person will allow. All of that reduces the heartbreak and a lot of the loneliness of living. But it is damnably hard to do."

A change had come over his features, giving them a granitelike severity. He said almost angrily, "I am tired of the drama of unsaid things."

Saroj looked away from him into the fire and she saw an immensity of space and light, the dazzling dimensions of a world without pain. She thought, it was strange of him to say he had never worshipped in a temple. He had, she felt, worshipped in temples that other men did not know existed. And he would be a fanatic about what he worshipped. When she glanced up he was looking at her with a harsh urgency, the way a man looked when he took what he wanted of a woman, a kiss, or more. Only she knew Vishal did not want a kiss, and the "more" he desired was not the flesh of her. He wanted the bone and sinew of truth between them, the vital ingredient of his grand design, and from her nothing else would satisfy him. The distance between them seemed to press against her and she felt jolted into an awareness of every detail of the room. She thought, I've been in this room before, only I never knew exactly what it was like, this chair here, that picture there. Its shape and size leapt vividly to her new perception. There must be an entire world I've lived in and never really seen, she thought with a shock.

"Where have you been?" he asked gently, his face relaxed again.

"Everyone can't live like that," she said slowly. "Most of the time there's no other way but to pretend and hide. Your kind of world isn't possible."

"I know we have to hide at times, but there's no dignity in that kind of living and we know it even while we do it. I'm only asking that we do not do it with each other."

She sat very quiet.

"Try it," he urged. "Let there be one person with whom you need never be afraid to say and be what you like, and it may become a touchstone for living."

"All right, Vishal." It sounded like a pledge as she said it.

"And don't look so scared," he smiled. "The nicest part of this bargain is that you can dispense with it, and with me, whenever you want. Now if you've finished that horrible-looking drink I think I should take you home."

Inder looked up from the dining table as she entered and she felt a pang of guilt at being late.

"Where have you been?"

"I went for a walk with Vishal."

"In this rain?"

"And then for a drink at the guest house. We just escaped the rain. Sorry I'm late."

She was a schoolgirl again, apologizing for shortcomings of which she was suddenly conscious. Sham brought her dinner. We must talk, but what about, she wondered nervously. Which, after all these years, were the safe, unguarded topics between them, those without consequences? She searched her mind for a neutral subject that would keep the ground level between them.

"I've had one hell of a day," said Inder.

She was quick and eager with her sympathy.

"D'you think your workers are going to strike?"

"It's a peculiar situation," said Inder. "We've had no strike notice. Officially there's going to be no strike, so there's nothing definite to deal with. I don't know what to do about it. There's bound to be some kind of holdup. When Gyan's got everyone dressed up for his act, do you think they're going to be cheated of their performance? What did Vishal have to say about it?"

"We didn't talk about it."

Inder looked up from his plate. "How did you avoid it? No one seems able to talk about anything else."

She felt the precarious emotional balance between them rock and tilt, and the familiar, unaccountable tightening within her. He had finished eating and had lit a cigarette, waving out the match.

"Well, what *did* you talk about?"

She rummaged anxiously for the right words. "About people being able to talk to each other frankly, and life being easier because of it."

"A cure for the world's ills," he said, and laughed good-naturedly.

The emotional balance righted itself. She breathed easily again and went on eating, not sure what current had charged an ordinary remark and why for an instant she had felt so suffocated. She responded to his laughter and impulsively stretched her hand to his. It felt warm and strong. Are all the warmth and strength of a man contained in his hands, she thought. Does desire begin and end with his body? For if that is so then this—my hand in his, what I can see, what I can hold—is the solid ground between us. On this I can walk safely and nothing will go wrong. On such ground men and women build shelters and bring children to birth and grow old in the comfort that they will live on in future generations. Perhaps the rest—the mist of longing for all that remains unanswered—lies outside this cycle. Saroj knew she could not tear away the blinds between herself and Inder or take him her thoughts. In the labour of living together there had never been that intimacy between them. Perhaps, she thought desolately, it was not meant to matter.

Upstairs she looked forward to stretching out on her bed with the blankets over her. The room in the soft glow of bedside lamps looked inviting, its familiarity welcome at the end of each day. She loved to return to it. She opened the window Sham had kept closed all evening against the cold. It had stopped raining. A thin young moon hung in the sky, unimaginable distances from her, and tears filled her eyes for all of life that would not be denied.

When Inder could not sleep he resurrected the other man, the one who had known Saroj before he had, making her marriage a mockery and a betrayal. He had stalked the man down the dark alleys of his imagination, his thoughts about him churning, now sticking, now moving sluggishly, now flowing on unimpeded, like the filth in the city's sewers. *If I catch him I shall kill him.* Inder had lived with the decision so long that meeting and killing him had become almost a social event, an episode that one day would be smoothly enacted. When they were introduced, Inder would kill him. The scene had long since been washed clean of savagery, even of emotion. There would be nothing crude or clumsy about it at all. Inder's hands would close round the man's neck with precision. He knew exactly where he would place them, his thumbs at the base of the throat, snuffing life out with one lightning gesture. The act had not always been so cleanly conceived. In his early imaginings Inder had thrown the man to the floor and pounded and mangled his face to purple pulp. The mutilation had been necessary, filling and fattening the scene to perfection in his brain, until at its crescendo he could sigh and fall asleep satiated, his hands still smarting from sensation. The scream that night came not from his victim but from Saroj in the next bed. Inder was shocked awake. He was lying face forward, one arm flung heavily across her throat and grasping her pillow on its far side. He sat up and switched on the lamp.

"What happened?" he asked tensely.

"I thought I was being strangled," she laughed shakily. "I was so frightened."

His dream flashed back to him. "Were you? But you

weren't frightened when you gave yourself to a stranger."

His voice, always the first sign of his transformation, chilled her. After an interminable pause she said, "I've told you all about it. He was a friend, not a stranger."

"A friend? To go to bed with? How many times did it happen?"

"I don't know. I can't remember—"

He was sitting hunched in bed, staring straight ahead of him at the shadows the lamp threw on the opposite wall. Look at me, she begged mutely, speak to me, touch me. Even in extremity she had never said, Forgive me. For each time she had lived through a night's torment, she could wake to the sunlight and find herself unsullied in it. There's nothing but you yourself between us, she wanted to cry out. But she could say none of it aloud any more. She could only grope and stumble her way through his transformation until it was left behind and she trod a familiar path again.

"How many times?" he repeated in the flat, taut monotone of illness.

"Four, five. It was so long ago. I'm not sure."

"You're not sure." The voice, remote and dangerous, unpredictable as a rawhide whip, flicked at her nerves. "But it's such a signal event in a girl's life surely. The first man. A woman never forgets her first man. The experience must have been a shock, a physical shock. Wasn't it a shock?"

A part of her mind prayed, God, God, God, God, God. She had learned that terror was not external catastrophe. It was the failure of reason.

"Answer me. Was it a shock?"

"I don't know. I think so. I don't remember." She tried to keep the stammer out of her voice.

"But you didn't protest."

"No—yes—I don't remember."

"And then, there must have been others."

"There were no others."

"No other who went that far. But there must have been others."

"There were not." She turned to him wildly, "It's finished. What do you want me to do about it *now*? *What do you want?*"

"You should be ashamed of what you did. Aren't you?"

"I'm not, I'm not."

Frenzied sobs she hardly recognized as her own dragged through her, until a gleam of sanity within spoke lovingly to herself as if to a child. The sobs were not her own. They were part of the self that surrendered to terms and conditions to make living with Inder possible. *She* was a being of pride and purity with a face uplifted to the stars. *She* could not cry like that. And though she fell asleep exhausted and woke dull as an invalid, the morning was new and she could welcome it. Besides, she had to limp back to normalcy before he did, be waiting there when he arrived, accept the absolution she did not want when, worn out himself, he would say in his normal tone, "It was not your fault after all. You were very young. You were led astray." She wanted to cry each time, "I don't want forgiveness. I've committed no crime." But she had stopped saying it. She yearned to penetrate his inflexibility. "Look at me! I am clean and whole and yours!" But she had forfeited the right to radiance the day she had told him of her first experience and been branded sinner. From that day only the part of her he could not see and would not touch walked upright. The rest stooped and shrank in supplication to the man, her husband, who stood between her and the light.

"This is destroying us." She would say it only in the intervals she thought of as their convalescence. "Can't we put it behind us? Must it go on all our lives?"

How far behind should they put it, Inder would demand. To the past when she had given herself? The past when she had told him of it? The past rose in dreadful images to taunt his manhood. Jealousy had caught him unprepared. It had no place in an order that clearly demarcated the roles of men and women, unless that venerable order were breached, trampled, and mocked. He was maddened by it. When it came over him he sat looking at Saroj with a revulsion that had ancient, tribal, male roots. It forced him to focus on her a concentration he would ordinarily have spread over the whole area of their lives. There were people he knew who would have flung her out with the rubbish, considered her used, soiled, and unfit for marriage. Somewhere he had read there were primitive societies that demanded the blood of virginity as evidence of female purity. No man need be cheated of that. He had been cheated. And it was he, not Saroj, who paid the penalty, who suffered the secret disgrace, sickened into silence and turned to stone. The foundation he had thought rock had turned out to be straw and beneath it the unknown yawned.

"But I told you about it, Inder, I told you about it."

She had. But the queer thing was he had not believed it possible. She, just out of college, the ink hardly dry on her fingers, history and literature fresh on her tongue? She with the childlike mouth and eyes that brightened in anticipation of a treat? She, so enchantingly innocent, with a man? From the depths of his experience he had been convinced she must have dreamt it to give herself importance. It was not till she became his wife that the abomination took life and shape and exploded like poison in his consciousness. Unamuno, the Catholic philosopher, had said, "If your wife has a pain in her left leg, you shall feel that same pain in your left leg." And if the woman you had married, thought Inder, had slept with another man, knives shall twist in your vitals. When the mood came upon him he retreated from the knives into a bleak landscape that barred entry. There she would be, somewhere outside it, stricken with panic at his unending silence, and he knew he was where she could not reach him. At times she would beat against his numbness like a bird against a window pane, trapped in a futile frenzy. He would watch her from a great distance, enfolded in greyness, speechless and deaf. And when at last he came out as though from long, crippling illness, it was to the sound of her frantic pleas and the sight of her tears. Then they would lie down and make sad, despairing love.

But tonight the unborn child lay between them. Through her convulsive crying Saroj felt it tighten into a hardness inside her. Poor Flutter, she soothed. Did I frighten you? I won't any more. And she fell into a tired sleep.

"Saroj," Inder called from the bathroom in the morning, "there's no toothpaste left. Saroj?"

She heard it through corridors of sleep, the voice on which her peace depended.

"There's some in the medicine cupboard," she said incoherently.

"There isn't."

When would she remember to replace what was finished? He stood, a towel wrapped round his waist, a frown gathering on his face, in the doorway. She found her slippers and shuffled towards him, looking like a little girl with a big tummy, eyes full of sleep, hair straight as rain over her shoulders. She fumbled in the medicine cupboard, dropping a roll of bandage and a cake of soap into the basin. He followed her, repairing the damage.

"Sorry I woke you," he said.

It was not all right yet, then. She could sense the constriction in him as if it were round her own wrist or throat.

"I tell you it isn't there. Get back to bed. You're not awake."

"But I thought I put a spare one there," she insisted.

"You thought. What did you think with?"

She giggled and the constriction snapped.

They prolonged their shared laughter in the comforting domesticity of the bathroom. She laid her cheek against his chest.

"If I depended on you for my blades I'd have a ten-foot beard by now," said Inder rumpling her hair.

"Soft, warm, long beard," she muttered.

She sleepwalked back to bed, the good warmth of contact washing over her, safe in the intimacy they had just inhabited, safe as long as she did not sleep outside it, as long as she did not by accident or design utter a word, evoke a memory, or conjure an image that would put her in jeopardy again.

Chapter 7

Mara had woken from her nap and drunk her tea in a state of depression. Was there anyone anywhere, she wondered, who did not feel let down at this hour of the day? It was only six-thirty now but dark as midnight, and there was a thick sprinkling of stars overhead. The hour before dawn, when prisoners were executed, was supposed to be as melancholy, but she had never been awake that early. Her own sad hour came in the evening, especially in winter, and especially if she were alone. If you were nearly thirty, you wondered at such times what had become of your life, why the man you had met at a party and married eight years earlier had not, after all, been your destination. There was some sense to child marriage, she thought, to two people growing up and old together, gradually becoming moulded to each other's needs. There was some sense, too, in marrying late in life—now for instance—when you had discovered what you were and what you valued. But marriage did not come at either of these sensible times. It came instead when you were young and desire was ripe and easy to confuse with the more complicated need called love, and above all before there had been time to realize what you wanted out of life. And so you married the wrong man because it was time to marry—the sweet-tempered, considerate Jit, the young girl's dream of a romantic lover—when your own needs were both simpler and more profound. And some time years later, the true need, if it had not by then been blurred by the paraphernalia of living, burst through. You stood face to face with it alone on a dark evening with no glimmering of how to cope with it, and only the burning knowledge that it was there and you were utterly submitted to it.

Whatever had become of the past, there was still something to be made of life—now. Her hands tightened on the cold balustrade and she checked herself. That was the kind of urgency with which she had married, the headlong slide towards attraction, the transfiguring flare that ended at worst in an ugly clash of temperaments, and at best—as for her—in the mere unwinding of day upon day. She wanted no part of such an avalanche now. She would wait.

On the road below her balcony she saw a car turn into the gate. Jit was away and Inder had not come since the evening of her party. She wondered who it could be. She tidied her hair and went down to the drawing room to find Inder brooding in one of the deep chairs. He did not get up when she came in. She disliked his manners, but she remembered that she had good manners at home and that they were no substitute for what she craved. She would keep her peace.

Inder came out of his fog and said, "D'you think I could have a drink?"

"Yes, of course. Help yourself."

She sat down on a low pouf near his chair, her hands

clasped round her knees.

Inder came back with his drink and took a swallow of it, his eyes closed.

"I've never seen anyone drink the way you do," said Mara, "as if your soul depended on it for its salvation. The moment you have a glass in your hand you've entered a sacred precinct where no one may follow."

"How do other people drink?"

"Other people," she reminisced. "In Europe eating and drinking go together. Wine is part of culture. It isn't a big performance all by itself. Here it's a performance, a measure of one's Westernization, or the amount of money one has—and since fortunes among us are rather recent, they don't always go with culture. So it becomes a question of how many bottles are poured into a party and how quickly one can knock back one's drink and get on to the next. And that makes some few people scintillate, and most others noisy and quarrelsome. But I've never seen it work as it does on you. You get so morose."

"Thanks," he said stiffly.

She smiled, refusing to pander to his mood.

"Did it always make you morose?"

"No, damn it all, it didn't," he said violently.

"I thought not. Well, what's the trouble now?"

"What trouble?" He was instantly on guard.

"You remind me of those iron bands that go round wooden crates."

"What the devil are you talking about?"

"You know, those iron bands," she said pleasantly. "Even if the crate arrives in splinters, the bands are sometimes still in place, though a bit battered. Anyway, that's what happened to ours. Where's Saroj?"

"She's probably out for a walk."

"Good Lord. Alone in the dark?"

He said reluctantly, "Dubey goes with her."

"I rather like him," said Mara.

"He's all right."

Every topic is a dead end today, she thought. It might be amusing if it were not for the fact that she longed to know him better. Last time he had come he had relaxed and talked, for the first time, about his work and the problems he was facing. Today they had to start from the beginning all over again.

"What has Saroj been indulging in," she said lightly, "extramarital talk?"

He slammed his glass down on the table with a violence that sloshed the liquid onto the carpet. A vein stood out in his temple.

"Don't say things like that."

The outburst astonished her.

"That kind of remark disgusts me. The thinking behind it disgusts me. There was a time when such things couldn't be spoken, or even thought, except with shame. There's no shame nowadays, no barriers. Everything is taken lightly. And women talk and behave like men."

"Perhaps they just behave more like human beings and less like possessions," said Mara mildly.

"I have no use for that jargon," said Inder bluntly.

He leaned back in his chair and said with a savage irritation, "Put it in whatever smart new language you like, it's a lot of bilge. A thousand years from now a woman will still want and need a master, the man who will own and command her—and that's the man she'll respect."

"Thou shalt have no other gods before me," said Mara softly. "Is that what it's all about?"

"Yes."

"Well at least you're honest enough to admit it. But how does that help you to understand Saroj?"

He made an impatient gesture. "She is my wife and I am her husband, and whatever understanding there is has to come out of that."

Or not at all, Mara wanted to add. She looked at him wonderingly. She's your wife all right and she has borne your children, but she is not your woman and you are not her man. She flies from you apparently in search of comfort you cannot give her, and you are drawn here to me, almost against your will, for some reason you don't even understand. So where does that leave us all, husbands and wives though we be? And do our neat labels protect us from our private torments? She offered him another drink.

"I have to get back." He got up, and remembering the courtesies for the first time said, "I'm sorry about the way I barge in—as if it were my own home."

"Perhaps it is."

"Don't," he said roughly.

He left without saying good-bye. She heard the car door bang and the engine start and hoped he might come back. But Inder was not a person who had second thoughts. She sat looking at the wet patch on the table and the carpet where he had spilled his drink. She had not even reminded him about Christmas. Upstairs she listlessly opened the cupboard where she had put green wrapping tissue and scarlet ribbon. Christmas was three weeks away and she still had to buy presents for her friends and for Jit. She loved Christmas. It was a reminder of winter holidays in European countries with parents who were in the Foreign Service. They had observed Divali with small, private, token illumination, but Christmas had been part of the literature of childhood and later of a snow-marbled world warmly shared with friends in different lands. Since she and Jit had come to Chandigarh soon after their marriage she had made its celebration a tradition, inviting their friends and acquaintances to punch on Christmas morning. Jit had protested mildly at first.

"We're not Christians."

"Well, what are we, anyway?" she had demanded. "We're not Hindus either. What we know about Hinduism could be put into an acorn."

Jit wished she would not be so dogmatic in her pronouncements. When she made that kind of remark she ruled out half a dozen other possibilities. It struck him that this was the least Hindu thing about her, the final statement, the unwillingness to linger on the fringes of a situation.

"Well, couldn't it?" she repeated. "I knew as much as any Catholic child about the Catechism when I went to school at the convent, and since then I've learned more about the Bible than I shall ever know about the Shastras. And except through your grandmother, who said her prayers every day and went to the temple now and then and told you stories from the Ramayana, what do *you* know about your religion?"

"I don't know much," said Jit. "But one is conscious of it just the same as a background, and a very insistent one at that. We can't escape what we are, Mara, all that's gone into the making of us. It comes out in so many ways, even the most Westernized of us, in our thinking and our attitudes."

"I hate vagueness. I don't understand it. Either you know something and you can deal with it or you can't."

"How can you know it, my love, unless you make the effort?"

"That's just my point. It's a maddening state of affairs when you have to make an effort to know your own background."

"But that's what you and I and lots of others like us have to do. We are strangers to it, as you said, because of our education and upbringing. You especially, because of all the years you've spent abroad. Yet we live with it and always shall. It's ours and we have to make friends with it—and that doesn't come about by making downright statements and wholesale rejections."

She could not find fault with what Jit said. There was never anything to quarrel with. She had said mutinously, "I don't see anything wrong with having open house at Christmas."

"Who said it was wrong?" he said in surprise, and took her out to the nearest shopping centre to place an order for a tree from Simla and to buy decorations for it.

Jit looked continually for the source of her discontent and for ways of bringing it to rest. He had never succeeded. It was something, he decided, to do with the chemistry of their two characters, an insoluble difference, nothing that could be sorted out, even with patience. In fact, patience seemed the wrong ingredient for it. She needed at times to be pried loose from her attitudes, shaken into yielding, but he lacked the coarser grain of behaviour that could have accomplished it.

Mara opened Jit's cupboard, wondering if the Christmas cards she had bought were there. In a corner of the top shelf she discovered a brown paper bag and, opening it, an oblong shape wrapped in gold paper, tied with red ribbon. Scent, by the look of it. The small white card attached read: "For a determined celebrator of Christmas from her devoted husband." She sat down weakly on the bed, still holding the package in her hands, and booked a call to Delhi. It came through in fifteen minutes.

"What are you doing?" she asked Jit.

"Getting ready to go to drinks at the Imperial." His voice was crystal clear and gay. "I got a lot done today. Is everything all right?"

"Yes." She said after a pause, "I found your Christmas present in your cupboard."

"That's cheating."

"I know." She felt close to tears. "Jit?"

"What's the matter, love?"

"I don't know."

"Well, it'll be better tomorrow."

"How do you know?"

"It always is."

"Three minutes up please," said the operator.

"I'll give you a ring tomorrow," said Jit.

"When are you coming back?"

"Day after, probably," he said.

"Time up, please," said the operator.

"Can't you come tomorrow?"

Her urgency fell into a vacuum as the operator cut them off and left her holding the telephone in a tension of unshed tears. How could anything be better tomorrow unless one *made* it better? And how did one do that if one didn't know what was wrong? She felt a storm rising in her against placidity, inborn and ingrained, that would not recognize disaster unless the very roof caved in. She wanted to lash out against the belief that everything went on and on uninterrupted and unchanged as a matter of course. Suddenly there was nothing, no substance at all, to hold on to.

"I think you are incapable of joy." Jit had once delivered the bitter judgement which was as far as his anger had ever taken him. "You are determined not to be happy."

She only knew she could not belong. She did not even feel a part of her school. Even there in that place of her own creation she was an outsider looking in. And at every step in its creation there had been problems to face. The most tiresome thing about this country was that nothing got done unless one did it oneself. Even a house did not get built unless one sat on the site every minute watching and urging its progress. She had spent hours on the site when their house was under construction, just sitting there, wasting time.

Chapter 8

It had been a long and gruelling tour, ending at Bhakra. The dam had not been part of it. It had been forty miles off course. Gyan had gone there to revive himself as men seek muscular relaxation after sitting cramped at their desks for hours. There were ambitious hydroelectric projects in other parts of the country but Bhakra was unique. Seven hundred and forty feet high, it was Asia's highest and the world's second-highest dam. He liked to recall that the concrete used in its construction would have built an eight-foot-wide road round the earth at the equator. That was how men should think: big. And going there reminded Gyan of how far he had travelled from his own origins. He could almost measure his own progress from the village in terms of the splendour of the dam.

This evening he took an elevator at the side of the spill-way to enter the dam. He walked through its galleries and went to the top to look down on the sixty-mile-long storage reservoir. Govind Sagar impounded eight million acre feet of water and the magnitude of the conception never failed to excite his imagination. People took the word mechanical to mean without thought. Yet the power of some man's thinking went into producing what became a machine. It worked in a particular way because a gifted mind had decided it should. The machines at Bhakra had fascinated him, beginning with those that drilled into foundations to remove hundreds of thousands of cubic yards of rock, and going on to the erection of the highest steel trestle bridges ever constructed in India. The facts and figures connected with the project stood out like milestones in an arduous journey, each bit of factual data a thrilling victory of human effort over nature. He knew that the concrete monument he stood on had been constructed after making two of the largest river-diversion tunnels in the world, each fifty feet in diameter, lined with concrete several feet thick. He had come to the site periodically to watch the excavation and had seen over a hundred mounds of earth lifted at a time by giant shovels and loaded into trucks for dumping. At places the rock had been soft and had caved in thirty feet without blasting, and the tunnel had had to be supported by steel girders. He had watched turbines and generators installed, cranes working on high trestles, diesel cars carrying huge buckets of concrete, pneumatic machines drilling and thundering, and he had marvelled at the men, helmeted and roped to steel rods fixed into rock, who laboriously cut and scaled the rock by hand on the steep sides of the narrow gorge where roads could not be built for machinery to do the work. He had visited the workshops, the nerve fibre of the whole gigantic activity, providing the manufacture and repair of its equipment.

Other dams had been built in India but no other that had so exercised the resources of the builders, and at times been so hazardous and nerve-wracking. Gyan had followed its misfortunes. Heavy rains had damaged the conveyor-belt system a month before the formal concrete-laying ceremony. A section of the spillway wall had given way. And a structural failure in the hoist chamber had flooded the galleries and the left-bank power house with water. But each disaster had been faced and put right and Gyan had been present four years earlier when at its dedication the waters of the Sutlej, flowing across the Himalayas from the bowels of Tibet, had at last been released to gush over the Punjab's acres and start the wheels of industry moving in a great regeneration of vitality. The dam stood now, a massive tangible achievement, a source of inexhaustible power. Already it had revolutionized agriculture and industry, a far cry from the age-old historic repetition of famine and failure, and a triumph of human ingenuity over the meagre share of the vast canal network that had fallen to the Punjab's lot at the time of Partition in 1947. To do the solid practical things there was no need to be stuffed with a college education. The principal foreign construction specialist on the Bhakra Dam had had none. He had been trained on such sites, rising from foreman to chief constructor, and the Government of India had thought highly enough of him to pay him a wage higher than that of the President of India.

Gyan could not understand the stupidity of linking the peasant with the worker. The men who had done it had obviously not been in either category themselves. Could you link the Stone Age with the twentieth century? You could only shackle progress that way. The peasant, anyone knew, does not change. Leave him on his land, and leave the land to him. Let him feel secure on it. Land was not man's invention and the laws concerning it belonged to the blood and marrow of human beings, to conventions older than laws, that could not be tampered with. Leave the land alone, he had always felt, and change the cities. Build them upside down or sideways or backwards, whichever way made them prosper. Give them industries. Then the peasant would go to them for jobs and change come over the countryside.

It had been a long day and he was tired when he got back into his car. He was dozing against the back seat when something told him the engine was not behaving. He opened his eyes to the dark road and asked the driver sharply, "What's wrong with the engine?"

He was a new man, Gyan remembered, who thought that driving a car meant steering the wheel. He was deaf to its minute and sensitive functioning, never heard a fault, and tinkered with its mechanism with about as much confidence as an old woman with St. Vitus' dance. Gyan had a profound contempt for him, for any man who did not know his job thoroughly and could not use his hands to get it done.

"There seems to be something wrong with it," the driver complained.

"There's something wrong all right. What I want to know is what in the name of the Almighty is wrong. Where did you learn to drive?"

The driver, already nervous, was reduced to inaudibility at his master's approaching temper.

"Stop the car at once," Gyan ordered.

"Here?" said the driver nervously. "It's dark."

Gyan swore roundly and the driver pulled up at the side of the road. He fumbled in the glove compartment for a torch and, leaving the headlights on, went to look in the bonnet. Gyan, already there, pushed him aside. Five minutes of careful investigation revealed the fault. He told the driver to get the bag of tools and worked at the ob-

struction, then getting in he tried the engine until it produced the right whine. The go-slow programme of the car
factory did not respect special cars. The incident had its
amusing aspect. His humour restored, he got back into the
car and told the driver to carry on. He would arrive at
Chandigarh only a little late for his public meeting. The
smell of petrol and grease on his hands, the stain on the
white khadi of his kurta gave him a sense of solid satisfaction. A fit ending, he thought, to a good tour, and the
grease smell reminded him of the time, still clear in his
memory, when he had first sat behind the wheel of a car,
sneaking in while his uncle, a chauffeur employed by a
British company, was having it filled at the petrol station.

He could hear his uncle roar at him from the pump
where he stood talking to the garage mechanic, "Get out,
mule. Anything goes wrong there and I'll be strung up, not
you." The huge face with its ragged beard had suddenly
loomed threateningly in the window. Dhan Singh kept his
beard neatly combed and netted when he was on duty, but
otherwise it flowed unkempt, giving his face a leonine
ferocity. One end of his faded green turban blew sideways
in the breeze. His heavy hand swung open the car door,
reached inside to grasp Gyan's shoulder and dragged him
off the seat. The boy found himself rolling on the ground
from the force of his removal. Picking himself up he dusted
off the seat of his pants and looked at his uncle with a
pleading intensity. "I want to learn how to drive."

"Off with you," came the roar again, "before I warm
your hindquarters with the palm of my hand."

Dhan Singh got into the car, slid it into gear, and drove
off, and Gyan, his face screwed against the sun and the
dust, looked admiringly after the vanishing machine. Excitement for him lay among the men who handled
machines, the truck and taxi drivers who plied between

Delhi and the Punjab, the chauffeurs of private cars and the mechanics who had the servicing of these machines. The miraculous world of machinery—of coils and tubes and cylinders and throbbing whining engines, of speed along the highway, rose before his eyes. It was hundreds of years removed from the bullock cart and the wooden plough of the village he had left not long ago.

The drivers his uncle knew met in one of the garages to drink on their free evenings. Gyan sat unnoticed listening to the belly laughter that sounded like thunder claps in the night, watching their giant shadows humped around the kerosene lantern, heaving with life, larger than life. To make sure he would not be caught and flung out of their company he crept one night into the lavatory adjoining the garage, listening there, until the door was wrenched open and his uncle stood, a hulking shape against the dim outside light. Gyan's eyes travelled upwards, stopping enthralled at the belt of cartridges around the waist, at the black chest hair showing at the open neck of the crumpled khaki shirt, at the green-turbaned head lowered to avoid colliding with the door frame stoop. Eyes blurred with sleep, the lavatory stench in his nostrils, Gyan was awake enough to know that magnificence, not a man, stood framed in the doorway. Dhan Singh's thick voice rumbled inarticulately, "Well if it isn't the mule. I'd have pissed on him in another minute." The idea struck him as uproarious and his belly laughter beat mercilessly on the air. He reached for Gyan and lifted him outside. One of the men offered him a mug of liquor and Gyan choked and coughed over the mouthful of raw liquid.

"What happened to my father and mother?" Gyan asked Dhan Singh, with whose family he lived.

"Your father killed a man in a fight and then was killed by his relative."

"And my mother?"

"Your mother came to the end she deserved. She was a whore."

"But what happened to her?"

Dhan Singh collected a mouthful of spittle, rolled it on his tongue, and deposited it with expert aim on the roadside where it frothed and bubbled before the dust swallowed it.

"It does not matter what happens to a whore."

"What happened to my mother?" he asked his aunt, who stooped in an attitude of eternal weariness as she ground grain for bread, pounded the washing or leant over the string cot where her youngest child lay, immobile as a rag.

"She's dead."

"Did she grow old and die?"

"No, she did not grow old."

"Was she a whore? What's a whore?"

The tired face was raised in frightened recollection before it returned, expressionless once more, to its task.

"Your tongue is too long with questions. Go eat and sleep or you will not wake in time to go to school in the morning. Where have you been all this time? Hanging about with the men is not right."

Gyan was not listening. He was lying on the ground on his bed of cotton sacking, steering an imaginary wheel, while the road to Delhi flowed smooth as oil below him.

The weariness of his aunt, even the mystery of his mother faded before the primitive colourful reality of his uncle, the ruler of this shabby domain, the one whose lung power shook the rafters, before whom children trembled, food appeared and was cleared away, and the only bed prepared for the night. Dhan Singh was master of his environment, and never more than when he stood resplendent in uniform, starched emerald-green turban atop his great height, beard immaculate, cartridges gleaming in his belt, beside the long sleek car of his employer. Gyan had seen other drivers jerk their machines, tear a performance from them, bruise and batter them in their ignorance of their functioning. Dhan Singh understood every bolt and nut that had gone into the making of his. His car obeyed his lightest touch, responding to it with spring and a panther's fluid electric grace. Because he drove the car of a British company boss he was the dean of drivers, and contemptuous of lesser machines and the men who had not mastered them. He spat heavily when he said, "That son of a sow's sister doesn't know an engine from an ox. Sits at the steering wheel and calls that driving. One breakdown and he has to tramp to the garage. That box on wheels I could patch with string and glue and keep going on one tyre. Dare it not go when I drive it!" Gyan was convinced that if there was a half pound of machinery left in any vehicle, it would move when his uncle took the controls.

"When will you teach me how to drive?" Gyan insisted at every opportunity.

His uncle looked at him shrewdly one day and grunted. "No reason why you should not do a job of work, mule," and he handed him a cloth and a bucket of water and instructed him to clean the car. It was not driving but it was contact with a machine, the feel of metal under his hand.

"Leave a speck or a scratch on it and I'll hammer your hide."

Gyan's face cracked into a wide, ecstatic grin. Somewhere in that shining metal case was the magic to make it whine and drone and purr into motion. He spent his spare time at the service station learning about the cars that came in for repair. All machinery fascinated him but this happened to be at hand.

"In any other country," he heard a foreign voice say as

he stood watching a familiar car fill with petrol, "that boy would be training to be a garage mechanic, maybe one day own his own garage. All he needs is a chance. Have you seen the way he handles a car? I've been watching him for some time now. He's always hanging around this garage. Something should be done about him."

The speaker had grey hair and keen blue eyes in a gaunt face. Gyan had seen him often, earning a tip from him on occasion. He had not wanted to take the tip at first.

"I don't work here," he had explained.

"You did a job of work for me, didn't you?" said the foreign voice in surprisingly fluent Hindustani. "Any man that does a job of work gets paid for it."

And Gyan had grinned delightedly as he pocketed the coin.

The strict-looking woman in the flowered dress, her hair in a bun, seated beside the man, said, "Now John, you came out here to preach the word of God, not to take upon yourself the responsibility of every child you see on the street." She had been saying it for twenty-five years, ever since she and her husband had come to India to work in the mission in the Punjab which he now headed. She knew she would go on saying it. John Meadows preached God's Word from the pulpit, but he found God's glory on every street corner, in the village settlement where he taught while his wife tended the sick, in the hut of the peasant and the tenement of the town dweller. Above all he found it in the bright intelligent eyes of children, a brightness he knew would fade and disappear unless it were taken young enough and nurtured and allowed to glow.

John Meadows was an American, born where the wheat grew tall under cloudless skies. He had a lingering love and nostalgia for his native country, but the passion of his mind and his spirit had been expended on India—that strange amalgam where Christianity bloomed like a perishable springtime in bewilderingly exotic, scented gardens older than time. The mission had toiled unremittingly. There was a band of converts, some few from fine old families, but not nearly enough to justify a lifetime's labour. This was a continuing anguish to Martha Meadows, but her husband had at some time during those twenty-five years come face to face with the grandeur of God and his purpose. Age, she often thought, had worked at him like a remorseless chisel, paring away all but the hard gem of a human being, leaving his face a transparency of light. While she grieved over a friend they respected but had not been able to convert, her husband could say, "He walks in Christ though he does not know it."

John Meadows took Gyan, one more bright face that flowered neglected in the street, put him in the mission school and afterwards got him his first job as a factory apprentice. When he sailed from India he did not know he had prepared the ground for a tumultuous leadership, and ironically one that would sprout in direct opposition to what he had tried to teach. The missionary had tried to instil the boy with conscience but Gyan had been bred in a turbulence where honour had more meaning. He knew that manhood depended on it and all important choice flowed from it. Conscience was invisible, hidden under secret layers of bafflement and doubt. Honour like prestige was public. It was a badge, the insignia of hardihood, the sign of a man's standing in his community. It must at all costs be upheld and it could never be shared. Conscience was no match for it. And during his apprenticeship in the factory Gyan learned that if there was one thing more important than machinery, it was the men who controlled it.

Though he was soon leader of the men among whom he worked, he had no experience of women.

"Come on, let's go to the whoring alley. Come on, don't gape. You can gape all you want when you get there."

They took him unprotesting with them and brought him away uninitiated. He remembered a room at the end of a dirty lane, with one small iron-barred window high up in the wall. There were quilts piled in a corner on the ground. She sat on them, knees spread, picking her teeth, a long plait falling limply over each breast. He caught the dull red glint of glass bangles on bony wrists. He stood in the entrance, retching feebly and ineffectually onto the ground, his body shuddering with the effort. When he lifted his head she was still sitting there, as indifferent as he had found her.

Years later he was able to ask his companions, "Do these women ply an individual trade?"

They had guffawed in reply.

"Every other industry has a union," said Gyan.

"You stick to the factories," they told him.

But Gyan had not become a leader of men by taking advice. The succession of Congress candidates in spotless white khadi who stood up to address election meetings did not know how the Party manager swelled his funds. It was soon evident that the money was available and no one asked where it came from.

An enormous, handsome figure of a man, observed Dubey from his chair at the end of the front row at Gyan Singh's meeting. There were other men on the dais, but as Gyan took his place in front of the microphone no one noticed the others. Behind Dubey were the four rows of folding chairs reserved for officials and dignitaries. He always wondered what a dignitary was. A number of people who weren't, apparently thought they were, because there was a scramble for the chairs. Behind the chairs was a concourse of several thousand. The numbers, especially at night, were hard to judge. And Dubey had learned not to be impressed by numbers. Any street could produce its overflow at the drop of a hat. A crowd could always be collected for any *tamasha*. It did not take him long to realize, when Gyan began to speak, that this was more than a *tamasha*. It was a strange mixture of truth and imagination that had the lure of a revival.

Gyan was using history to weave an atmosphere. He was talking of irrigation but conjuring glories long past of a state no longer in existence. The twice-truncated vanished Punjab blossomed on his tongue into the Land of Five Rivers again. Once more it became the pivot of India's most turbulent development, the playground of heroes. Against that he traced the history of irrigation, from Ferozeshah Tughlak's Jumna Canal to the seventeenth-century Shai Nahar, creation of Ali Mardan, Shah Jehan's famous engineer. It was this canal, he told them, that had been reconditioned to carry water to the Golden Temple of the Sikhs at Amritsar. And then there had been British attempts to extend irrigation against famine. Just before the independence of India and Pakistan, he said, the undivided Punjab had owned this vast network of canals, the world's finest. But at Partition the Indian Punjab was given a meagre, niggardly share, some areas of it hilly, some unirrigated. That was what they had been left with. But they had also been left with Punjabi peasants, Punjabi engineers, and a Punjabi determination to set their crippled economy to rights. And so the work on the Bhakra project had begun and through the years the use of electric energy had changed the face of the Punjab.

Now They were telling us, he said, that Bhakra was not ours, that we should not control it. It should be controlled, They said, by the Centre. This was not something we would stand for. If necessary we would demonstrate against it.

Dubey left the meeting with an air of unreality as if the words he had heard had been "The moon is mine. The Milky Way belongs to me." What he had heard had been as audacious, an inverted genius blazoning an equally fantastic legend. Men could be convinced of almost anything. And men like Gyan usually won their game. Their very narrowness gave their arguments a crude strength that no larger vision could ever have. Between Gyan and Harpal, he now realized, there was more than a political battle. It was a battle of philosophies. The juster but vaguer range of possibility could seldom hold out against violent immediate claims supported by the obvious.

The crowd surged towards the exit, blocking Dubey's way, and he was still trying to elbow his way through it when it parted to make way for Gyan and his colleagues. When Dubey reached the archway with its red-lettered welcome, Gyan caught sight of him and hailed him.

"Waiting for a lift, Mr. Dubey? I will take you home."

"Is your car in working order, then? Everybody else's seems to be having trouble."

The remark produced a burst of infectious laughter. The faces around Gyan split into smiles.

"I like your Lucknow brand of humour," he said. "Yes, mine works, Mr. Dubey, because when it does not I put it right with my own hands."

Dubey grinned appreciatively and got in beside him. And now, he thought ironically, there was nothing for him to do either, but wait with Harpal Singh for Gyan to choose the day for his strike.

Chapter 9

Dubey studied the pattern on the floor. "You've lost a piece," he told Bunny. The child shook his head solemnly.

"Yes you have. It's not here."

Saroj looked up from the letter she was writing at the dining table.

"Are you still at that jigsaw? It's time the children were in bed."

Dubey was sitting cross-legged on the carpet, puzzling over the colourful cardboard mosaic. He had been coming to the house every evening. She was continually aware of his existence in a way that did not interrupt her life but added to it. She felt it as she went about her house, as she put the children to bed, their sleepy warmth filling her with a bursting tenderness. And it flowed over her every minute of pause in the day. Yet with all its gentleness it was oddly compelling. She did not know what was happening to her except that she occupied a sweeter and more satisfying world. The bargain she had entered into with him had released a delirium of talk between them. It made her look inward at the whole dim, untidy complex of living, each corner suddenly floodlit, every cobweb exposed. No one had even wanted any of it before, not even she herself.

"It's the wrong jigsaw," said Dubey at last. "The one I bought for Bunny must have been picked up by the other customer in the shop and I came away with this. Bunny is managing all right with the shapes though I don't think he has any idea what the picture's about. Do you, old chap? That's the piece we want." He took the section the little boy had found caught in the fringe of the carpet. "How did it get that far?"

Bunny looked mystified. He sat back on his heels, smelling of bath soap and talcum powder, his small fists stuffed into dressing-gown pockets already bulging with hoarded treasures.

"There, that's half done. We'll do the rest tomorrow," said Dubey. "How do you like it?"

Bunny beamed.

"He'll never be a Member of Parliament," said Dubey. "He never says a word. Do you, Bunny?"

"Doesn't he? He screams and shouts when I touch his things," said his six-year-old brother scornfully. "He's stupid."

Bunny's placid mood dissolved into fury and he rushed to butt his brother in the stomach.

"Man of action," said Dubey, scooping up the small fighting bundle. "Bedtime."

Saroj came down after putting the children to bed.

"You've been at that thing for half an hour. What do you get out of it, Vishal?"

"I like jigsaws," said Dubey as he lifted the completed section into its box.

"No, I mean just being here like this. It's so dull and domestic. What a way for a man to spend an evening."

"But all right for a woman?"

"Well," she said helplessly, "it's my house and they're my children."

"And that's how I like knowing you in an ordinary way. The high spots come and go. They aren't most of life."

Comradeship, he was saying, was a concern with the ordinary. Out of that could grow relationships closer and more powerful than any that the fevers of passion could conceive of. For there was a passion of the mind that far exceeded any other kind. When you shared that you could see the stars on a morning walk through the fields or over a cup of tea in your drawing room.

Inder came in. The scene in his drawing room was pleasant, yet somehow disturbing. The fire had been lit and Dubey was poking it to encourage the glow. Saroj sat, as she did nowadays, in a high-backed chair near it, wearing the familiar brown cardigan she wore when she gave the children their baths. It had become her uniform. She looked as she always did. Yet it was her face that stabbed him. It was very attentive and alight. He spoke more abruptly than he had intended.

"Where are the children?"

"They've just gone to bed," said Saroj.

"Is it as late as that?"

"You lose all track of time at the mill." She spoke without resentment and the lack of it grated unreasonably in him.

"Why didn't you ring up and tell me Vishal was here? I'd have come home earlier. I've been working overtime to get things organized and a consignment ready to send out before the workers decide to strike."

"Oh, Mara rang up," Saroj remembered. "She says she's

sick of this crisis talk and wants us all to go on a picnic to
Pinjore tomorrow."

"Good idea," said Inder.

Dubey was standing before the fire, his shoulders
slightly hunched, his hands in his pockets. Inder realized
Dubey and Saroj were talking animatedly and that he had
no idea what they were saying. He had not heard a word
of it.

He cut in. "I'm going to have a drink. How about you,
Vishal?"

"I'll have one too," said Saroj.

Inder looked up in surprise. She was fussy about avoiding alcohol during her pregnancies. He brought her a
drink. They were talking again. "I feel like celebrating," he
heard Saroj say.

"So do I," said Dubey, "I think one should during a
crisis."

Inder said, "No celebrating for me. I'm dead tired. I
want an early night."

In the second of silence that followed Saroj roused herself to his need. "Then I'll order dinner. Vishal, stay and
eat with us."

She left her drink untouched and listened quietly to their
talk at table. When Dubey left she stood holding the door
knob where his hand had rested, while Inder went out to
his car with him. She was still there when Inder came back.

"Hello," he said.

The stranger in him she had never understood excited
her as he stood, just a shape in the darkness. His voice was
close and rich.

"Aren't you speaking to me?" he demanded.

"Of course," she said breathlessly.

"That's better."

He put an arm about her shoulders and they walked

upstairs, jostling each other in the narrow space, her nearness kindling him. His hand slipping lower encountered a damp patch over her breast.

"What's this?"

"I've started oozing," she said, pleased.

She had always been proud of her ooze, as she called it, a sign that she would have plenty of milk for the baby, and for Inder a reminder that for months after the birth Saroj would be drenched in the smell of human milk. He decided he did not mind her pregnancy. He minded its effect on her. Her absorption with it tantalized him. It made him feel he was borrowing her from her real occupation.

"Does Vishal have a family?" he asked.

"No. His wife died a few years ago and he hasn't any children."

"He must be lonely."

"No, I don't think so." She tried to explain it, "He's so at home everywhere, with all sorts of people—and things."

"Things!"

"Like the lake, or the way the sky looks. He notices, and he has a sense of wonder."

"Good God. He sounds like an animist."

Just now, she thought, he's driving home under the stars, but he's not alone. It all belongs to him, the whole bewitching universe. We're the lonely ones, you and I.

"He certainly feels at home here," Inder remarked shortly. "What's the matter? Out of breath?"

"I'm all right." She sat down on a divan in their room and pulled him down beside her. "Don't go away."

"I'm not going anywhere except to the bathroom to brush my teeth."

"Promise you won't go away."

He laughed. "Where in heaven's name would I go?"

"Anywhere," she pleaded, clinging.

She trailed her fingers across the comforting expanse of his chest. Where wouldn't you go, she thought, far off into your wilderness where I can't reach you. Don't go and be lonely out there and don't leave me lonely here.

He stroked her hair. "Here I am as large as life. Come on. We can't stay here all night."

When he got up she followed him into the bathroom, leaning against his arm while he brushed his teeth. He put an arm around her.

"Let's always be like sticking plaster," she crooned.

"When are you going to grow up, infant?"

He helped her to undress and put her to bed, then yawned, stretched and changed into pajamas himself.

"Wonder how much longer to that bloody strike," he said getting in beside her and holding her close.

"I'm not the right shape for a picnic," Saroj grumbled in the morning, examining her reflection in the mirror.

At this stage she had to decide where to tie her sari, above or below the bulge, and it didn't make much difference in the end as Flutter shifted it around. She could feel his movements against her ribs. She thought of him swimming around like a fish, like life since the world began. The doctor had said if he did not behave and stay head downward he'd have to be massaged into position.

"All these thousands of years and no one's designed a maternity sari."

She pulled hers off and started all over again.

"It's so much easier in the West. Everything hangs from your shoulders and there's a big hole cut out in front for your tummy. Mara's sister said it was bliss having a baby in France. And she drank red wine with her meals. The doctor said it was body-building . . . four, five, six."

"What are you counting?" asked Inder from his desk.

"My pleats. There used to be nine and now I can only make six. It's funny about stomachs. Some go right back to normal and others never do. Dr. Varma said you could almost pick some up and let them drop."

Inder stopped writing. "The doctor said that?"

He felt uncomfortable at the thought of the doctor talking that way to Saroj.

"I asked him about it. I think mine's midway. Mara's sister didn't look as if she'd had two children, did she?"

"I didn't see her stomach," Inder pointed out.

"I did. It was lovely. I'm ready," she announced.

She looked at her profile in the mirror and felt like dissolving into tears. She sat down on her bed. "I can't possibly go. I look so *large* today, Inder." The children's shouts drifted up to them. "Oh dear. We'd better leave."

They were to meet Dubey and the Sahnis at Pinjore. The children were put, protesting, into the back seat. It was too long a drive for everyone to be squeezed in front.

"Besides, can't you see how *large* I am today? I'd be squashed if we all sat in front."

"You look just like always," said Muff, crossly, "and the front seat is closer to everything. Why can't Bunny sit on your lap?"

"Because I haven't got a lap," she said decisively as they drove away.

Bunny and Muff relapsed into silence.

"You were given a lot of freedom—weren't you?" said Inder.

Now what made him ask that just now, she wondered. Though it was a day to think of freedom, the breeze balmy, loose brown earth upturned in fallow fields, a lovely distilled morning light.

"I wasn't given it. It was just there. I took it for granted." She added with affection, "My parents didn't know there was any other way to live."

"Still, it was unusual—for a girl. Your meeting with that man couldn't have taken place if you hadn't gone about so much on your own."

"That was just by chance. I told you I met him at a play the university dramatic society organized."

"And normally a girl wouldn't take a stranger to her home."

Saroj burst out laughing. "Where else would I have taken him?"

"You were attracted enough to take him home."

"But that was what home was for," she said. "I took everything I liked home. Stray dogs and wild flowers and of course my friends. Don't you remember I asked you to come to the house very soon after we met?"

"Yes," he said dryly. "At the time I thought I was something special."

"You were."

"Along with the stray dogs and—what else did you say —and that other individual."

Saroj searched for something to focus on outside her window but the landscape rushed too swiftly past. She felt she could halt the menacing current if only there were something solid to focus on. Instead she kept thinking of her father's face as he asked the only question he had about Inder: "Does this young man share your frame of mind?" But the whole courtship had been much too brief and exciting to ponder on that commonplace.

"Did your parents like him?"

"Yes they did."

"Did they have any inkling what was going on?"

"No, of course not."

"But they trusted you, didn't they? They let you come and go as you pleased?"

Far up there was a herd of cows crossing the road, with their owner urging them along with his stick. She clung prayerfully to the sight.

"Didn't you feel you were betraying their trust?"

"No."

"But you were, weren't you?"

"I don't think we should go into all that just now," she begged. "We're nearly there."

"That's what I can't get over. You always make such a point of trust, about the way you were brought up, how close you were to your parents and all that. But you didn't mind cheating them. You knew perfectly well they would have been horrified if they had found out. Or would your father have approved of his only daughter behaving like a tart?"

"No, of course he wouldn't have."

"Well, why did you do it? That's what I keep coming back to. Why did you do it?"

"I was fond of him," she said wearily, "and I was curious. Is that a crime?"

"Good God. Didn't you have any inhibitions, any sense of modesty? Couldn't your curiosity wait till you got married?"

Bunny and Muff gave a shout as the gate of Pinjore came into view. Inder turned the car into it and parked in front of the arched gateway of the Moghul garden. The children tumbled out, exclaiming over the cloud of butterflies settled over the wall creeper.

"Get down," said Inder.

"Please, Inder," she implored. "What will I tell them?"

She started to plead but the words died in her throat and she stood in an agony of indecision as he drove away. Dubey came up the steps into the archway.

"Was that Inder? Where's he going?"

"I don't know," said Saroj.

"Where's Papa?" asked Bunny, coming to join her.

"He'll be back later," said Saroj.

Muff opened his fists to show his mother a butterfly caught in each.

"Oh the poor things. Let them go."

"Where's Papa? I want to show them to Papa."

Saroj looked helplessly at Dubey.

He said, "Papa had some work to do. Let's go down and have our picnic."

He took the children ahead, letting her walk slowly through the archway, down the steps and along the paved path where the fountains played. Saroj went to the stone pavilion at the end of the walk and looked out over woodland to the plain beyond. The explanations were over by the time she arrived in the mango grove where Mara had spread a carpet.

"I almost didn't come," Saroj said, "I got so discouraged when I saw myself in the mirror. I look so *large*."

"As Shah Jehan told Mumtaz Mahal," said Jit, "thou art ravishing in thy largeness."

Saroj looked at him unsmiling.

"He must have told her something of the sort since she was always pregnant and we know he thought her ravishing."

"I wonder what he really thought of her," said Saroj.

"The twentieth-century female needs more proof than the Taj Mahal," said Jit to the mango trees.

"Oh the Taj," said Saroj. "He built that after she was dead. What did he do for her while she was alive—besides give her thirteen children?"

"We're in that kind of mood, are we," he sympathized. "Let's have a drink and cheer ourselves up."

Mara said, "Jit thinks if you pat a woman on the head

and say 'There, there' it should be the answer to all her problems. And if it isn't, she's abnormal."

Jit looked bewildered.

"Did anyone see the papers this morning?" asked Dubey. "The Electricity Board is threatening to go on strike next week."

No one answered.

"I hope there's a good supply of candles in Chandigarh," Dubey went on tranquilly.

"Why don't we just go back to living in caves?" suggested Mara. "That would be the end of all this bother. Saroj, aren't you going to sit down?"

"I can't get down on the carpet," she said. "It's too uncomfortable."

"We'll move to that terrace and you can sit on the parapet on a cushion."

They trekked to the terrace with the carpet, cushions, and picnic basket. Saroj sat down on the parapet, declining a cushion. Mara stood, her arms crossed, looking over it onto the plain.

"I'd call this a kind of cave," said Dubey.

"What's a cave?" demanded Mara without turning around.

"The four of us here—in total ignorance about what's happening to each other."

"I'm going to have that drink," said Jit.

"You can't have a drink and certainly not whiskey. It's only eleven o'clock," Mara objected.

"When you are a manufacturer of whiskey, my love, you can have a drink at any time, and the oftener anyone else has one the better."

"Like the British dumping opium on the Chinese," said Mara acidly.

"Anyone else care for a drink?" Jit held up the bottle.

"Well, there are times obviously when a man has to go it alone."

He raised his glass in a silent toast and took a swallow of his drink.

"The Government," he announced, "is like a backward parent. It's No to everything. Drinking is a sin. Making money is evil. Betting on the race course is for loafers. Eventually they have to concede that normal people do these things the world over and their souls don't burn in hell. Only it's one long misery for everyone till they concede it. Now what makes Government think we are, or should be, such a hallowed species. What would you say, Vishal?"

He did not wait for Dubey to reply. "The point is, do we or do we not eat, drink, make money, do a good or a bad job of work, just like other people do?"

"Oh for heaven's sake Jit," said Mara irritably. "No one's in the mood for a lecture."

What were they in the mood for? Jit decided his own even temperament was a handicap; a few black moods, some table-thumping, a little thunder might get better results.

He looked at Saroj. Sulking, he decided. He wondered why Inder had not joined them. Her sulking probably got on his nerves. Spoiled rotten she was. Too much money, which must be another thing Inder had to put up with. And too much attention. Expected everyone to commiserate because today she didn't feel like having a baby. And the sight of Mara's unrelenting back needled him. Another one spoiled rotten. By him. For years he had done everything in his power to make her happy. He had racked all his resources to get some human response from her. That stiff ramrod back was the sum total of her response. Back to the caves, she had said, and that was what would suit her best. You gave a woman the perfection of which you were capable, the finest flower of your most evolved instincts, and it was a waste. She didn't even know what it was. She didn't want to be cherished and affection made no impression on her. He thought bitterly that she'd understand brute force. She wanted some man to drag her by the hair to submission, bring her to a gasping shuddering climax in sex, and brand her personality with his own every waking hour. Jit knew as he thought it that it was not true. Mara was fine and intelligent. She was conscious of all that she did. She had pride. She would never be an object for anybody's use. And he loved her. He wanted to turn her around to face him and offer her a companionable sip of his drink. It was his misfortune that whatever else she wanted, it was not him.

"This cave theory of yours," he said to Dubey. "If people can talk to each other, they're not in a cave?"

"How can they be when there are no dark, unmentionable subjects between them?"

Mara turned around. "Which people should talk to each other?"

"Parents and children. Husbands and wives."

"Rot. Husbands wouldn't like it a bit if their wives talked to them frankly. That's why women don't."

Why in God's name does she say things in that flat, downright way as if no other point of view existed? Jit's irritation flared again, and with it a sense of failure. He had never been able to convince her she was his equal, and tenderly held. She could have come to him with anything.

"That was my point," Dubey was saying. "When people are afraid of each other they don't want to show themselves. It's too risky."

Jit got up, waved his arms in the air, and shouted.

"It's Inder," he said. "He's looking for us."

The children playing under the trees ran towards their father. Inder came closer, waving a greeting. He knew as he came up to them that he had come back too soon. He had to be alone longer for his revulsion to die down and the day to become benevolent again. He tried to divorce the revulsion from Saroj but it had got hold of him again at the sight of her troubled, delicate-featured face. The paradox of her tore at him. There had been no such nightmare to contend with until his marriage. He had been precocious and successful in sex, robustly collecting experience where he found it. Saroj had plundered that robustness, made a tortured image of the body's surrender, and nailed him to the inquisitor's chair.

"It's a perfect day," he said to the four on the terrace, "I think I'll take a stroll before I settle down with you lazy people."

He walked away into the dense seclusion of the mango grove. He did not wait or turn when he heard footsteps behind him. Mara caught up with him.

"That leaves three of us," said Jit. "Sure you won't have a drink?"

Dubey shook his head.

"It's a good view, isn't it?" Jit remarked.

"Glorious," Dubey replied. "Such a sweep of country-side."

In the distance, grass grew luxuriant and cows moved slumbrously through the green-turfed carpet of it.

"All the more glorious probably because of the human flesh that fertilized it. No it's not the drink," he held up his glass cheerfully. "I'm talking about that spot there under that grove of trees."

There had been a well there once, he said, though it had long since been filled with lime, its mouth sealed with earth and covered with a layer of loosely packed bricks. Later

these had been cemented, and children playing on the platform were reminded it was not as even as the rest of the
ground only when a ball bounced off at a tangent or a
pebble got caught in a crack. Oh, yes, it was quite a smooth
surface now. Only the village elders, too feeble to leave the
village and run away, too old even to tempt the blood lust
of the attackers when frenzy had swept the countryside,
talked of the well now. Most of the village had fled in
terror, on bullock cart, on foot, any way they could propel
or drag themselves, to the nearest town, and finding it in
flames had joined the long desperate march to Delhi. The
survivers among them had straggled back when it was safe
to plough their fields and graze their cattle again, and they
had not seen the sight for themselves: of bodies unloaded
from public-transport buses in the fierce heat of an August
day. With gaping mouths, staring eyes, and stiff lifeless
limbs, some still looked astonished at the death that had so
suddenly overtaken them. They had been lowered one by
one, with the careful precision of expertise, into the well,
neatly arranged to circle its inner curve, one layer on top
of another . . .

"Please don't," said Saroj. "You're making me quite ill."

The well had been deep, Jit continued blandly. It had
taken yards of its human consignment. It had been a re-
prisal, people said, for the slaughter of an equal number of
Hindus just across the border, a kind of mathematical,
matter-of-fact revenge. An eye for an eye, a tooth for a
tooth, a life for a life. Not a single more Muslim had been
butchered than the exact number specified. And the stink
of rotting flesh had putrefied the atmosphere for miles and
weeks through the merciless heat of August 1947. It had
taken some time for the authorities to arrive at it through
the death and devastation of the border districts and vil-
lages. This was, after all, some considerable way inside In-

dian territory. When they did, a team of sanitation inspectors came to burn the contents of the well and to treat it with chemicals. In time the grass grew on it, the air cleared, and the living returned to their land.

"And now," said Jit, "it's a lovely view so let's drink to it."

He got up to refill his glass.

"Did it happen?" Dubey asked.

"Does it matter?" said Jit. "If it didn't happen to this village, it happened to some other. It was all too common. That's a cave for you, Vishal, people having great orgies of slicing each other up as if they were Genghis Khan's blood brothers. And less than that doesn't seem to make any kind of impression, on women least of all."

"What does the woman say?" asked Dubey.

Saroj was looking ungainly today, the fine modelling of her face and throat incongruous above her bulk. There was a line of strain between her brows that he wanted to erase with his finger, and he found it hard to remain passive in sight of her unhappiness. She had not heard him.

"Bunny and Muff have wandered off somewhere," she said anxiously. "I'd better go and find them."

The woman had no conversation whatsoever, thought Jit. She must drive Inder round the bend. You could expound for half an hour on the world's most fascinating subject and at the end of it she'd tell you Bunny had a toothache. He wondered what she got out of life and thanked God for Mara, though he wanted to shake her at times.

"What does a woman like that get out of life?" he asked Dubey.

"I've wondered about that myself," said Dubey.

"Husband, children, and all that, I suppose."

"Very much all that and more," said Dubey. "She's the

kind whose natural climate is affection and one who'd give it back in sweat and joy a hundredfold—"

Dubey stopped as he was going to say "if she had the chance." He realized that there was something aspiring and painstaking about all three of them, Saroj, Mara, and Jit. It was Inder to whom he had no clue.

"I'm afraid. This idea of yours that people should talk to each other," said Jit, "is like nuclear disarmament. It doesn't work unless both sides do it. It's a monstrous gamble otherwise."

"It's a gamble someone must take, whether it concerns bombs or a conversation. Someone must be willing to be destroyed."

"That's a large statement."

"There was a time when this country took that gamble. A whole generation went into battle with no weapon but its will. When you gamble for the big things you have to risk everything."

Mara demanded, "Why did you come so late?"

"I went for a drive."

She said icily, "It never occurs to you to give an explanation for anything you do, does it? You accept an invitation to a picnic, then you just dump Saroj and the children here like sacks of potatoes and go off without so much as a word. When you turn up again you haven't even the decency to apologize for coming late."

Inder reached for a loose end of mango branch above his head, snapped it in two and flung the pieces away.

"I didn't go to finishing school in Switzerland," he said.

"Then you wander off on a walk," she went on, furious. "Doesn't it strike you there's anyone in the world to consider besides yourself?"

The shutters were down on his face. He was rigidly

inattentive. She stopped, defeated.

"I'm sorry. I shouldn't have said that. Only I wish I knew what goes on in you. What does she do to you? Whatever it is, it's horrible. There's something under that bland innocence of hers that's destroying you."

He was stung to retort, "What are you talking about?"

"About you and Saroj. Inder, I can't bear to see you go through this. Get away from her."

"You don't understand," he said stiffly. "She belongs to me."

"*Belongs* to you? So do your shoes."

"Even my shoes are special to me because they are mine."

"They're special because they fit you. If they didn't you'd throw them away. And you can't own a woman, even if she's your wife."

"You're a foreigner," he said harshly. "You wouldn't understand."

"Does *she* understand?"

He thought of Saroj, clinging, dependent, responding to the unpredictable law of his emotions and living in obedience to it. He could truthfully say she understood.

"Then that's the most terrible part of it," said Mara. "Sometimes I hate this country," she added with passion.

"What do you know about it anyway?"

"That's what I hate—the fact that I wouldn't, even if I tried. When I try I can't believe what I find. It's like coming up against—the ages." She stopped and faced him in bewilderment. "Old, useless, impossible ideas going on and on. We carry them around like deadwood on our backs. It's all ours all right, but some of it is rotten. We'll die if we go on like this. Sometimes I think we're already dead."

His unwilling attention was captured. She was the only

one who could do this to him, force his interest and hold it.

"I didn't have to live here, Inder. I chose it. That's why I'll never be satisfied till I get the hang of it and somehow make it mine." She said impulsively, "Well, whatever's annoying you, come out of it. This picnic has been absolutely wretched. Let's enjoy the rest of the day."

Her words brought back distant days when a coaxing voice had recalled him from temper. It was not always the same voice. It was his mother's or his grandmother's or a servant's—whoever was at hand. Someone, unconnected with what had upset him, had waited patiently at the edge of every child-crisis for his return to cheerfulness and been grateful when he did. He felt the knots loosening, his stomach relaxing. Suddenly he felt hungry.

"Let's go and open that lunch you've brought," he said.

Chapter 10

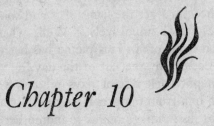

Accident had played its part in Gyan's life. If he had
not attracted the attention of an American missionary at a
petrol pump he would have grown up uneducated and
chauffeured a truck or a car like his uncle. More fateful
was the conference that had carved out the new state of
Hariyana, giving him the leadership of the Punjab. It was a
truncated Punjab, but his to rule. He had gone to Delhi to
argue for a state where the Punjabi language would have
pride of place, and astonishingly he had been given it. He
wondered if the protagonists of Pakistan had been equally
astonished, even dismayed, when a country had been
dropped into their laps. John Meadows' training had made
little impression on him but now and then a phrase from
the Bible struck him as apt: Ask and ye shall receive.

He had cut an impressive figure at the conference, his
great bulk and resonant voice dominating it. He had been
the Man of the Week in the nation's two leading journals
and had figured along with Harpal, but always over-

shadowing him, in the editorials of the leading newspapers. He realized why when he read one of them. He was, the editor commented, a living monument to the urban working class, a man who had risen from the ranks, yet remained one of the people in his dizzy rise to power. In an age that was alive to the needs of the common man, Gyan was its most distinguished representative in the country.

He had been invited to speak to the Journalists' Association in Delhi and had gone there expecting a critical reception. But when in that crowded hall he had thrust away the microphone and stepped forward to the edge of the platform, he knew his personality had sent an electric current through the room. He described himself as a simple man fired with a simple purpose: to call his soil his own in the language of his forefathers. He had, he said, no inheritance but that. He had been born in a village and grown up in the streets. Gyan sensed the prickle of guilt in his audience, guilt at opportunity, and comfort, and a desire to redeem that guilt. He discovered at question time that the language fever ran high among them. Any man among them who denied him support for his Punjabi-speaking state would find himself unpopular in his own Tamil- or Bengali- or Marathi-speaking one. He knew they were with him.

There was something about the atmosphere of the proceedings on the first day of the conference that Gyan could not quite grasp. It took him a little while to place the elusive element as anxiety. The men around the table were anxious, from the pale, tense Prime Minister to his Cabinet colleagues. They wanted a speedy end to the controversy. But more than that they were anxious there should be no disagreement on the decision, and the delay in announcing it was the Home Minister's opposition to the formation of a new state. It was rumoured that he and the Prime Minister had fallen out over the issue and the P.M. had hoped he would resign. Not even the P.M. could ask him to resign. The old man was an institution. It was known he had a single fierce allegiance: India, and the invisible regard of an electorate far wider than the one that regularly elected him to Parliament. Ministers came and went but Indians had a way of creating their own leaders that had nothing to do with a man's office. In his lifetime the old man had already joined such a legendary handful. No government could dismiss him, for fear that where he lived would then become the seat of power. But it could overrule him.

The other man who spoke against division was, of course, Harpal. His arguments were precise and down to earth. And they were dull. Economy, and the strength and security of a border region, could not hold out against the colourful emotional appeal of the mother tongue. Any government that further divided the Punjab, said Harpal, would reap the whirlwind. But his arguments fell, one by one, dry as dust into a vacuum. The conference was waiting for a sign that would give it the courage to announce what it had already decided. Gyan gave it when he rose at the end to remind them eloquently of the ardour of a people for identity. Let those whose mother tongue was Hindi, he said, form their own state.

No one thought it strange that Harpal Singh, also a Sikh, was chosen leader of the new Hindi-speaking state. There were Brahmins who ate beef, and evidently there were Sikhs who did not feel the tug of their heritage enough to include all others.

The Home Minister, whose views were known, was stopped by reporters on the steps outside the conference building. One of them, the correspondent of a foreign paper, asked him if this meant his resignation.

"Certainly not," was the tart response.

Gyan Singh had come up behind him and they had looked absurd standing side by side, the towering figure smiling down on the meagre one. The old man had told the photographers with a twinkle that they would not get such an unlikely pair on film again and to make the most of it. He was, he said, an admirer of brawn. One of the most vivid memories of his younger days, he said, was of a thrashing. The statement evoked amusement all round.

"You thrashed someone, sir?" the correspondent was writing down the recollection with a smile.

"I did not," was the indignant rejoinder. "*I* was thrashed. By a sergeant or someone of the sort in uniform and on horseback. *We* were on foot, lots of us, demonstrating against the Prince of Wales' visit. The sergeant looked magnificent on his horse. A most beautiful sight."

"Were you badly hurt, sir?"

The old man, lost in reminiscence, came back to the gathering.

"What? Yes, yes. Black and blue. My poor mother nursed my bruises for days."

And he went off down the stairs, leaving Gyan to face the battery of cameras alone.

Gyan did not know when the language issue had blended in his mind with his religion. But how could it ever have been otherwise, he thought? His next official act would be to start religious instruction in the schools and he had already mentioned it last evening to a press gathering. He had asked them why it should be considered strange. He had spent years—hadn't they all?—listening to and repeating the Lord's Prayer in Christian mission schools. No one had said, "This is a Sikh boy. He should be exempt."

To begin with, Harpal had not wanted the state called Hariyana. Punjab revived and swaggering with its post-independence prosperity had been good enough for him, and, he was convinced, for the millions now boxed into Hariyana. He had realized as he sat with his delegation at the conference that had forever mutilated that Punjab that he was being backed into a corner and presented with an ultimatum. Take it or leave it, they had said, and he had taken it. He ought to have resigned. Why hadn't he? He didn't know, except that the decisive action had always been a problem for him.

He remembered the case of the industrial complex Gyan had started years earlier when Chandigarh was being built. Members of the Assembly had come to Harpal with complaints about the way plots were being distributed. Men who had paid their deposits and waited years had not received theirs, while others had had theirs mysteriously released. Gyan, Minister of Industries at the time, had claimed he had cut through all the red tape to get the state's life moving. There had been some opposition to his methods. A group of earnest young legislators had come to Harpal urging him to spearhead the attack in the Assembly against corrupt practises. They wanted a clean administration. They believed Harpal was their man, one who would take up a cause. Harpal had made a speech about it but it had never been followed up. The day afterwards two of his men had been found beaten up in the empty lot near one of the sold plots, and Harpel had counselled caution. And caution had continued to be his watchword. Because of it he sat at a desk stacked high with newly printed files and manila covers stamped with the new name, the unbelievable fact of Hariyana. Plans had been put up to him for a reorganization of the educational system of Hariyana. He would have to reward with suitable cash prizes the poets and authors, the growers of the most wheat and breeders of the best cattle of Hariyana. The Secretariat where he now

sat, the city he had lived in all his official life were now a
battleground between Hariyana and Punjab. He had
thought the feeling of fantasy would abate and make it
possible for him to apply himself to his work with some
conviction. But it had not. It still seemed grotesque that a
metaphoric line had been drawn through the Punjab, that
millions who had till yesterday been Punjabis had suddenly
become Hariyanis, sanctifying another language and spout-
ing another nationalism. Whatever it was all about, he did
not want any more to do with it. A revulsion that had as
much to do with his own caution as with the march of
events swept over him.

Each day brought some new statement about this dis-
puted capital. Yesterday the Punjab Assembly had passed
an unofficial resolution declaring that Chandigarh and the
Bhakra Dam belonged to the Punjab, and now Gyan had
thrown the bombshell into their midst that there would be
religious instructions in the schools. What would the next
step be, an army and a flag for the Punjab? The spectre of
states stuffed with power rose before his eyes.

In his own Assembly that morning Harpal had already
faced the demand for a larger Hariyana. An eminent Hindi
poet had spoken powerfully for a movement to extend the
state's boundaries, concluding his speech with a recital of
some of his own recent verse celebrating the birth of
Hariyana. It had evoked a spontaneous cheer which the
Speaker had had some trouble quieting. Produce an idea,
thought Harpal wryly, and it would generate its own
quota of fanatics to clothe it in colour, put it to music, and
fire a whole population. It had been difficult not to be carried away by the poet's lilting lines, but he had sat determinedly silent, chin resting on his hand, secretly appalled
by the enthusiasm for so outrageous a concept. His silence
had been noticed and would be remarked on in the lobbies

where the poet was congratulated on his performance. Harpal had avoided the throng. He had been impatient to get back to his desk to the scheme for making land and power available at lower rates for industrial development.

Talking to Dubey later in the morning Harpal said, "I don't believe in theatrical gestures, but I lack the conviction to handle all this. I don't think I can serve this situation any more. I am going to resign. I should have offered my resignation before I left the conference room in Delhi."

Dubey said nothing.

"You disapprove?" Harpal prodded him.

"No, I approve entirely," said Dubey. "I was thinking that we should all—civil servants, politicians, doctors, lawyers, armed forces, everybody—have resigned in 1947 when India was divided and the very foundation of this country's belief, that religion was a private affair, torn up. But I don't suppose that would have been a practical thing to do."

Harpal smiled faintly.

"In 1947 there was still an India left to serve. Now there's no such loyalty to bind us. The big vision has disintegrated. At any rate, let someone who believes in the existence of Hariyana, and to whom carving out this extra state makes some sense, look after it. I have no heart for this job."

He had intended merely to inform Dubey of his decision, not to discuss it with him.

"What will you do?" asked Dubey, interested.

Harpal noticed that the question ignored the uneasy politics of this border area.

"Myself?" he frowned. "I would have to think about that. This has been my whole life. I suppose one imagines, or at least hopes, that one will die at one's desk. I've never even considered retirement. Now I may have to."

"I envy you," said Dubey unexpectedly.

"You wish to retire?"

"I'd like to lead another sort of life."

"What would you do?"

"I'd have to make a living so it would have to be something dull, like growing vegetables, that would leave my mind free to cope with what I really want to do, which is write."

"I don't want to grow vegetables," said Harpal emphatically. "I just have no feel for this job any more."

Conviction was what he needed, he thought, as he went down in the lift, and where did one pluck it from when it was sucked dry? What motivated the men in politics today, merely power? He was convinced it was not enough to be a politician in India. The lot of them should resign—grow vegetables—and let others who could love their work take over. As he waited for his car at the entrance a group of young men surged towards him, surrounding him.

"We won't take no for an answer," one of them said.

"What's this all about?" Harpal demanded, looking at their eager faces.

"The University Union wants you to address them on the first of January."

"My young friend, I don't know where I shall be on the first of January. The Union had better find someone else."

"But we won't take no for an answer. It's you we want."

They clamoured around him, lanky and bright-eyed, affection in their faces. A thoroughly unruly lot, he knew, who made life a misery for their professors, who did not even know how to make an appointment, but in whose faces the lamps still burned.

"I will let you know," he said.

"But promise you will consider it."

"Very well, I promise."

They broke their circle to allow him to reach his car. He could, he knew, retire from his office, but not from the feeling that he was needed and had a job to do.

We're all dissatisfied, thought Dubey, back in his office. He with his job and I with mine, and both of us for the same reasons. There was still the matter of the policeman to be cleared up, sticking like an untidy scrap to his agenda. And Dubey had to admit that administration now had untidy ends. The British had severely penalized incompetence. They had had to. Power over a huge country had depended on the knowledge and efficiency of the few who had governed it. And nothing had so reflected this thoroughness as their land policies. Dubey remembered his own training under Trivedi when he had learned not only about the land but all the intricate psychology woven through its laws. A farmer and his earth, he had thought, were a simple concept. But there was nothing so complex, so caught up with the drama of personality and the past as an acre of Indian soil. The Mughals had recognized the fact and the British too had had to square their account with it, for here was history that could not be ignored. Region by region the land had been surveyed every forty years and its record brought up to date.

"Ownership itself is no simple matter," Trivedi had told Dubey. "There are types of ownership, and its shades and variations are endless. I may be the legal landowner, but you may have equally recognized rights under customary law. The relationship between our two families may go back twenty generations or more. So a type of ownership, traditional and unshakeable, passes to you."

And then there had been the intricate structure of the village to be taken into account. There were members of the village community who had nothing to do directly with the land, but they were tied up with it just the same—

the cobbler, the repairer of ploughs, the barber, the scavenger, men who were paid in kind through the harvest. All their rights had to be considered.

"The British entered into an alliance with the past because they had to," said Trivedi. "They could not just collect revenue. It was a question of understanding the system to keep the good will of the people. Any government, British, Hottentot—or Indian—will have to understand it."

But the Indian Government had let the surveys slip. Things were changing, of course. Cash was taking the place of payment in kind. The village itself was changing. But efficiency had fallen into that chasm between old and new. Meanwhile life went on as usual, perhaps because everybody, had become used to a slower, more inefficient pace.

A phone call from Delhi informed Dubey that the Centre, in shape of the Cabinet Secretary, was disturbed by Gyan's latest announcement.

"We'd like to know what it means," said Kachru.

"It means the Sikh scriptures will be taught in schools," said Dubey unnecessarily.

"I know, I know. Have you spoken to Gyan Singh?"

"I have. He says it is a part—sorry, he said 'an integral part'—of Punjabi culture. I have his statement here on my desk. Do you want me to read it to you?"

"No," said Kachru. "We'll be getting it."

"Shall I convey the Centre's disapproval?"

"No, not yet. We'll have to think over all the implications." Kachru added doubtfully, "Of course, there's something in what he says. And it's a touchy subject. We can't do anything in a hurry. We must be careful."

One of these days, thought Dubey, we're going to be so careful we're going to have Bunny's jigsaw instead of the map of India to administer, every bit of it jumping. He wondered why he did not feel more agitated over this latest development. He supposed that he, like everyone else, was becoming a victim of inertia. He pulled himself together and spoke urgently.

"I think we should protest immediately. There's danger in this development."

"We'll let you know. Don't do anything yet."

In fact, in a critical situation don't do anything at all for as long as possible, Dubey thought. He put the phone down and in exasperation drew a small cat threatened by a huge mouse with enormous whiskers on the top sheet of a new note pad. He had shaded the cat's chest and was pointing its ears when his P.A. came in carrying a rolled newspaper.

"If you are not busy—"

Man Singh drew the newspaper from under his arm, holding it between thumb and forefinger as if it were infected, and spread it open on Dubey's desk with the same distaste and economy of gesture at a page where he had marked a corner item in small print with a blue pencil. Dubey read: "A senior official now among us is seen often in the company of a lady not his wife. We would like him to know we do not approve of—" Dubey read no further. He looked at the name of the paper. Inspiration.

"What a picturesque name."

His P.A. looked grave. "It is not a nice paper. I see it because a copy comes to the office."

"Well thank you for showing it to me. Do cats arch their backs when they're pleased or only when they are angry?"

"Excuse me?"

Dubey turned the note pad towards him. Man Singh did not smile.

"If you're worrying about that item," said Dubey, "don't."

Man Singh looked relieved. "Then you will deal with it? It is not a decent thing to discredit a gentleman, and so many people read this paper. What will they think?"

What people called morality touched their oldest and most cherished prejudices. I was, Dubey knew, an inflammable subject. For him it meant one thing alone, the proper use of life. It was not a matter of doing what one valued. It was a matter of being what one valued, and being was a daily affair, not an occasional activity. To live one's truth was both glory and disaster, but every particle of such living had been his strength. Whatever Man Singh saw in him of worth was because of it. Dubey watched Man Singh's face change as he spoke to him. That, he thought, should be the limit of one man's power over another, to be able to change a look of doubt to one of belief.

"There's a man called Hansa Ram waiting to see you," said Man Singh as he left.

When the man was admitted to the office, Vishal remembered he had seen him on the bench outside. The wifebeater. Only now he looked more embarrassed than obsequious, as if apologetic about his mission. He owned a restaurant, he said, and wanted his bar licence renewed. He had had no answer to several applications, and his business suffered when there was no bar.

Vishal made a jotting on his pad. He was busy and wanted to get on with his work.

"You will excuse me, sir," the large liquid eyes focussed on him, "but through the normal channels they will not renew it. I would not have come at all had I not heard there was a new official—yourself—here."

"I don't understand," said Vishal.

"No sir," Hansa Ram humbly conceded. "That is what I must explain. Perhaps you would rather hear it at my house, if you would honour me there with your presence.

Then you could decide what to do."

"I'd rather hear it here," said Vishal.

"As you wish, sir."

"Wait a moment," said Vishal. "Tell me where your restaurant is."

Hansa Ram wrote the address down for him and told him how to get there. His gratitude was boundless. Today had been the right day to seek admission to the Secretary Sahib's office.

Chapter 11

The letter was from Gauri. She was arriving, she wrote, on Friday night for the weekend and staying with Inder and Saroj. Nikhil was away in the south for a textile conference and she wanted a change from Delhi. She was sitting in a reclining canvas chair under the garden umbrella when Dubey arrived for lunch, the lush pink of her sari making her skin glow.

"You look terribly healthy," she told him.

"It must be the air," he said, "cleaner and colder than Delhi. And you look beautiful."

"That's different. I spend a lot of time and money to look beautiful."

Dubey sat down on the grass. "How you cling to that myth when you know you wake up beautiful."

"Vishal, you never will understand women. No woman past seventeen wakes up beautiful. Whom have you been meeting here?"

"Harpal Singh mostly."

"I meant women, silly."

"Oh women. Saroj and Mara."

"Saroj is pregnant," Gauri dismissed her lightly. "And Mara. What an odd name. What is she like?"

"Rather unusual like her name and very intelligent. She has a mind of her own."

"Never mind her intelligence," said Gauri.

"She's tall and slim. She and her husband are coming to lunch."

"Yes I know. Is she good to look at?"

"Decidedly," he said.

"I'm a little jealous," said Gauri.

"Don't be," he said gently.

He lay down flat on his back in the sun, the warmth and brightness on his face, his arms crossed under his head. Gauri looked at him thoughtfully.

"Well, I'm not actually. Except that—" she stopped.

"Except what?"

"Well you are a very attractive man—and I've often wondered why you don't make more of it. I'm glad you don't," she added, "but I've wondered why. It isn't as though you're plagued by a lot of conventions and principles."

"But I am plagued," said Dubey, "not by conventions, but by principles. I always have been."

"Right from the start?" she asked. "Tell me about the start. No other man ever will."

Dubey laughed. "Have you asked any other man?"

"No of course not. I've wanted to ask Nikhil about his start but I know he'd be horrified. But tell me, how *do* men start?"

"I don't know about other men," he said, "but I didn't know much about these matters until I went to Oxford, and then I started quite matter-of-factly to find out—and did."

"Oh," said Gauri, "who with?"

"A very capable lady who obliged—and educated—quite a large clientele of students and didn't mind Indians. Some of these women were finicky about colour and one didn't want to arrive and be turned down. As it was, one wasn't very brash and bold at that age. I certainly wasn't and if skin colour had been an added complication it would have been hard to manage any savoir faire."

"It sounds so cold-blooded," said Gauri with a shiver.

"It was," Dubey agreed. "That's the pity of these episodes, and the way most young men go about them. It's a curiosity, an urge, nothing more."

"And then you had other urges!" she prompted.

"I did. I went to Germany with a friend for the summer vacation. We motored and I remember we got quite gay and picked up a couple of girls at one of these roadside restaurants and took them along with us. They were on a holiday too. We took rooms at an inn that night—and after a while we swapped girls."

"You did what?" asked Gauri scandalized.

"We exchanged girls. One of the girls suggested it."

Gauri went into peals of laughter, and Saroj looked out of the window.

"What are you two up to? I'll be out as soon as I've finished in the kitchen."

"Vishal has been telling me about the lighter side of the political situation," said Gauri. "And then what happened?" she gasped.

"Well, then we all went back to our various studies and eventually came back to India and coped with life, so to speak."

"But what happened to your sex life?" she insisted.

"It was there—sort of sporadic and stealthy—the way it

has to be. It all turned my stomach somewhat."

"My poor supersensitive Vishal."

"I mean the noninvolvement of it. I'm not a person who gets much out of a situation unless I can give my affection or my loyalty to it. It's just a blank otherwise. I found that out fairly early."

He sat up and chewed meditatively on a blade of grass.

"Vishal, I have a horrible feeling I'm in love with you."

She spoke lightly but there was a new serious note in her voice, or had it been there before and escaped his notice?

"It's a good thing to be in love," he said.

She looked at him appraisingly. "I can't make up my mind whether you are the simplest or the most complicated man I've ever known. It's maddening. Are you going to ask me to dinner tonight?"

"Yes, of course." He waved to Jit and Mara as they came through the garden gate. "Would you like to come for a walk first?"

"I would not. You can pick me up after your tramp."

Saroj came out with a tray, which Dubey took from her.

"Lunch is going to be a hodgepodge," she said. "There's the usual stuff, dal and veg and so on, and then Gauri has brought a heavenly boxful of goodies. Lovely imported things we never see—here they are."

There were a jar of black olives, a mound of cheese, and two bottles of wine on the tray. Dubey set it down on the table Sham had laid under a tree.

"Black olives!" breathed Mara. "What bliss."

"The Greek ambassador sent those," said Gauri.

"And the wine?" asked Saroj.

"Toni—the Greek ambassador—sent those, too."

"Hasn't this Indo-Greek relationship sprung up rather suddenly?" Dubey murmured to Gauri.

Gauri raised innocent, long-lashed eyes to his. "Why no, Vishal. It goes rather far back—326 B.C., I think, was when it began."

By the time Inder came from the office they had settled down to a feast of cheese, olives, and wine.

"Not that I'm interested," said Gauri amiably to Inder, "but how's business?"

"Business is all right," said Inder. "Cotton is in a slump but our mill is flourishing because we're producing nylon and new mixtures of yarn, and there are enough people here to buy them. There's nothing wrong with business. It's the atmosphere outside it that's worrying. I'm damned if I know what to make of it."

He looked at the table in amazement.

"The Greek ambassador," explained Saroj, helping her husband to cheese and wine.

"Why didn't you bring this wonderful man along?" asked Inder.

"I had to explore these wilds for myself first," said Gauri.

"Is this your first visit here then?" asked Mara. "How do you like it?"

"Oh dear," said Gauri, watching four pairs of eyes fasten on her, their possessors obviously dedicated to Chandigarh.

"You mean you don't?" asked Jit, incredulous.

"Well," she began helplessly, "all these ramps and things. Nearly every building in one of the sectors I passed had one on the outside. And I'm told some of the public buildings have them *inside*. It's all a bit preposterous."

They sat in an accusing semicircle around her.

"But Gauri," puzzled Saroj, "you're so keen on modern things. You're always opening modern-art exhibitions. I thought you'd love this."

"That's quite different, pet," said Gauri. "A painting is

on a square of canvas. If you don't like it you can put it away in the *godown*. What can you do with a building, with a whole *town*?"

They stared at her in consternation.

"It's a revolution in architecture," said Jit, "and what's more a revolution in people's thinking."

"That's just it," said Gauri. "Revolutions are so—sudden. And they have such peculiar results. Now why on earth has that funny-looking thing like a funnel been stuck on top of the Legislature?"

"It's to let in the light at a particular angle," Inder explained with unusual patience.

Gauri shook her head unconvinced.

"The High Court," Mara volunteered unasked, "is one of the most magnificent and dramatic buildings I have ever seen. It has a kind of immense antique grandeur about it, like an ancient temple."

"Well, I haven't seen it yet," Gauri conceded, "but Mr. Justice Ahmad who used to be here—he's at the Supreme Court in Delhi now—said it was positive hell inside. Hot as blazes in summer and freezing in winter. And they'd hung up the most bizarre looking things they called tapestries on the walls."

"Those are Corbusiers," said Mara reverently.

Gauri turned to Dubey. "Well, what are you sitting there tongue-tied for? Say something."

"You're the one who hobnobs with the diplomatic corps," said Dubey. "Think of something diplomatic or you won't get any lunch."

"I can honestly say the weather is divine," said Gauri, relaxing in her chair again. "If we had your Chandigarh winter all year round we'd be a different breed of people. And I've never seen such roses."

Saroj beamed. Magnanimously they forgave her and

called for lunch.

"There's nowhere decent to dine out," said Dubey when he picked up Gauri in the evening, "so I'm taking you back to the guest house for dinner."

"That's what I wanted," said Gauri.

She exclaimed in dismay as they entered the long sitting room.

"Why get a world-famous architect to design a building and then furnish it with junk? All this frightful P.W.D. furniture!"

She sat down on a sofa covered with dingy upholstery. "The fact is we aren't ready for Chandigarh. We should carry on with dak-bungalow style living till everyone is educated and has some taste. Revolution indeed! What kind of mess do your ministers make of their houses, I wonder."

"I haven't been invited to their homes," said Dubey. "Do you want a fire?"

"Naturally. I'm freezing."

She was wearing a cardigan of soft grey wool embroidered with sequins over her sari and looked like an expensive and exquisite work of art in unlikely surroundings.

"I didn't realize what a commotion I'd start when I casually mentioned a ramp," she said.

Dubey attended to the fire. "What I like about these four young things is that there's nothing casual about them. There's character there and a natural concern with what goes on."

He sat down with his drink. "They've made new beginnings in this town, built their homes, struck roots. It's something of an adventure for them in the personal sense aside from the fascination of a whole new city coming up around them. The first thing Jit ever told me was that he had thought for a while it would be the only place in India where politics wouldn't take over. Now it's the centre of the arena. It's a great pity."

"You like it here," said Gauri.

"Yes, enormously. It's like a shot in the arm after Delhi. And these four have been very hospitable. I don't know why I link them up. They seem somewhat on edge with each other."

"I don't know about your unusual girl and her husband," said Gauri, "but Saroj and Inder certainly are. She has more or less petered out since she married him."

"In what way?" Dubey asked.

"She was a bright girl, with a college degree and all that. You'd never know it now."

"She doesn't assert herself much," said Dubey.

"It's worse than that. She doesn't express herself at all. Inder belongs to the he-man school and I suppose someone has to bow before the blast or there'd be an explosion. They're two entirely different kinds of people."

"They're two different cultures," said Dubey. "That can only happen in a country like this which produces people of such vastly different traditions. And a thin veneer of Westernization succeeds in fooling people they come from the same sort of past. Get two people so unlike together in marriage and every effort at growth on the part of one can look like an act of betrayal to the other."

"How true," said Gauri. "You walk into a home where people eat with knives and forks and you think it must be the same sort of home as yours. Thank God it didn't happen to me. There's only one safety in India for some time to come, and that is to marry in your own state into a background you thoroughly understand."

"Yours was arranged?" asked Dubey.

"I never expected anything else. And I had no college

degree either. I went to a convent in Calcutta and then sat around for a couple of years until Nikhil was found for me and then I married him. That kind of thing endures. You look doubtful about something, Vishal."

"About your saying a minute ago that Saroj has petered out. I don't think she has. There's a definite core in her that's all herself, like something held on to, waiting to flower, if it has the chance."

"She'll never have a chance at anything if she goes on producing babies," said Gauri. "It's years since I've been able to persuade her even to come to Delhi. She simply won't budge from here. And look at the way she lives, everything falling to bits from her chair covers to that impossible servant. She could have found an ayah by this time if she'd made up her mind to. And she refuses to take a penny from Nikhil outside of Inder's salary."

Gauri would not leave the fireside when dinner was announced and they had it served on trays.

"At least the food is good," she said.

"The cook used to be on the Maharaja of Patiala's staff."

"Well no wonder. Good cooks are petering out too."

"I have no liqueur to offer you," said Dubey. "Want some coffee?"

She shook her head. "What's the use of keeping awake when there's nothing to do in town? But take me for a drive first. I can't possibly go to bed yet. It's not even ten."

She sat close to him in the car.

"That noninvolvement you were talking about, this morning, Vishal—did it apply to me too?"

He hesitated before replying, "Yes it did."

"You'll never be a success with women if you go on regaling them with the truth. But I've told you that before."

Dubey smiled and said nothing.

"For some reason," she went on, "I am terribly fond of you. In fact I'm sorry to say that everyone else seems rather insipid in comparison."

"What about this ambassador person, the one who's so generous with his olives?"

"Oh he's charming. That's what I mean. Everybody is so full of charm and the social graces, uttering little compliments and politenesses. It adds up to exactly nothing. I'm tired of it, and I'm not as contented as I look, Vishal."

"I know." He put a hand on her knee and she covered it with her own.

"Well, what do you prescribe, doctor?"

"You have everything in the world a woman could want," said Dubey. "Make something of it."

"Good works?" she said dryly. "I'm not the type."

"You are just the type. You have the generosity of spirit and the interest in others, besides the means."

"My poor misled creature. I'm a social butterfly with positively no interest in life beyond my own comforts and pleasures. Hasn't anyone told you?"

"No, no one has and I must have missed that side of you myself. The Gauri I know is different and worthwhile."

She groped for a handkerchief in her bag and wiped the moisture from the corners of her eyes.

"Now you've made me smudge my eye makeup."

Dubey put an arm around her and drew her head down on his shoulder.

"If you had told me I was cut out to be a nun," said Gauri, "I'd probably take my vows without a moment's hesitation."

"No, don't do that, though you'd make a lovely nun. You weren't meant for burial of any sort. Live. And be happy."

He drew up outside the gate of Inder's house. He was getting down to open it when Gauri put a restraining hand on his arm.

"I'll get down here," she said. "Vishal, you won't disappear, will you? I couldn't bear to lose you—altogether."

He took her face in his hands. "I won't disappear," he said.

He felt her soft lips on his cheek before she got out.

It poured the next morning.

"Snow and ice would be kinder than this dismal downpour," said Gauri, sitting up in bed as Saroj, followed by Sham carrying a tea tray, came into her room. "It chills me to the marrow. Don't expect me to get up till it clears."

The room did not add to her warmth, with its sparse furnishings, handspun curtains, and coloured cotton rugs on the floor. Its only adornment was a big picture of a battleship slightly askew on a stormy sea, painted by Muff in nursery school. Saroj had tacked it on a piece of cardboard and hung it on a length of ribbon.

"That may be all day," said Saroj, sitting down on the edge of her cousin-in-law's bed. "It's awfully good for the crops."

"No doubt," said Gauri pouring tea into a cup. "Where's that Paragon china I gave you last year?"

"I've locked it away. Sham would have smashed it up in no time. It's pointless keeping anything valuable out in the way of china or silver nowadays. You can't get a trained servant any more."

"I think you ought to get Sham a proper uniform. What does he think he looks like roaming around in that outfit?"

Sham, in a sleeveless sweater worn over a once-white shirt and blue-striped night pajamas had just left the room.

"He has a uniform. He saves it for when there are

guests."

"I'd like him to think of me as a guest," said Gauri. "He looks quite disgraceful. And I'm going to send you two big English heaters I have at home. I'm not using them and that one there doesn't heat a square inch let alone a room."

"No don't. We like the cold." Saroj got up.

"Sit down. It's time you and I had a talk."

"Yes Gauri," said Saroj meekly.

"Now don't pretend you're deaf," said Gauri severely, then softened at the sight of Saroj's face. Really, she looked about sixteen. It was ridiculous her having all these children. "Before you get any larger, pet, you must plan a trip to Delhi. A few days away from housekeeping will be good for you. In fact, I've been thinking, why not come back with me this afternoon?"

"I couldn't. The children—"

"The children can go to Mara's. It'll only be for a few days. And you need the change."

"Do I?"

"Everyone needs a change from routine now and then. Well, that's settled then. Go and pack a suitcase and make whatever arrangements you have to."

"I couldn't," said Saroj. "Inder wouldn't like it at all."

"Well, we aren't going to consult him," said Gauri firmly. "I'll just tell him I'm taking you along with me. He's a big boy now. He'll get along all right for a few days."

"I couldn't," repeated Saroj, distressed.

"You're beginning to sound like a broken record, pet. And now that we're on the subject I may as well come out with the other things that are bothering me. I've hardly slept thinking about them. Chandigarh isn't in a very settled condition. Suppose it gets worse? I don't like the idea of your having your confinement here. Have you a decent doctor?"

"He's wonderful," said Saroj. "He takes such an interest—"

"I don't care whether or not he chats with you about genes and chromosomes," interrupted Gauri, "the point is, is he competent?"

"Of course he is," said Saroj shocked at the suggestion. "He's the head of the gynaecology department at the Medical Institute here."

"That doesn't make a bit of difference," said Gauri. "In fact it makes me a lot more nervous. These government institutes are a mess. The best people can't do a competent job in them. Everything moves at snail's pace. They have to wait months to get anything, from a bottle of ink to an x-ray machine, sanctioned."

"Gauri," said Saroj patiently, "millions of women have their babies at the Medical Institute, women who'd have died in their huts without any kind of care at all."

"That's another thing. Millions of women shouldn't be *having* babies. And *you* certainly shouldn't be having one alongside the teeming millions. Saroj, do be sensible. Come to Delhi for your confinement. The children will come too and I'll be able to look after all of you. You needn't stay a minute longer than you want to afterwards."

Saroj traced a careful pattern on the coverlet with her finger.

"Gauri, you're so sweet—"

"I'm not sweet, I'm frantic. Now for the love of heaven say you'll come—at least for your confinement—and we can think about your in-between trip later."

Saroj looked up after a long moment.

"I know this isn't Delhi, Gauri, but it's home. Of course Mara would look after the children. She'd be glad to but I'd hate leaving them. But the main thing is, Gauri, that I *want* to have the baby at the Institute. I *want* to be with all those women. Don't you see, I want to belong to the human race?"

Gauri sighed. "You won't belong less to the human race, dearest, if you have your baby in a comfortable, quiet nursing home with a room to yourself."

"Yes I will. People—ordinary people—don't have those things. I'd be wretched in an expensive private air-conditioned room. What on earth would there be to notice and enjoy, all walled in like that? And anyway, Inder—"

"What about Inder?" He stood in the doorway in his dressing gown. "Is her ladyship receiving?"

"Persuade this wife of yours to have her confinement in Delhi," said Gauri, "and to come with me now for a few days for the change."

"What does she want a change for?"

"For all the usual reasons. A different scene, new faces, a little fun, a hair style."

"What's wrong with the one she's got?"

Gauri gave up. "Go away, both of you, and let me get dressed."

She heard Inder say as they went down the passage, "What do you want a change for?" and Saroj protesting, "I don't."

Gauri rang up Dubey after breakfast.

"Are you coming over? I have to talk to you about the political situation. No, not that one. The actual one. Good, well stay to lunch. I'm leaving soon after in any case."

She took him aside when he arrived.

"I've been so worried about Saroj, Vishal. I can't persuade her to have her baby in Delhi. And if Gyan Singh launches his strike, there may be all sorts of upsets here."

"No need to worry," said Dubey. "It'll be over long before she has her baby. We expect a showdown any day now. What Gyan plans is a demonstration to show the strength of his demands. He'll call it off once he makes his point. It's a political trick, not a mass movement."

"Are you sure?" She was still doubtful.

"I'm certain. Besides I understand babies have been born in air raids and taxis and all sorts of places, none the worse for wear."

"That's neither here nor there."

She stood, resigned, beside the window, watching the rain slant against the pane.

"It's just as well I'm leaving today. I'm itching to turn this house upside down. I'd change these chair covers and curtains, burn the carpet, donate the crockery to an orphanage, and send Sham to be dry-cleaned. Anyway, you think it's all right to leave Saroj to the tender mercies of this Institute and these politicians who can't make up their minds when they're going to come to blows? What a collection."

"This 'collection' will tell you all the history that counts was made in these parts," said Dubey, "from Kurukshetra to Panipat. It's the cradle of Indian civilization."

"The cradle of fiddlesticks," said Gauri.

Chapter 12

There were days when it soothed Mara just to arrive at the school and look at her own handiwork. This was not one of them. Her batteries needed recharging. She was in her office, smoking her midmorning cigarette, piano music and sunlight from the schoolroom just beginning to weave a pattern of peace, when Inder arrived, filling the doorway with his restless brooding energy.

"I left office early," he said unnecessarily.

"Have you come for the children? It's not nearly time, but I'll call them if you like."

"No," he said quickly. "I'll wait."

"I can't give you a cup of coffee here but I've got some sticky raspberry syrup the children drink. Want some?"

"No thanks." He sat down, facing her.

He must have been a Russian in some previous birth, she decided. All that gloom. Only she knew he could never have been anything but Indian. In him she came up against every irritant she had ever encountered in this country, her country, though she had spent so many years away from it. The people she knew had become clues to India, to be fitted together to make some sense of the bog of her inheritance. The people were different from one another—who could be less alike than Jit and Inder? But they all had in common endless layers that admitted of no pith. There was never the final answer that would explain why a man functioned as he did, what the core of him was. The children were her comfort. In five or six years of life a creature was still part instinctively animal, and altogether refreshingly natural, belonging to the whole human race and not some baffling ration of it.

"What a mess things are in," she said, squashing out her cigarette. "At this rate I'll have to send out notices closing the school until the strike is over. I wish politics wouldn't interfere with everything."

"You can't get away from politics in this country," said Inder.

"Why ever not? You can get away from anything if you make up your mind to, and really want to."

"That's childish nonsense, Mara."

"No it isn't. Some part of a person has to stay free and make decisions."

Of course remarks like that came too near the bone. Only one had to get to the bone to understand, and how did one get near this man, she wondered. Trying to know him was like walking on a soapy surface. It was sheer chance if one got safely to the end of one's conversation. It would be sheer chance if more than conversation came up between them. And that really shouldn't be left to chance, she thought in distaste. It was indecent just to slide into situations. They were not adolescents.

"Can't you leave the school for half an hour?" he said suddenly. "I've got a painting just arrived from Delhi for the office. Gauri sent it—along with a vanful of things from kitchen utensils to heaters. And I have no idea where to hang it."

She considered this a minute. "I suppose I could. The children have singing from now till the end of the hour."

It was the first time she had been in his office. It was smaller than Jit's with no attempt at elegance. Jit's had personal touches. He created an atmosphere around himself, with his pipes in a rack, a few of his favourite books, a photograph of her, and snaps of his nephews and nieces. This room was strictly for business, with just enough furniture, plainly upholstered and no adornment. Suddenly she wished she had not come, wished intensely that she did not live two lives. Inder and Jit. Jit and Inder. The duality of it tore her apart, yet people would laugh at her saying so. Two lives, one of which was in her mind? A life built on a vague insistent yearning, with no more substance than that? Even the man, above all he with whom she lived it, would not understand it. This was a man who would understand only flesh and blood and its promptings. She went up to the canvas leaning against a chair and turned it around.

"It's beautiful," she said with pleasure, "but then one would expect Gauri to know what was good."

"Where should I hang it?" he asked indifferently.

"Inder, for heaven's sake *look* at it."

Exasperation made her tone peremptory. She wanted a spontaneous reaction from him, at least about this impersonal object.

"I'm not interested in it. It's just something to hang on a wall."

Her temper rose. "What *are* you interested in, apart from yourself?"

He stood looking at her fixedly, unhappily.

She could not keep the anger out of her voice. "Aren't you human enough to step outside yourself even to quarrel?"

He crossed the room and pinned her arms to her sides. "Stop talking like that, Mara."

They sat down clinging on the sofa in a terrible, longed-for intimacy, and the frantic thought flashed through her, What are we going to do? What's going to happen to us? She knew the excitement of his nearness did not wipe out the questions in her mind. She could not make love to a mystery. She could not be lost to the world. With an effort she struggled up, but he had his arms around her, his face against her hip. She put a restraining hand on his head.

"I don't know what's happened to me, Inder," she said, and then with difficulty, "That's not true. I do know. I've longed for this—to be near you like this—"

"Then what's the matter?" He pulled her down beside him.

"You're too important. I don't want to stumble into lovemaking with you, by accident, here in this place. It wouldn't be good enough."

"What do you want then?"

"Something different, not so haphazard. Let's meet more and get to know each other." As she spoke she despaired of convincing him. She was afraid of his rough refusal to understand, and above all, of losing him. But she did not want him any other way.

"When can we meet?" he demanded.

"Come over on Monday afternoon."

"Not till then?" He was incredulous.

"It's only two days away." Inwardly she panicked again. "And it'll give us time to realize what's happening."

She felt stronger as soon as she had said it. She could lean against him, feeling his urgency relax. They kissed tenderly and looked wonderingly at each other. She knew now they could wait, for waiting would have value. She had not believed she would be able to make him understand.

"This is what I've needed Mara, a resting place."

She had wanted just those words.

"You won't escape me, will you, Mara?"

"I don't want to. I want to build something with you."

"How can we? We're both so tied."

"We can—between us—for what it's worth."

"I don't know anyone like you. What kind of woman are you?"

"Odd, I suppose," she said.

"Your name is odd too."

"Yes, it's short for Tamara. I was named for my god-mother. She was Russian and a very dear friend of my mother's."

"Was?"

"She died last year. She lived in Paris."

"I don't know anything about you, Tamara."

"We must learn about each other."

He traced the curve of her cheek with his finger, and encircled her narrow wrist in delicate cautious caresses foreign to him. He had never known there was exquisite pleasure in such things. An aimless fever had dropped from him like a worn-out garment, and he recognized a new feeling, respect, that had never played much part in his relations with women. He knew that he was in the one place where he could be himself. And Monday was not too far away. He wanted to savour each moment till then.

"The first time I met you, Inder, you looked at me as if I were a trade union."

His laughter exploded in a sound of sheer uncomplicated enjoyment. He put both arms around her, careless of their hard grip, and they rocked and laughed together like children, coming out happy and carefree into the bright morning. A group of men at the gate watched them as they got into the car.

"Better roll the glass up," said Inder quickly.

His own went up not a minute too soon. A handful of wet brown dirt plastered the pane for an instant before falling off, leaving some sticking. Mara gasped.

"It's all right," said Inder. "It's a good thing we had our windows up."

"Why did they do it?"

"There's a nasty mood about. That was cow dung. Stone throwing is an offence and they can be penalized if they break anything, so they use cow dung. It's more messy and it proves their point, whatever it is."

"Inder?" she turned towards him.

"Not now," he said on a note of warning. "When they're in that sort of mood it's better not to give them an excuse to break out. And this man-woman business riles a crowd more than anything."

Would this newborn thing between them last even two days, she wondered, as she got down at the school. She knew it had when he came to see her at home. He sat down beside her on the wrought-iron bench by her pebble pond and took her in his arms.

"Do you know the strangest thing about you, Tamara? Talking to you and kissing you are the same. It all blends. I don't know where one leaves off and the other begins."

When she laughed he drew his forefinger along the edge of her teeth. Suddenly all the differences between loving and not loving had become apparent to him. He was in no hurry to possess her. He wanted to keep the softly glowing intimacy between them alive.

"Would you like a drink, Inder?"

"No. And don't get up. Stay close."

It was some time before he realized they were in the courtyard, not in the privacy of a room, and that anyone could have walked in, and when he did, it did not matter. The need for rigid secrecy seemed to belong to another lifetime.

"We didn't decide where to hang that picture," he remembered.

"I know. Pictures are just something to hang on a wall. When you said that I wanted to ask you what really touches you."

"You."

"But all these years?"

"Nothing." He crushed her hands in his. "I need you. Don't leave me."

For the first time in his life no demons plagued his imaginations. The sight of Saroj, still asleep when he woke, touched a chord in him. Her blankets had slipped. One hand lay on the mound of her stomach, some part of her conscious of its burden even in sleep. Her nightie had climbed up her legs and they looked awkward, flung out like a doll's, her thighs crisscrossed with fine white lines where the smooth skin had stretched. Carefully he drew it down and straightened the covers over her. She barely stirred. Filled with a contentment he had never known, Inder got up and went downstairs into the garden.

The gardener they shared with two other families in the neighbourhood sat on his haunches weeding the flower border. He looked round surprised to find Inder up so early. Inder walked over to him, seeing as if for the first time the pastel mixture of hyacinth, larkspur, and foxglove.

"Did you select these flowers for the border?" he asked.

"No, memsahib did," said the gardener.

"And those roses?"

"Memsahib did." The gardener looked at him curiously.

Inder remembered that Saroj had joined the Rose Society when they had moved here. He had heard her speak with pride of her own, looking sculptured now in their perfection, even the dew on them held still. It was an odd quirk of personality that led Saroj to bother not at all about an untidy house, yet drove her to demand beauty and order in her garden, to take infinite pains with a stray animal, and to spend hours in company with her children, though she did not mind if their socks needed darning. Sofas and chairs and socks were not alive, she had told him, they weren't important. The breath of one's body was for the living things. She had sent for seed catalogues from Poona last year and pored over them, deciding what she would order, her brows puckered in concentration. And now her flower-bed looked sweet and prim in the honey-coloured morning light. It was the way Saroj herself looked in a drawing room when she was among strangers, like a good little girl minding her manners, the way he liked her to look. It was the expression of shy reserve that had appealed intensely to him when he had met her. His mind suddenly braked as he thought of that apparent innocence, and he waited for the familiar knife blade of memory and association to cut into him. It did not come. A surgeon's knife had to cut through layers of tissue to locate the canker in the body. And that torturing memory would now have to cut through his new-found contentment to get to his wound. Perhaps the wound itself had healed and vanished, lifted out of him by Mara. He had been deeply at peace since they had become lovers.

The word had a curious new fascination for him. He had believed that if you took a woman to bed it made you her lover. Nothing, he now knew, could be further from the truth. With Mara the sharp distinction between bed and not-bed did not exist. He wanted to linger over her, to carry on in laughter and conversation what he had begun in lovemaking. The act of love, so final and complete with other women, a thing with a beginning and an end, was never ended with Mara. Its culmination brought a flood of tenderness that flowed into a hundred different newly awakened channels of his being. And with her, every act was an act of love. She stimulated his mind and involved him in ways no woman ever had.

Bunny and Muff came out of the house in their dressing gowns and made for the opposite corner of the garden, kneeling in front of two boxes of moist earth. He went to them.

"Nothing much to look at there," he remarked.

"It's too soon," said Muff. "We've planted seeds and we're taking them to school to watch them grow. Mara says they'll only take a few days."

"Do you like Mara?"

"Of course," said Muff.

Inder picked up his sons one after the other and kissed them with an exuberance that astonished them. They wriggled out of his grasp and he chased them all over the garden.

The sun had banished the mist and light lay like warm oil along the treetops. It melted over the lawn and onto the front porch where Saroj stood shading her eyes. Inder crossed the grass to her, wanting to cosset and humour her, his wife. He put an arm around her and took her indoors. There was a lightness about his bathing and shaving ritual, in his footsteps down the stairs, in the way he handled his car. He had not lived in any other country, but there could be no season anywhere as beautiful as the winter in Chandigarh, no place on earth like the Punjab—or Hariyana—or whatever they liked to call it. And whatever they called it, it was his, this soil and everything on it a precious possession. Anticipation mounted in him, making the last few yards of the drive to his office intolerably long. He went straight to the telephone and, still standing, picked it up and dialled her number. Her voice came over calm and clear. Relieved, he sank into his chair, the receiver close to his lips, his eyes on the painting she had hung on the wall facing him, surrendering himself to the few minutes that would give purpose to his day. He could never begin work any more till he had spoken to Mara.

Chapter 13

Dr. Varma's hands expertly probed the length of Saroj's child. She could tell by his touch exactly where her baby began and where it ended, and she found the look of worry on his face oddly reassuring. It had nothing to do with her case. It was the professional harvest he collected every day. She herself transferred her cares to him once a month for ten or fifteen minutes and always left his consulting room feeling refreshed. How often we put ourselves into the hands of others, she thought. All our lives, in routine ways. Trust is natural. We eat what the cook puts on the table, confident we won't be poisoned. We get into taxis, certain of reaching our destination. We believe our friends. But then it stops. The small islands of trust stay separated in a sea of suspicion. On the big issues, marriage and war and peace, people eye each other warily and walk with caution.

"Everything's all right," said the doctor, completing his

examination, "except that you don't look as if you've been getting enough sleep."

"Am I looking haggard?" she asked with interest.

He looked up from the pad on which he was writing a prescription for vitamins at the candid face and the fine childlike hair spread over her shoulders.

"No," he said emphatically. "Neither old nor haggard. Are you disappointed?"

She smiled as she tucked the prescription into her handbag and rose. In the small domestic world she inhabited his was the surest and kindliest touch. She would have liked to talk to him longer but there was a roomful of women waiting outside, against a wall lined with family-planning posters. It was a tableau she could never pass without a knot of misery in her. They were like blocks of woods, like *things*, without lustre, without animation, just waiting to submit to the moment of expulsion, for the dark waters to close over their heads, and for the deliverance that would follow. And when it was all over and their bodies restored to them, they would live without joy, inert to the miracle. It would be just an extra cry in the night for tired arms and flaccid breasts to cope with. The one next to the door, her tummy very round, held a small monkeylike creature against her trying to quieten its whimpering. Saroj bent to touch the ugly wizened little face and felt a rush of fullness to her own breasts as the baby gripped her finger. She had not known till then that one's milk was a form of compassion, that it had to do with love, not for one's own child but whatever needed it. She drove to Sector 22 for the vitamins and heard Dubey's greeting as she parked.

"Aren't you working today?" she asked.

"This is work. I have to hear a tale of woe at the Sea Shell. Come along and have a cup of coffee."

"I must do some shopping but I'll join you afterwards."

Dubey pushed open a heavy door of opaque glass framed in carved wood and it swung soundlessly shut behind him, cutting off light, fresh air, and escape. In the musty dimness he saw faded wine-red velvet hangings and a huge chandelier and felt thick carpeting underfoot. There was a scattering of couples at widely spaced tables and a four-piece band on a dais against a large oyster shell. The band crashed into sound and Hansa Ram emerged from the gloom.

"So kind of you, sir. Only your good self would have come. Mr. Prasad did not respond to my invitations."

Dubey gathered that news of Prasad's departure must have got around. Hansa Ram led the way to a corner table and followed Dubey's glance.

"People like a Western atmosphere," he explained.

He signalled a waiter, who brought a three-tiered carrier of brightly coloured pastries, a plate of sandwiches covered with pink potato chips, and coffee.

"I bought that chandelier fifteen years ago at an auction of the Dowager Maharani of Jharna's palace furnishings. At that time this place was in fine condition, everything new. That bar, too, I bought at the auction." He pointed to a heavy teak bar at one side of the room. "It was in the downstairs drawing room of the Dowager Maharani's palace. Her Highness honoured me with her patronage. I was sole supplier of gin to her."

"Only gin?"

"Her Highness drank only gin. The finest."

"And why did you stop?"

"Her Highness went away. That is why she auctioned her belongings. She lives in the South of France now and meets many film stars. She's an old lady now but she loves life. And it is her patronage that started me to success. Such orders she gave me. But please help yourself." He paused and said eagerly, "Perhaps you would prefer something stronger than coffee, that is, if you drink?"

"I certainly drink," said Dubey, more categorically than he need have, because it irritated him that in the Establishment it was an admission of moral decay, "but I won't have one now, thank you. And I'm expecting a friend in a few minutes. Why not tell me your story first?"

"Sir," said Hansa Ram, "it is a matter involving politicians so one dares not say too much. The floor above is owned by Sadar Gyan Singh. He hires out those rooms to couples. His business continues to flourish but my licence has been held up, I don't know why."

"That's a serious accusation," said Dubey.

"It is not an accusation. It is common talk in the marketplace. Everyone knows of it. Yet nobody stops it. But that is no business of mine. All I want is my licence."

"What sort of reputation does Gyan Singh have?" asked Dubey.

Hansa Ram said piously, "Who am I to judge another?"

"Of course you must judge another," said Dubey impatiently. "We all judge other men every day of our lives, or if we don't, we should. It's too easy not to."

"Yes sir," Hansa Ram was respectful, attentive, and eager to please, and Dubey regretted his outburst.

"Well sir, Gyan Singh is a man like any other, and every man needs money. A politician needs it more than most. So who worries where it comes from? I only worry about my licence. Do me the honour of eating something."

Dubey bit into vividly iced stale sponge cake and took a swallow of coffee.

"So you think money is his driving force? I wonder."

"Power, sir, and money. And the two go together. Is there some third force that drives men?"

"From time to time," said Dubey, "men have been driven by other forces."

"Indeed sir," said Hansa Ram respectfully, "I am not an educated man myself and have little knowledge of such things. Yourself is a graduate." He looked intently at his guest. "What other forces have they been driven by?"

"There have been saints and prophets and—"

"Ah, *religious* teachers," Hansa Ram acknowledged, back in familiar territory.

"And others," said Dubey, "but perhaps there isn't time to talk of all that just now."

"No sir," agreed Hansa Ram in relief.

"But what kind of man is Gyan Singh?" persisted Dubey. "What do people say of him?"

Everybody respected his authority, Hansa Ram said. There was no doubt about it, he was a man all right. He could keep law and order, or even upset it if he wished. Unquestionably a leader.

"Married, I suppose?" asked Dubey.

Yes indeed, and very much the head of his household too. Oh yes, he was a man all right. He was obeyed. The head of his family and no mistake, and that was how it should be.

Was it? wondered Dubey. Was the seed of violence, of one will trampling another, to be planted and to take root from generation to generation, because it was the medium of exchange between people, because they knew no other, because it had always been so? Did tragedy have to pass unnoticed in everyday life, even by those who suffered it, because they believed that was how life had to be lived?

"And then," Hansa Ram was continuing, "he has money, too. The place upstairs and a printing press he took over last election for printing pamphlets but now it brings out a newspaper—more a scandal sheet—"

Hansa Ram stopped abruptly, looking embarrassed.

"Yes I know," said Dubey, "I believe I have been mentioned in it. This is good coffee. May I have another cup?"

"With pleasure, sir," said Hansa Ram with alacrity, and added hesitantly, "The matter of the licence—"

"You'll get it," said Dubey.

"I do not know how to thank you."

"Don't thank me. There's no reason why it should have been held up all this time. There's no prohibition in this city."

Hansa Ram looked too moved to speak. "Any service for me, sir?" he said gratefully at last.

Saroj came in and he got up. "I will take your leave, sir."

"What a horrible place," said Saroj.

"The chandelier belonged to the Dowager Maharani of Jharna's downstairs drawing room."

"Well, what's it doing here?"

"She had no use for it any more. She lives in the South of France where she drinks excellent gin and meets film stars. Have a sandwich or one of these cakes."

Saroj shuddered.

"Is it the light in here or are you really looking put out?" she asked.

"I'm irritated," said Dubey

"I don't wonder. What a place."

Dubey said, "I'm irritated at a taboo-ridden system that makes one want to declare oneself a drunkard for no rhyme or reason."

She looked puzzled.

"And I'm angry with myself because I didn't make anything of this talk with Hansa Ram or get to know him better. I was too busy telling him what I thought, and now I've lost a good opportunity with him. As far as he's concerned I'm just another official and what with his licence held up for months for no reason he can understand, I don't think he has much use for officialdom."

"Didn't he discuss his business with you?"

"Yes he did. It's the man I'm talking about." Dubey called a waiter and ordered another cup. "At least the coffee's good. Where have you been?"

"To the doctor. And my flutter is about nine inches long."

"How do you know?"

"I guessed from the doctor's feel. About that long." She put her forefingers apart on the tablecloth, "And it's started growing fingernails. The doctor didn't tell me that. I read it in a book. Imagine being just nine inches long and having fingernails."

She was like a child herself, reaching for the moon, for something forever out of reach, a quality that contrasted touchingly with her earthbound sheltering motherhood.

"I'm impressed," said Dubey, "though I should have thought other things would have priority over fingernails."

"I suppose it has other things too. I must look up the book. But it's amazing about fingernails when babies are born. Some look jagged and uneven as if they'd been at manual labour, and others look as if they'd just been manicured. Have you ever seen a newborn baby?"

"I'm afraid not."

"I love them," said Saroj. "I love their lolling heads and their mewing cries. Do you know Bunny's head smelt like orange blossom? I love everything about them."

"You love everything about them even before they're born."

"Yes." Her eyes shone. "How did you know?"

She drank her coffee and added reflectively, "I can't understand people who don't, people like Chintamani, for instance."

"Who is Chintamani?"

"She was the doctor I went to when I was expecting Muff. She made me very angry. She was—unconcerned." Saroj brought out the word with feeling.

"You mean she wouldn't discuss fingernails?"

Dubey pictured a harassed doctor, working round the clock, coping with floods of pregnant women. But it was not the moment to express sympathy for Chintamani.

"One felt exactly like a pork sausage or a tinned sardine or something in an assembly line with her: All right, out you go, next. And so on. Oh, she didn't actually say that but she never showed the least interest. She had children of her own, neglected-looking things, and a 'what's-all-the-fuss-about' attitude. The curious thing is that you can have six children and not know what it's all about. And you can have one, and know. It depends how you have them and what the process means to you."

"What *is* it all about?" asked Dubey.

Saroj took a deep breath and subsided into silence.

"Too big an order?" smiled Dubey.

"Tremendous," she said. "You can have babies like a dog or a cat does, just produce them without being involved. Or it can be grisly because you don't understand what's happening to you. That's humiliating, like being at the mercy of a tyrant, and it's the way so many women do have their babies. Or you can understand every step of the process. And then it's not lonely and frightening. It's dignified. You're not just pushed around by the pain and longing for it to be over. You're in charge and it's your experience." She added in discovery, "It's probably the only time of stark no-pretence in one's life, when there's nothing one can be but oneself. But what do you want to know all this for?"

"I had to sew a missing button on my shirt this morning," said Dubey.

"What's that got to do with it?"

"Nothing—except that if I could convince one person of my acquaintance before I die that the world consists of human beings and not of men and women in watertight compartments, I'd count it an achievement."

"You treat it like a personal crusade," said Saroj.

"That's the way to treat what matters. Ideas move slowly until they become someone's personal passion. Think how long people took slavery for granted. It shocks us today because we don't think in those terms any longer, but we harbour some equally barbaric ideas without turning a hair."

"Yes, but it seems to devastate you, doesn't it?" she said. "I mean, more than it need. It's as if you—suffer for other people's sins."

Dubey had seldom been at a loss for words but he did not know what to say now.

"I'm not made of the stuff of the martyrs," he said at last. "I'm greedy for life. That's what has helped me to do whatever I've done, whether it was helping to run a government or making a friend. I don't believe in suffering and death."

"They believed in life too. They died for the living."

She was right. Even dying for a cause was done for love of life. It needed involvement. But his own involvement led him to live, even tortured, but to live and bear the scars of what men did to each other.

He said, "I still think I'd rather live for the living. You know, something like the experience of childbirth—the stark no-pretence you were talking of—is possible between people. It's only when you don't pretend, when you are determined not to pretend, that you get a relationship of supreme worth."

She knew it was true. She had tried it with him. It had

made the difference to her life that light made to a painting. She had been confused till now, even a little panicked by what he meant to her. But there was no confusion any more. It was luminously clear. In the presence of what one admired there could only be one feeling: acceptance. And that included gratitude for its existence on earth and that one had recognized it. She drank her coffee and said, "Let's go. It's so stuffy here. Have you been to the forest?"

They left their cars on the road and walked down a dusty embankment past the lake where sailboats were jaunty with the sun on their red, yellow, and multi-striped sails. The smoky line of the further hills changed to the pale coffee colour of the closer range. Hard yellow berries grew wild on clusters of thorn bushes. Beside the water thick caked layers of ground cracked into pieces, and further on ploughed fields turned up their soft fresh earth. They took the path away from the water into the woods where shisham trees stretched bare branches to the gleaming day and trod a carpet of crackling brown leaves. Deeper in the wood the path became dusty and uneven, winding through groves of kikar, some stripped, some with narrow fanlike leaves.

"This is my forest," said Saroj.

"I can tell it is by the way you walk in it, as if it belonged to you."

"But please feel free to use it at any time," she said gaily. "Oh, I'm glad to get out of that dismal restaurant and I didn't like that man's face. He looks as if he beats his wife."

"I thought so too," laughed Dubey, "but then we all beat our wives, or our husbands, in one way or another. And what Hansa Ram does, if he does it, may be the kindest way of all."

Saroj looked stern. "I didn't expect *you* to talk like that. If any man raised a hand against me—"

"I considered myself a good husband," said Dubey, "but I seemed to do Leela damage for no reason I could understand. And there were times when living with her left me feeling I'd been pulled through a wringer. I think most couples face that kind of problem over some area of their lives. There are things they can't talk about to each other, and those become a burden they carry alone. They have to be watchful about them, and it can become very wearing over the years. Has it never happened to you?"

Because it had, she hesitated, held fast by long habit and older tradition to the inviolable secrecy of marriage. He was talking about himself with ease as they walked, as if his own private domain knew no boundaries and he could wander through it in freedom. I'll have to watch him from here, she thought wistfully, watch him walk away over the hills—and stay where I am. The thought left her forlorn and she knew she would have to go at least part of the distance with him or lose sight of him forever. Her decision was so definite she felt like calling out, "Wait for me. I'm coming." But the words, wrapped in the tight dark embrace of habit did not come. Instead she said, "But you look happy in spite of your trials," and knew at once it was not what she meant. He looked as men might if they lived in a climate where the spirit's bondage was unknown, in serene possession of themselves.

"I've been happy since I came here," he said. "Partly it's getting away from Delhi, and partly it's meeting you. There's a great freshness and innocence about you that's very reviving."

"About me? Why?"

"I don't know," he said. "Why should anyone who has lived, and been used by life, as we all have, still have the dew upon them? How is it possible? It's like finding dew on the grass when the sun is high in the sky and the day half over. It is astonishing."

"I've never thought of myself that way, Vishal."

"No, you haven't, all tied up with Bunny and Muff and the size of your flutter. But that is what you are."

There was a wealth of affection and belief in his tone and she was filled with an anxiety not to betray it.

"But I'm not like that at all," she insisted, "not a bit like your dew on the grass."

She stopped, torn between reticence and a longing to bring the thing she wrestled with in secret out into the fresh air, to exorcise it once and for all from her being, at least never to struggle with it alone again. But it was the one thing impossible to put into words.

Dubey had no use for martyrdom in any form but the kind bred into women outraged him. It was even elevated to a mystical importance, glorifying their acts of self-effacement and never more than when it demanded the sacrifice of their essential selves. He thought of his own countrywomen as the subdued sex, creatures not yet emerged from the chrysalis, for whom the adventure of self-expression had not even begun. Whatever womanhood had once meant in India had been lost in the mists of antiquity. In its place there had long been a figure of humility, neck bent, eyes downcast, living flesh consigned to oblivion. Women had served a hard apprenticeship and few things roused Dubey's ire more than their own continued acceptance of its rigours.

It was a subject he would have talked a great deal about if anyone had given him the opportunity. No one did. Women were not a subject for discussion. They were wives, daughters, mothers. They belonged to their men by contract or by blood. Their sphere was sexual and their job procreation. They were dependents, not individuals. When you wanted them it could apparently only be for sex. You could lust after their bodies and that was all right and the way of the world, so long as you did it clandestinely and never pierced the façade of respectability. The one thing you could not crave, the thing that was a crime, was that they should inhabit the world as your equals, with the splendour and variety of human choice before them. They themselves were afraid to for they had no preparation for it. They did not believe in themselves. And here was one with the freshness of a rose who did not believe in her own purity. The word had different meanings, but in the vocabulary of the established order that Dubey had discarded long ago, it had only one: the fable of flesh unpolluted by man. A woman was not entitled to a past, not entitled to human hunger, human passion, or even human error. In the fires and desolations of living she ranked as not quite human. Dubey decided that at this moment and with this woman he was not going to pander to this ridiculous cult. She would have to leave all that glut of other people's unformed thinking behind if she wanted to come walking with him.

He said brusquely, "We're not talking of the same thing. I meant the quality of you as a person. I think you mean chastity."

He was not prepared for her reaction. The mixture of gay candour and earnestness he had found so attractive faded before the sudden beauty of this pale, fearful woman. He felt a new, unaccustomed desire, to lift her up and carry her somewhere to safety, and once there, to understand what brought such a look to her face. He had spoken with vehemence because reform, he felt, never came softly. It blasted its way through the jungle of superstition, through pretence, even politeness. It had to find its mark and that could be painful. The end of a cult was always a shock, stirring racial memory to the dregs. And male dominance was the most formidable of cults.

"If chastity is so important and so well worth preserving," he said more quietly, "it would be easier to safeguard it by keeping men in seclusion, not women."

Saroj was amused. "That's a new point of view."

"But sensible," said Dubey. "The biological urge is supposed to be much stronger in men, so it is they who should be kept under restraint and not allowed to roam free to indulge their appetites. The entire East might flourish under this sort of reversal of purdah."

"Do you say so to your men friends?"

"Yes. Though I haven't had much enthusiastic response to the suggestion. And it would probably be quite coldly received in Saudi Arabia, for instance."

"And you'd be put in the madhouse for making it," she added.

"Well that would be all right," said Dubey. "One would have to expect a little unpopularity. New ideas are never received with open arms."

"I can't think of any man I know who'd agree with you, even outside Saudi Arabia."

"Nor can I," said Dubey cheerfully. "On the contrary, there are men who might say: 'This is a dangerous man. Our wives and daughters aren't safe with him.'"

But life, Dubey told her, was bigger than any system. Life could remould or break the system that lacked righteousness and reason. It was life's precious obligation to rebel, and humanity's right to be free, to choose from the best light it could see, not necessarily the long-accepted light.

Freedom. Funny, she thought, we apply it everywhere except in daily living. What happens there? What makes us so timid, or so tyrannical towards one another? Jerked back to an awareness of the man beside her, she knew that marriage to someone like him—but there was no one like him—marriage to him would not be a shaky affair. It would take not only the best one had to give but the trivial and absurd as well. Even the dirt. It would recognize that somewhere within the desirable woman, behind the eyes, the mouth, the breasts, there was a struggling, imperfect human being to be valued for her own sake. A marriage like that would be uncommonly strong and uncommonly pure.

She stopped and looked up at the treetops. Sunlight filtered through the slim, thornlike branches of kikar, touching its paper-brown leaves with gold. She felt enveloped in the peace and radiance of the day.

"This is where I always stop and look around," she breathed. "I drink it all in and take it back with me till the next time."

"I've always loved myself," she went on. "One should be able to. I've been able to say I mattered, that I was whole and clean. But today, for the first time, someone else has said it. It's like seeing a rainbow."

Whatever blind alley she had been in, thought Dubey, she would find her way out now.

She had not expected to find Inder at home. He did not usually come back for lunch. He was upstairs on the divan when she went in.

"Where in heaven's name have you been?"

"I went to the doctor for a checkup and then to Sector 22 to buy vitamins and met Vishal there—and we went for a walk in the forest."

The coffee, she thought, her throat closing painfully. She had forgotten to mention she had had coffee with him.

"In the middle of the morning? Doesn't that man do any work?"

"He had to see the proprietor of the Sea Shell on some business. And I didn't know you'd be back for lunch."

"It's Saturday."

"I forgot. I just—forgot," she said lamely. "And it's getting late. I'm awfully sorry. Why didn't you start yours?"

"Because I didn't know where in heaven's name you were."

His voice was taut. It warned her to say nothing. But she said mildly, stubbornly, "I've told you where I was."

"Yes. Out for a walk at high noon with Dubey."

He had risen from the divan, hands balled in his pockets, eyes glazed, and the prospect of a long exile from him unnerved her. It would be all right in a minute if she didn't say the wrong thing, if she just kept quiet. She stood mute, conscious of her heartbeat.

"What the devil is this all about?" said Inder.

The silence grew heavy with dread and guilt, with all the things she refused to own.

"I like to talk to him," she said in desperation. "He's a good man."

He flung at her, inflamed, "I don't give a damn if he's Jesus Christ."

The flicker of light in her face checked the flood of words that were rushing to his lips. The flood turned back, pounding in his ears and his head, filling his chest to bursting. When he came to his senses he saw her struggling for balance, her hands ineffectually shielding her face from his blows.

The children's voices came up the staircase. Muff burst into the room noisily with Bunny trailing solemnly behind. Saroj noted dully that their knees were grubby. You could scrub knees till you wore out but they were still grubby. Their shoes left dirt on the rug. She was reminded again that it was Saturday when they all had lunch together.

"I'm hungry," Muff announced.

"Your face is red," said Bunny.

"Oh is it? Well, I've been in the sun," said Saroj.

"Does the sun make your eyes water?" asked Bunny.

"Let's go and have lunch now. Aren't you hungry?"

"Not for lunch," said Bunny firmly.

"He stuffed himself with toffees in school. I saw him," said Muff. "Anyway, he's never hungry."

Bunny burst into tears.

"Oh now, darling," Saroj bent her head to the child's, her hand gentle against his face, her ache extending to Bunny, whose joys and sorrows were so bound up with her own. The feel and smell of his mother's hand seemed to reassure him. She held out her other hand to Muff, who stood apart, friendly and curious, waiting for calm to be restored.

"Let's all go and eat. Coming Inder?"

It's all over, whatever dreadfulness there was. Let's be together again, her tone entreated.

"In a minute," he said.

"Now," she pleaded urgently. "Let's all go down together. It's Saturday—"

"That has just occurred to you," he said.

She turned away with the children, the leaven to get her past the next hour already working. At lunch meat, vegetables, rice, what had happened at school took over. It was soothing as Vaseline on a grazed surface, never reaching the mortal wound beneath. But it held her together.

Afterwards she walked out of the house. The forest was too far away. She took the main road, looking for a place to be alone where she could hear herself cry. She wanted her shock released in sound, the satisfaction of hearing it leave her body. Suddenly she understood the dry-eyed insistent wail of the professional mourner. The sun was hot for December, the road poured wide and blank before her. It didn't matter if she cried right here, she instructed herself, but no sound left her. When a long time later a car drew up to the pavement and the door swung open, she stood looking at it.

Inder said distraught, "I've been worried to death about you. Get in. . . . Are you all right? Get in." His hand reached out to grasp her wrist and draw her in. He turned the car round.

"Why did you walk off like that? Saroj, for God's sake say something. I'm sorry I hit you. I didn't mean to. I didn't know what I was doing. Tell me you're all right."

"I'm all right." She sounded queerly unlike herself.

He drew the car up to the kerb and put his face down against the wheel.

"Saroj, what gets hold of me?"

She cleared her throat.

"The thing is," she said carefully, "that I can't do anything about it now. It all happened so long ago. I don't even remember what he looks like. I really don't. So you see, you'll have to stop punishing me."

Inder raised his head and looked at her with concern.

"Something—dies—every time," she said distinctly.

"Never mind about that just now. You must get home and get some rest."

It was cold out of the sun. Exhaustion spread through her. In the house she stood, dead tired and swollen-bodied at the bottom of the staircase, the baby twitching beneath her ribs. Involuntarily she put a hand to her side to pacify it, and imagined herself borne magically up the flight of stairs, laid sweetly to sleep. Then she slowly began to climb.

She lay down and logic, cool and alert, detached itself from her tired body. There were apparently generations of men behind her—fathers, brothers, husbands—who would have killed at the very suggestion of what she had done. Why had she never known such people existed? She cast about for some hint of strain between her parents, some sign that fierce intolerance was usual between men and women. There must have been some strain, but it must have belonged to the wear and tear of living, been part of the stuff of the relationship, not something separate that brutally mauled it and made each disagreement a journey to the dungeon.

She thought of the man she had known before Inder. She often thought of him because Inder so often revived him. Otherwise she would not have thought of him at all. And he hadn't been a man either, but a boy. They had laughed and talked a lot with the abandonment of the very young. She had forgotten the meaning of abandonment since then, except as an act of her body in the desire to give and find fulfilment. The boy had meant so little. It was Inder who had inflated his importance. And it was the long line of inbred reaction before him that had poured a woman's emotional and sexual nature into one rigid mould from which nothing—no mortal thing—would liberate it. She knew quite clearly before she fell asleep that she would not give that fantasy her allegiance any more. Nor would she ever stumble sightless and begging through her subterranean maze of anguish again.

Chapter 14

Inder did not know how long he had sat there in the failing light while his wife slept. The outlines of the furniture dissolved into the brown evening gloom. The low ceiling acquired the shadowy illusion of height and the room began to resemble a vault. The dark upsurge in him gradually subsided and he had a sinking sensation as he sat beside her bed. If this was a vault, it was their vault, and they were confined to it, belonging together beyond reason. She had cracked that exclusiveness with a flicker of light across her face. He had caught her in the act of worship. It had vividly shown him the terrible potential of this situation, the stirring of something worse than disaster, the beginning between them of death.

It was not her fault. He had said so again and again ever since he had known her, to wash her image clean. He wanted it clean. He had not hit Saroj. He had struck out at an elemental darkness that shut out more than sight. He had hit out at treachery, not hers, but at something be-

tween them that had no right to be there. When he got up
to go he realized this was the afternoon he was to have
spent with Mara.

When Saroj woke she remembered the kink between
Inder and herself. Her sleepy mind groped for the cause
and out of habit fastened on the boy, the act it was impossible to undo, the canker that would continue. No, it was
something else, not that, something recent. It was a new
kink on an old and troubled landscape. It was Vishal. Was
it only this morning he had told her, "There are men who
might say: 'This is a dangerous man. Our wives and daughters aren't safe with him.'?"

Her next waking thought was of safety. A strange thing
to be thinking of in her own house. Danger belonged to the
unfamiliar, the outside world, not one's own. But the
thought persisted and it was not entirely new. If I'm not
safe in my own home, I'm not safe anywhere in the world,
she told herself. The theorem did not reassure her. It made
her wary. She lay still, frowning over it. She felt there
must be some very simple way to deal with it, but it eluded
her. She began again. She was safe here, within the rec-
tangle of her bed, with the blankets over her. Nothing had
gone a step further, not another word had been spoken
since she had lain down on it hours earlier. But she had to
get up, go from the bed to the bathroom and from there
into square feet of space, through minutes and hours of
time and events not yet enacted, into the unknown.

She heard the bedroom door open and saw Bunny's head
appear and vanish round it, far beyond her safety zone.
The small anxious face appeared again and remained. There
was nothing unknown about Bunny.

"Hello."

The first word she spoke was round and full, brimming
with love and gladness, and she found simplicity as she

uttered it. The unknown would have to be safe because Bunny stood in it. She would make it safe for him. That, she supposed, was what must be meant by making the world safe for democracy. How safe it actually was one did not know, but someone, some millions, had cared enough to fight for it.

"You didn't get up for tea," Bunny accused, coming across the gulf of time that had separated them.

"I just woke up." She patted the side of her bed and he sat down cautiously.

"Are you sick?" he spoke at last.

How could anyone so chubby, wearing so bright blue a sweater with a dancing bear knitted into its pattern, be so immeasureably old?

"I was just tired, but I'm all right now."

"Then get up."

The urgency of it caught at her. Get up so that the sun can shine and the birds sing again. If the most precious one was not in it, the morning was bleak. Only it was evening, she remembered, the daylight hours blotted out while she slept.

"Where's Muff?"

"He went in the car with Papa to fill up the tank."

"And you didn't go in the car?" she asked, incredulous.

He shook his head as he must have shaken it when they tried to coax him to go with them. Saroj could see him standing resolute and alone in the drive, scuffing the gravel with the toes of his canvas shoes, sacrificing the cherished car ride. They belonged, he and she, to the same sphere of intense, sharpened sensibility. The deep intuitive current that bound her to her son flowed out to him, re-creating the unity that was theirs alone. The questions and answers, the search to ease relationships, to find understanding, all dissolved in this the fact of love. She had a flash of perception that in the years to come the earth he trod would feel firm and friendly beneath his feet. He would treasure beauty, use his reserves of strength to protect all fragile, fleeting things because of the light remembered in his mother's face.

She was having tea on a tray when Inder came in. Bunny ran down to find his brother, leaving them in the room together. A yearning to reach Inder possessed her, stirring a desire she recognized as old and unfulfilled. She wanted to love him in unpermitted ways, to make love to his doubts and dreams, to the private worlds within him that were locked and barred from her. He was at the writing desk, his back to her, rattling the drawer. At a sign from him, at their first nonchalant resumption of talk, they would slip back into routine and go on as before, the mutual unspoken pact between them inviolate, the danger dissipated for the time being. Only they could not go on as before with the kink between them. This kink belonged to the present, not the past. Saroj felt agitated, yet strangely at peace. Her spirits rose in preparation for their encounter. They must talk out what lay between them. She did not want any longer, or ever again, to live in uncertainty with him.

"This damned drawer is stuck."

She got up and went to the desk and tried ineffectually to open it.

"There's a wad of paper caught in the back," she said.

Together they manoeuvred the drawer open with exaggerated care.

"It keeps happening," said Inder. "I'm going to file down the side a bit."

"Yes," she said.

"You slept for hours."

"I know."

"Come down. I'm taking some papers to work on."

He laid a finger along her cheek. The gesture welcomed her back to him. After he had gone she waited, suspended, in the middle of the room, the familiar warmth and security enveloping her once again. It had been dark outside the circle of his arms. Yet somewhere on the rim of that darkness lay the light of a universe where candour was possible, if they had the courage to travel the distance to it. Vishal was right. There was only one way to live, without pretence. It would be the ultimate healing balm to the lonely spaces of the spirit, beyond which there would be no darkness.

Downstairs the children had built a card fortress on the carpet and Inder was working at the dining table.

"Inder, let's go for a walk when you've finished."

"Haven't you done enough walking for one day?"

"Well, just outside for some air. I'm rested now."

He put down his pencil and closed his file. The garden, neatly oval with its dainty flower border, looked too small and trim to contain what she had to say. She took his hand and drew him along the road beyond the gate. It was so hard to say the simple colossal sentence.

"I've needed someone to talk to."

It came out breathless, sounding like a deception. He did not answer. Perhaps it needed none. Perhaps he had understood the great hunger behind it.

"Please tell me you understand," said Saroj.

"I don't know what you mean. I've never prevented you from talking to anyone."

The deception began and she floundered. "I know you haven't, Inder. But after all we're so unlike. And it's natural we should need friends who share our interests."

"What do you mean by friends?" His hand had become wooden in hers.

"People to talk to."

"Talk about what? What is this mania for talk?"

He took his hand from hers. He had never been able to love her through an argument. There were breaches and pauses in his love. Love was granted as approval and reward.

"Haven't you ever longed to—about yourself?"

"*What* about oneself?"

"Ordinary things. Nothing special. Oh, you know what I mean."

"I suppose I spend too much time at the mill and you haven't enough company."

"No it's not that. Everyone needs friends. That's why it's such a blessing knowing Vishal—"

"We'd better get back. You shouldn't walk too far."

"So I'd like to go on seeing him," she brought out in a rush.

"Yes, ask him over—"

"And going for walks with him."

Through the forest, she wanted to add, in sight of the fields and the hills and the sky. Right out in the open.

"You can't do that," he objected. "You have to draw the line somewhere."

But where in the open, in the guiltless soaring expanse of discovery, did one draw lines? Unable to express it, she could only say childishly, disobediently, "But I like going for walks with him."

She felt his withdrawal and for the first time could not plead for his return. In the code they had lived by it was treason not to. But she was empty of sensation, of guilt, of danger, even of compassion, of all but the desperate need to settle her own problem. Without realizing it she had renounced her begging bowl and with it her capacity to be broken. There was nostalgia in the thought for she had been a good beggar, grateful for his alms. On the soundless walk home she puzzled over the past as if it had been a long time ago, not only just ended. Through layers of light sleep she heard him pace the room, go down the stairs and return, and sensed him beside her bed, staring down long and strangely on her. His unhappiness was part of an agony to be borne for the sake of the small steady flame that burned and glowed in the shelter of her being.

Chapter 15

Dubey sat facing Harpal Singh across his desk. It was weeks since he had arrived and first mentioned the police officer and a week since he had reminded the Chief Minister about the case. Harpal now said, "I think we had better leave the matter alone. I spoke to Prasad about it before he left and he agreed. This is no time to stir up old difficulties. We can deal with it after the strike is over."

When that would be no one knew. All they knew was that it would start in four days' time, and that for some freak reason, perhaps as a warning, the State Electricity Board had gone on a day's protest strike today, supported by other government employees. The Secretariat was deserted when Harpal's Cabinet met to discuss the situation. The Chief Minister had made a joke of being lift boy to his Cabinet as he brought some of his colleagues up in the lift. And they had tramped down an empty sunlit corridor to the conference room. Somewhere in the city ten thousand employees marched in a mock funeral of the Electricity

Board with a brass band playing a funeral march. Chandigarh's light and water supply, unlike those of the smaller neighbouring towns, had remained normal because officers of the Board had patrolled the lines for breakdowns. In fact Chandigarh's lights had not gone out at all, even when they should have. As the sun rose over the hills in the morning, the street lights were still on, paling to anaemic strips of opaque glass. Later the officer on duty had switched them off.

The Cabinet meeting had lasted all morning and Dubey had found himself looking out of the window for relief at the graceful, perpetual line of hills against the sky, then back to Harpal, who listened with weary patience to the proceedings. Several impassioned ministers had held the floor, indignant at Gyan's stand. The speakers would go home in cars that no longer ran' efficiently, and come across the major and minor irritations of industrial paralysis every hour of the day, but no one had injected a note of emergency into the gathering or made a concrete suggestion. Not even Harpal. Dubey wondered at the difference in temperament that made some men seize a problem foursquare and others ignore it in the hope that it might vanish.

He said to Harpal, "I'd like to make a suggestion."

The Chief Minister looked harassed. "Why didn't you make it at the meeting?"

"I wanted to put it to you first."

"We seem to have discussed this from every angle."

"Except this one," said Dubey. "I think it would be a mistake to yield to the strike threat."

"We have tried talking to Gyan Singh. So have you. He says the strike will go on."

"But you need not yield to it. Face it. Keep the works going. Appeal to your loyal workers and officers. Enlist their support." Dubey added urgently, "Make a stand."

Harpal said dryly, "Have you any idea what keeping the works going will mean in terms of strategy and planning?"

Was strategy the stumbling block, Dubey wondered. Leadership that had survived a shattered economy, lost granaries, and the rehabilitation of millions of refugees did not balk at a bit of strategy.

"Then dealing with a strike in the public sector is not quite the same thing as in the private sector," Harpal went on. "These are Government's own employees, even Government's own trade union. And in any case it's never easy to handle a mob and stick to your principles at the same time. Even with the best effort we are likely to fail."

The fear of failing in this situation seemed an echo of some deeper failure with which Harpal still grappled.

"It's a risk," Dubey said, "but there are greater risks: the prospect of the machinery of two states running down at the behest of one man, without any kind of stand made against him—and that a man who believes, and correctly, that he has only to call the tune. There is no room for such men among us. Let us take the risk."

A shadow of a smile lit Harpal's face at the "us."

"So the Centre's representative takes sides?"

"The Centre is on the side of the country," said Dubey, and it sounded pompous, as the simple truth sometimes did.

"A strike situation is ugly at the best of times," said Harpal. "We have enough experience to know. But to try to keep the works running for even a day in the face of a hostile labour force around which Gyan has mustered public support is almost out of the question."

"Public opinion changes. You can win it tomorrow, if you make a stand."

Dubey knew he was saying too much, but it had become necessary to bring this man to grips with a problem that Dubey believed reflected a graver disease, in the man and the nation. There was a time even in the most weighed and calculated of judgements when the next step was a risk. He wondered why he felt so certain it must be taken in this case and knew it was for the simple reason that the tempo of ordinary life must not be interrupted. The business of government was to see that it was possible for people to live their lives and get on with their daily work in peace.

"The strategy will not present an insurmountable problem. Bhakra is seventy miles of excellent road away. It won't be difficult to move police up. But the first thing will be the appeal to the workers. Everything will depend on that. It'll have to be done soon. We must know what strength we can muster."

Harpal got up and walked about the room for so long that Dubey wondered if another interview had ended inconclusively.

"Then that is what you advise?" he spoke at last.

This is the moment, thought Dubey, when the noose tightens round my neck. There was no need for him to say any more. He had said what he had to say, given his advice. Let the politicians decide what they wanted to do.

But he said with emphasis, "I most definitely advise it."

"Then you had better work out the strategy."

Dubey was at the door when Harpal called him back. He looked uncomfortable.

"I don't know if you have seen this."

He drew a folded newspaper out of his drawer and opened it on the desk. A corner item belying its unimportant placing by its heavy black print read: "It has been noticed and mentioned before in these columns that a senior Government official keeps company with a married woman. This official, an outsider, does not understand the importance we, in this state, attach to the sanctity of marriage." Dubey did not read the rest.

"Gyan Singh seems to have taken a dislike to you. This is his paper."

"I think he likes me," said Dubey, "but he doesn't like my presence here. He thinks it's an interference. This is his way of protesting."

"Would you like to issue a contradiction?"

"That would be difficult," Dubey pointed out. "I have been 'keeping company,' as it says, with a married woman. On the other hand I am aware of the 'sanctity of marriage.' Well, I'd better get back and start making arrangements—"

Harpal said hesitantly, "I don't mean to intrude in your personal affairs, but people here get worked up about this sort of thing. I thought you should know."

"It's good of you," said Dubey.

He went back to his office, pulled a note pad towards him and wrote on it: Facing the Strike. Under the heading he wrote: "Power houses not labour based. Check number of officers and number of junior supervisory staff. (J.S.S. not allowed to strike under the law, therefore appeal to them most important. If they are kept on side of management work can go on in spite of strike.) Chief engineers can talk to J.S.S. in groups. This may be better than talking to all of them at once as crowd apt to get emotional. Prepare ground for C.M.'s appeal. Personnel, technical and nontechnical officers all to be approached. Officers must be prepared to do menial jobs, even clean latrines during strike. Above all Government must give sign of decision and action. No dithering." He stopped a moment before going on: "All personnel and loyal workers should be housed within power houses twenty-four hours before strike, in fact as soon as strike threat received. All to be fed within. This precaution in case workmen strike in large numbers and prevent entry to loyal workers. Buses to operate to collect loyal workers and take them to P.H. as soon as strike threat received. Important to start well ahead as striking staff will otherwise block roads. Police arrangements."

He booked a call to Delhi and went on writing, realizing he would have to type the note himself in the afternoon since no member of the staff had appeared. The call came through in a few minutes.

"The strike is going to affect the four power houses, sir."

The Home Minister's thin voice came over the wire succinctly. "Don't let it."

"That is what I have advised. Sardar Harpal Singh is addressing a workers' meeting at Bharkra tomorrow at five o'clock."

"I have a morning appointment. I can't cancel it. But I can get there in time if I leave immediately after lunch."

"Don't do that, sir," said Dubey hastily, calculating the number of hard-pressed policemen that would be required to keep the Home Minister safe.

"The dam project happens to be a concern of the Centre," said the voice tartly.

"We'd be glad of your presence later, but just for the time being—"

"All right, all right."

Dubey put the phone down, intensely relieved. Thank God he would not be on his way here tomorrow, making more anxieties for the police, and thank God he was there at the other end of the wire when Dubey needed him. Now there was a man, somehow different from those around him, a creature with a defined inner structure and a sense of unfaltering discipline. One who did that dull, old-fashioned thing, his duty. A frail old bag of bones who was paradoxically a rock of strength. The few minutes' talk with him had bolstered his own confidence but the coil of inner tension had not unwound as he went home for lunch. He went up to his room and took a bottle of whiskey Jit had sent out of his cupboard. He poured a peg, filling it with water from the bathroom tap. The taps were working. One gave fervent thanks for the oddest things nowadays. He came back into the bedroom and held the glass up to the light, remembering he had signed a temperance pledge at the age of fifteen. An excellent thing to do at fifteen, like being a Communist at eighteen. Almost essential for balance later. There had been a sweater with holes in it he had gloried in wearing during his "Workers of the World" phase. Whatever had happened to it? Probably had rotted right on his back, he'd worn it so much.

He sat down in an armchair and stared moodily at the cupboard. He had never liked it. It was supposed to be "built in" but it stuck out—a good six to eight inches, he'd say. Parts of Chandigarh were like that. Things intended to be built in stuck out. Dust blew and the Indian sun shone brazenly through the exquisite lacelike cementwork of walls, and imprinted acres of glass. Why was modern living synonymous with glass, showing every fingerprint, stain, and flick of dust in a country where dust and dirt abounded? This was architecture transplanted, not conceived here, and he wondered how successful it was. Or for that matter how successful democracy was, superimposed on illiterate masses, exploding millions of them.

A worry nagged at him. He walked over to the wall and put on the switch. The overhead light shone palely. The electricity was working. That was something. Things had to work, buses run, lights go on, water flow. And people had to be fed. There could be too much argument about the why and the wherefore; an argument was a luxury for people who had time. The Cabinet had sat there manipulating words as if they were going to be there till eternity.

Whole localities would be in darkness in parts of the state when the sun went down that evening. How long would these incredibly patient people have patience about things like that? Just get every damned thing working, Dubey had wanted to announce at the meeting. The Secretariat is empty today. Tomorrow it may be the city if people start the long trek to where things work, or take the law into their own hands to make them work. Dubey stared hard at the cupboard. But that could not happen, not here, not to us. People would not just take the law into their own hands. He knew in his heart it could not happen, just as every tingling nerve in his brain told him it might. But we're civilized, he argued. Didn't it all come down to that? The Russians had not been. And the Chinese, though civilized, had never been gentle. We had committed excesses, it was true, but no other people so revered the quality of gentleness. If we could hold on to that a little longer there was still time. Was that asking too much of this country? But for as long as he could remember Dubey had asked too much of his country.

He had asked too much of everything that had crossed his path. There were times when Leela had considered his intensity a lapse of taste, a travesty of manners. She had never said so. She never gave a name to any emotion. But the chasm between them had opened early and never quite closed. That particular evening she had been standing in front of her cupboard quite unlike this one; it had been one of those old-fashioned almirahs. Memory played queer tricks, fading out the rest of the room but letting the cupboard remain, only her cupboard had been open, her saris hung in a brilliant row on the rod. She had been deciding what to wear. She had always shied away from directness, so it was a good time to ask the question, while her face was turned away and her attention divided. He had chosen the occasion with care, because he had to know, quietly and naturally, without startling her, yet not allowing her flight. Life with her had made him cautious and premeditated, even in the bedroom where they both stood half dressed, getting ready for a dinner party.

"Hari rang me up in the office a few days ago," he said.

Had he imagined it or had she stiffened at the name?

"He said there was something urgent he had to talk to me about."

"What was it?" she asked.

"He didn't say, except that it concerned you. And he sounded very overwrought."

"What could it possibly be?"

She took a sari off its hanger and laid it over her arm while she closed the cupboard, meticulous, tidy, perfect. She would have an affair like that, sealed in secrecy, with not a crack in her façade of perfect wife, nothing admitted. The thought struck him that that, of course, was the way of affairs. Was it asking too much, was it a perversion to want to know about hers, to share even that with her, if it was an expression of herself? There was no way to put it but bluntly.

"Leela, the man is in love with you."

"Yes I know. Everyone knows. He has been for years."

"Do you love him?"

"Don't be absurd."

The shimmering silk unwound as she tucked one side of it into the slim waistband of her petticoat.

He continued quietly, occupied with his cufflinks, "I don't want to hear about it from him. I'd rather hear it from you. That's why I keep putting off his coming to see me."

He noticed her breath came faster, that one hand flicked nervously at the pleats she had arranged with such care.

He could not help noticing. He noticed everything about her. It was the way he had lived with her, in depth and detail, and had wanted her to live with him.

"Give me something to get hold of, something real," he said harshly. "I don't care if it's good or bad, as long as it's real. If you're fond of him, tell me."

She faced him, her poise restored. "That's monstrous. How can you say such things?"

His mood shifted out of control. He gripped her wrist to compel her attention.

"Forget all the rules, what is and isn't done. Don't you understand what I want is something of *you*? For God's sake give me your natural self."

She twisted out of his grasp. "You're insane, Vishal. What are you talking about?"

To the last she had released only the emotions appropriate to "wife." To the last she had maintained her fiction and he had left it undisturbed, even when he heard the truth in anguished detail from her lover in pleas that implored him to release Leela. Only Leela had said nothing at all. Dubey had sat with Hari, a disciplined exercise of emotional withdrawal perfected during the weeks that Hari had haunted his office. It had enabled him finally to say with composure, "Fidelity isn't something either you or I can demand of Leela. That kind of exclusiveness can't be forced or conferred by her as a favour."

"What kind of monster are you? Don't you have any feelings?" Hari had thrown at him in desperation.

A strange charge, for Dubey had recoiled from hurting. Pacing the lawn outside their house by the hour in an effort to make sense of his wilderness, it had seemed to him that even his feet shrank from crushing the grass beneath them. He did not want a blade of it bruised. There was no meaning to his life if everything around him did not bloom, if he could not add lustre to it. But it was a charge he often faced, for feelings apparently had to be flamboyant to be recognized. No one suffered who did not disgorge that suffering in great bleeding bouts of grief and violence. Control was inhuman.

Hari had looked curiously caved in, as if the whole rational side of him had been blasted away by dynamite, leaving a palpitating debris. Dubey had understood Hari. He had not known what to make of Leela. Between Leela and himself there had been no outward change. She was dedicated to the cult of conformity, to observing forms that his most intense pleas had not been able to penetrate. She clung to the façade of a fidelity that had no meaning for him. A tumultuous rage had filled him that would not erupt. The rules. The regulations. The laws that made people fearful of each other. The whole mindless mess going on down the ages with never a shaft of new light on it. Men and women contorted into moulds, battered into sameness, the divine individual spark guttered out. If the spirit had a shape, what shapes would emerge from the grotesque twilight people called living. Somewhere under the sun there must be another way to live, with relentless honesty, where the only cruelty would be pretence.

He did not know what lives Leela lived outside their common orbit. Within it though they lived and ate and slept together, he believed she suspected him of an unnatural zeal for corrupt causes. It troubled her that he did more than honour his contract. Even his generosity frightened her. It did not seem quite possible, Dubey wondered himself whether he was flesh and blood or just a mind, an intensity willing to be consumed by the fires of his belief. In his isolation he knew that the character he had laboured to build was not proof against hurt, though she believed it was. And at times he wondered whether his ardour for the truth between them had done her actual harm, made her lose her bearings, so that she was like a lost soul wandering in a land not her own.

Saroj's car drove into the portico as he came down the stairs on his way to the dining room. He held the door while she slid awkwardly off the seat, and they stood with the door open between them.

"I don't know why I got out. I can't stay. I just came to tell you I can't come for a walk this evening."

In his preoccupation with the strike he had forgotten about the walk. Now he felt a pang of disappointment.

"Are you going out?"

"No, it's Flutter. And I shouldn't call him that any more. He kicks. He keeps getting turned around. I've been to Dr. Varma and he says he'll have to massage him into position every day if he doesn't stay put, and I'll have to stay in bed for a few days."

"What does it mean?"

"He'll be born feet first if he isn't made to stay in position now."

"Would that be very serious?"

She said in a small tired voice, "It's not natural. It would be difficult."

"He would get turned around just when I've got this strike to cope with," said Dubey. "It gives me two things to worry about."

Tears filled her eyes and she began to laugh unsteadily.

He made no move towards her, but said clearly, "We have to keep our nerve—about everything."

The "we" so unfamiliar in her life braced her.

She smiled, restored a little. "It'll only be a few days' bother. I'll be able to go to Mara's party on Christmas morning."

"I'll see you there, then."

Today, thought Dubey, he had made choices. He had identified himself with Harpal, and with Saroj and that unborn child of hers. The remedy always lay in what had to be done, and they were doing it, this woman tending the flowering in her womb, a man preparing to face a threat. Old Bones, too, on the job in Delhi. People steadfastly doing what they had to do, continuing the adventure of being man and woman in the confusion of living.

It was not until he got back to office after lunch that the full impact of the day struck him and his whole orderly conception of government and administration collapsed. It happened when he sat down at his desk in the empty Secretariat to type out his own note with two clumsy fingers on his P.A.'s typewriter. It was difficult enough to hit the right keys without this new anxiety for Saroj blocking his concentration. He began to feel feverish and restless. He wanted to phone her but she would be in bed upstairs. He could not even go and see her this evening for the same reason. He tore the page out of his typewriter and crushed it in both his hands, feeling trapped in a conformity he detested.

Images he did not want crowded his mind. The whole mysterious process of childbirth flowered dark with blood in his imagination like a primitive rite. Suppose she died? Only women did not die in childbirth any more. Not a woman who nourished life, every aspect of it in and around her, as Saroj did. Leela had been different. She had not wanted her child. She had died because her abortionist had been less than expert, less than sanitary, because his knife had slipped and perforated tissue it should not have touched.

Dubey had never known what had driven her to it. She had been cheerful and normal when he left for office that morning. He had come home to find her dying. Her eyes had flickered across his face and closed. Only her hand had caught convulsively at his and remained in his until the end. The bitter end, he thought, for she had died the way she had lived, a stranger to him. He had been horror-struck at her needless death. For months he had groped blindly for the reason. Why had she done it? How had he failed her? Her answers might have been numerous, had she lived, had she talked, had she ever given him her confidence. In his mind there was only one answer. He had lived with her without love, so in the end perhaps the crime was his.

Dubey shook off the memory. He felt very tired. The typewriter, devilish and obstinate, would not obey his fingers. He would damned well write the note by hand. He was about to begin when his P.A. walked into the room.

"I tried to come earlier," said Man Singh, "but the road where I live has been completely blocked by demonstrators, and I finally had to sneak out from the back."

Dubey sat back in immense exhausted relief. "If you valued your skin you wouldn't have done that. Why did you?"

"I knew you would need me," said Man Singh, and, looking down at the page in his machine, "Here. I'll do that now."

Chapter 16

Christmas Day and open house, the drawing room decorated with holly from the hills and greenery from their own garden, had become an intolerable burden. The centrepiece of scarlet roses sent by Saroj in the morning was a blaze of colour against the black, white, and green. Mara felt leaden. She was standing beside the punch table with Inder, as they had one night an eternity ago, as if nothing had happened in between. The strain of being normal was beginning to be too much for Mara.

"I haven't had a word from you all week," she said, though she had decided to say nothing.

"I've had a lot to cope with."

The cold explanation shocked her.

"Couldn't you have rung up?"

"I'm sorry."

"Inder, I've been beside myself. What's wrong between us?"

His expressionless face told her there was nothing

wrong, in fact, nothing at all between them. Someone was playing the piano, voices carolling. Mara remembered there was a party at her house. A guest, wreathed in smiles, disentangled himself from the singers and came towards her, cup in hand for a refill from the punch bowl.

"Mara-ji, this morning party is a fine idea."

Mara's mouth smiled. She dipped the ladle into the carved Viennese silver bowl, exuberantly baroque in design, with clusters of grapes forming its two handles. It brought back Vienna, childhood, snow outside, people gracious in manner, easy to talk to, people one could understand.

"Mara-ji, pardon my asking, are you a Christian?"

"No," she said sharply.

But her guest, helping himself to a sugar-topped pastry, had not noticed. Why did everyone have to have a label? Couldn't one just be human? The barriers that crisscrossed and ate through daily living like white ants suddenly nauseated her. She felt physically sick. Turning abruptly from the table she went upstairs and flung herself across her bed. She heard someone come in and Inder sat down beside her. Every nerve in her recoiled from this assumption of familiarity.

"What's the matter?" he demanded.

She stared at him.

"I said I was sorry. Everything has been in a hideous muddle at home and at the mill."

"But I haven't had a word from you. I haven't known what was happening."

She tried to get up but he pulled her back to the bed. With an effort she flung his arm off.

"It's gone," she whispered, "the thing we were trying to build. You've torn it down. I should have known you would. Please leave me alone."

"What are you talking about?"

He had come to life suddenly and followed her, baffled and desirous. He took her by the shoulders, forcing her attention.

"Don't touch me," she blazed.

Anger boiled up in Inder. She wanted him all right. For all her airs and graces she wanted him like any other woman. But she had to call the tune. He had catered to her whims long enough. He let her go with a suddenness that caught her off balance. The click of the door shutting behind him had the finality of a blast, wiping him clean of all emotion. And then without warning the enormity of what he had done hit him. He wanted to sit on the floor and sob, go back and push open the door, not just to Mara, but to the oxygen of understanding, to the growing thing between them he had killed. He went downstairs instead.

Saroj had seen Inder come down the stairs and walk out of the house. Suddenly she wanted the children, the softness of a face beneath her hand, a child's insistent need filling an aching void and continually stirring the mother-core in her.

She bent down to retrieve the silk purse that had slipped off her lap, her hair falling over her face. When she straightened, her face set in a pale perishable composure, she found Dubey watching her. She sat motionless, even when he said, "I'll take you home." He took her arm and she got up obediently, dropping her purse again. He picked it up and flung it by its twisted silk cord on her wrist and took her out to his car.

He did not take his eyes off the road or his hands from the wheel.

"I can take you straight home," he said, "or for a drive. Which do you want?"

She started to tell him but the words did not come. Tears

ran down her face and into the corners of her mouth.

"Home, Vishal," she said with an effort.

He turned the car towards the sector where she lived.

"It's not true, Saroj, that people can't help each other. They can. No one need be alone. I'll be with you."

Would he, he thought. And of what use could he be to her in any case? He had said it nevertheless, knowing what she needed most was the strength of his spirit, and that would be hers wherever he was. He left her at her house, driving away before she entered it, unable to rid himself of the feeling that he had sent her into battle alone. He parked his car at the point in the road where he and Saroj had, the day of their forest walk. Only today he took the opposite direction to go around the lake. The walk skirted the lake over uneven ground, going from shrub to clearing and in places over ridges and cracked earth that looked as if it had been refashioned by the wind. The sky was a lavish blue, the wind a constant companion, whipping his scarf loose, tugging at his hair. It came at him tumultuously, binding him to the landscape. He was part of it as he had always been of the life around him, not dragged into it against his will but an active embracing part. He had never been a man to let well enough alone. He was by nature a trespasser. The ground he walked on, the problems he tackled, the people he befriended had become his own in a curious ecstasy of involvement. If it had gone wrong, as it had with Leela, was it because ecstasy was not intended for daily use? It had to be confined to acts of creation, to what a man could invent with his mind, mould with his hands. The world forgave the overflow of the spirit if it resulted in a masterpiece of music or marble, something it could see, hear, and understand. Otherwise it said "This man is different" and crucified him. Even devotion to God had to be taken out of the pale of ordinary human contact into a monastery or onto a hilltop. The human spirit was allowed to burn bright only if its fire did not sear those around it. But Dubey had not known any other way to live.

He climbed a mound and found himself in an alcove sheltered by thick foliage from the wind. He could look down on a curve in the lake that seemed to have collected the entire day's sparkle, and an extraordinary sense of peace and happiness pervaded him. He wondered what there was in this impossible situation to be happy about—a woman, not his, for whose well-being he was racked. But he knew his joy was for the fact that he had come home, and that a lifetime's longing could now be concentrated on loving Saroj.

Saroj went in and the house was empty. She had forgotten Bunny and Muff were spending the day with a friend, and Inder had not returned. She sat down to wait for him. The sudden vista of years to be spent waiting for his return from wherever he had gone, without explanation, stretched aridly before her. Of course he would be back, when he chose, and resume life with her without a word about his impetuous departure, and they would go on, their give and take reduced a little each time. She saw the human substance between them dwindling until in old age they would just be two people who had happened to live under the same roof, no real bond between them, only the accumulation of a lifetime's living habits. The enormous waste of it appalled her. She did not think of Inder coming down the stairs at Mara's house, from Mara's room. She thought of him walking away without telling her why, leaving her, as he always did, in frantic helplessness outside doors forever barred.

Sham hovered in the doorway of the pantry. She had forgotten about lunch too, and it was already past two o'clock. She asked Sham to bring hers and told him he could go. She would heat Inder's herself when he came home. Later she went upstairs and lay down. The baby, lodged head down now, shifted restlessly in her, not letting her fall asleep. She did not know she had slept at all when she woke to the sound of the doorbell pealing. It was Vishal at the front door, his shoulders hunched against the cold wind, his hands in his pockets. The wind had whipped colour into his face.

"I should have offered you a third alternative," he said. "A walk. I've been around the lake. Can you give me a cup of tea? And how about you and Inder dining with me tonight?"

"Inder isn't back."

"Well, can you give me some tea?"

"Yes. Sorry, Vishal, I'm half asleep. Come in."

"I'm already in," he pointed out.

"I'll get the tea," she said dazedly and stayed where she was.

"It's awfully quiet. Where are the children?"

"They're out for the day. There isn't a soul in the house but me. Hasn't been for hours. It's like that a lot." The words suddenly spilled out. "I'm used to it. It's not being alone I mind. I enjoy that. It's the loneliness. I'm alone even when Inder is here."

"Yes I know."

"Do you?" she said sadly. "I expect he feels that way too."

"He probably does."

"The enormous waste of it," she said. "Oh your tea."

"I'll make it."

He followed her into her kitchen, took a box of matches from his pocket, and lit the small stove. He took off his jacket and unwound his scarf, filled a kettle and put it on to boil. He felt weighed with her distress.

"I suppose I should have some ambition—*do* things, you know, paint or write or something," she said.

"And have you no ambition?"

"Well yes, I have," she admitted with reluctance. "I want—don't laugh—I want to be a virtuous woman."

"Darling," the word was torn from him and he took her hands in his. "What do you think you are?"

The intimacy was so natural she hardly noticed it.

She told him her story while he measured tea leaves into the pot and poured boiling water over them. It was like telling herself only telling him made it a simple, not a tortuous thing, the sort of thing that could happen to anyone, not a punishable offence, not a guilt.

"It didn't make much impression on me," she ended, puzzled. "These things are supposed to."

"Who supposes them to?"

"Men," she said. "At least, Inder insists they do."

"It has suited men to suppose such things," he said severely, and added, "The sad thing is not that it happened, but that it made, as you say, so little impression. We don't indulge in pointless conversations with people, yet we go in for pointless sex experience, contact without communion, without rhyme or reason. *That* is shocking."

"Anyway, that is a mountain between me and Inder. Silly, isn't it? I mean, what can I do about it now?"

"It's for Inder to accept it."

She shook her head helplessly.

"Oh Vishal."

"Not just this, but to accept comradeship with your past, all of it, and with all of you. That is the meaning of living together. Is there anything on earth to compare with the great glory of communication, and that is only possible when people accept each other in truth."

"Everyone can't be like you, Vishal, as free in your thinking."

"But there's a yearning for freedom in everything that lives. The way plants grow towards the sun. No power on earth can prevent that happening. And in people, since time began, sooner or later, in one way or another, the yearning bursts out and spills over. We haven't begun to realize that yet. Freedom is just an isolated political achievement for us. It hasn't become a habit of mind or a way of life. We are still bound by meaningless doctrines and we show no mercy to those who don't conform." He carried the tea tray into the drawing room and put it down. "As for virtue—"

"I thought you'd laugh at that," she said.

"I don't laugh at it," he said abruptly. "I kneel before it."

He began walking the room.

"You bring back words—and ideas—a whole under-graduate storehouse of them that gets put away in moth-balls when one leaves university. Good God, Saroj, who talks of virtue any more?"

He stopped pacing and looked hard at her.

"Now you listen to me. You must stay as you are."

Her glance moved away from his, unable to bear the scrutiny. She said tiredly, "What does it really matter how one person more or less lives, Vishal?"

"It has taken a million years of evolution for a person and his cherished individuality to matter," he said, "and no terror must be allowed to destroy that."

"I don't want to destroy it in myself," she said. "I know it's there, hidden away somewhere inside me, safe. Like museums in Europe stored away their art treasures in their basements to keep them safe from bombings during the war."

"Only people should not keep their qualities in storage. There is such a limited time to live. I don't mean that life is short. I mean that every minute of it is priceless. It's for use, not storage."

His words illuminated her predicament, as they had a way of doing, not like the powerful searchlight that scoured the skies at Chandigarh's air base, but with a steady quiet radiance in which her heart healed. It made her feel life need not just be got through. It could be taken into one's own hands and understood, even changed. There was even such a thing as suffering with one's eyes open. Strange that she had understood that so well during her labour at Bunny's birth, and never outside that experience.

Inder had spent the afternoon in his office in desolation more scalding than anger. Unexpectedly it had been magnified by the newspaper clipping that must have been left on his desk yesterday. His head throbbed and the room filled with a tension that he felt would explode if it had no outlet. It did not surprise him when he heard a sharp crack of sound behind him. He wheeled round in his chair to find the glass pane behind him split. Another crack dislodged pieces of glass and they fell in splinters on the floor in a shower of pebbles. A stone struck his temple, sending a wild pain drilling through his skull. Stunned, he saw men outside smashing other windows, and one man leading the way through an opening into his office. They stopped, momentarily taken aback, to find him there, and then poured in. Inder saw the glint of steel through the painting Gauri had sent. Within seconds knives flashed through the sofa and chairs, expertly ripping upholstery. Stones smashed the light bulbs on the walls and brought the bulb covers crashing down, their ground glass crunching underfoot. Then they were in a semicircle around his desk. At the same instant he heard shouts and running feet and knew the mill had been attacked. His mind leapt to the bales of nylon. Black roses on a yellow background, he catalogued idiotically, sari-width, hundreds of metres of it, thousands of rupees' worth, lying stacked, numbered, labelled, ready to go to Delhi tomorrow. One more day it had to be protected. He knew what they would do if they got to it. They would set fire to it, burn up months of their own labour. And in agonizing impotence he knew he would not be able to stop them. The pain in his head pounded systematically, savagely, nearly blinding him. He snatched up the brass table lamp high above his head, feeling the plug wrench from its socket, and brought it down with all his force on the man nearest him, saw him buckle to his knees and crumple to the floor. Inder could not focus clearly any more as with a huge effort he overturned his heavy office table. Swiftly they crossed over it and his fists smashed out as they closed around him, driving him to the wall. When he opened his eyes the office was empty and he lay in its ruins. He raised his hand to his mouth, wiping away the blood. The pain hammered in his head. His telephone wire had been cut and the instrument smashed. He dragged himself up, limped out to his car, and examined its tyres. Strangely, they were intact, and there was no damage to the car, perhaps because it was not parked in its usual place and they had not expected he would be in office today at all. He drove to the police station.

An hour later he was on his way home. They had shown concern for his condition. They had taken down his report. An investigation would be made. The workers' version would have to be obtained. What had been their grounds for attack? No grounds, Inder had said. They had attacked without provocation. But surely, there had been some warning that all was not as it should be. Had he not known of any grievance the workers had? They had complained of the food they were getting, that was all, Inder said. Ah, they were being inadequately fed. No, Inder said monotonously, labouring the words through his pain, they hadn't liked the quality of the wheat flour, but that was an excuse. They were in the mood to make trouble.

"People don't make trouble for no reason," the inspector had said, with maddening imperturbability.

"I'm here to report damage to my mill," said Inder, "to the tune of what figure, I cannot yet tell. These men are responsible for it. Furthermore I am reporting assault."

He was in a towering rage by the time he drove home. He had forgotten what he looked like as he entered his house, saw Dubey and Saroj and the tea tray, and the consternation on their faces. He heard Saroj's cry as he went up the stairs. By the time she reached the bedroom he had locked the door.

The children came back full of their day, to be bathed, fed, and put to bed, claiming Saroj's attention. She attended to them, feeling strong and serene, armoured against loneliness and most of all against futility. There was a child to be borne, a life to be lived, hers to mould. She moved quietly around the children's room, folding clothes and putting away toys while they drifted into sleep. The wind had dropped and the filigree network of stars made her catch her breath. I hope it's a girl, she thought for the first time, brimful of excitement. She tried her bedroom door again. It was still locked. She spread a mattress on the floor of the children's room and went to sleep full of bright, unvanquishable hope.

Jit felt he was following a trail of someone just gone whom he could catch up with if he tried. Upstairs the white bedspread still bore the imprint of her body, the pillow dragged out from under it was dented where her head had rested. A red wool dressing gown lay flung across Mara's chair, one long sleeve forlornly trailing the ground, empty of Mara. She had thrown it off and gone—where? Jit, standing in the middle of the room, wondered why he was allowing himself these thoughts. She had gone, obviously, into the neat modern kitchen where she liked to make herself a cup of tea after a nap. She hadn't put a comb through her hair before going down, he noticed. Her brush and comb were untouched on the dressing table. There was not a speck of powder or spilled lotion on the polished blond walnut surface. Kashmiri walnut furniture ordered because dark teak did not do her flawless looks justice. Bottles of perfume stood neat and stoppered. But she must have sat at the dressing table and stared long at herself in the mirror, filling a heavy crystal ashtray with cigarette butts.

He went down the curved staircase through the empty immaculate drawing room from which the servants had removed all traces of the party, into the kitchen. That was unusual, for Mara liked the holly decorations left for several days. A small tin of the fragrant green tea she preferred stood open on the kitchen table, beside it the Chinese tea set of willow-patterned porcelain with the remains of the pale brew still in the cup. He had given her the set when he discovered she loved China tea. Jit sat down on the kitchen chair she had vacated, feeling disembodied, suddenly powerless even to protest.

If I were a different sort of man, he thought, I would go through this house shouting for Mara, out onto the road, into other people's houses, if necessary, overturning obstacles, clearing obstructions, getting to her—if she had gone. But he had never been that sort of man and he did not know if it were his blessing or his curse. High drama was not his instinct. He would never set the world on fire or plunge it into darkness to match his moods. Yet nor would Mara. He had described her to himself when he first met her as a thoroughbred and recognized in her the quality of restraint he prized so highly. She would not just disappear. And he did not know why, on this day, he should return home from a walk along the lake to think about her disappearance.

He poured tea, still warm, into her cup. It was not that he had never lost anything, he thought. In fact, depending on how you looked at it, he had lost everything. But it had never struck him that way. His father had died, but of age and a life lived in fulness, and his going had been a culmination of living, not a tragedy. Lahore had been lost too, emotions uprooted, a whole past destroyed, and with it a substantial inheritance. But he had found Mara and gained Chandigarh, started a new business and built a home. He had never said so but he believed that the Partition with all its horrors had in the end been good for the Punjab. It had brought out the energy and the drive of the people and revolutionized their lives. Women had started to work and that would have been unheard of in the old Punjab. There was education for them. And again, Chandigarh had come about. Old familiar channels had run dry but new ones were flowing and there were opportunities for the young. People like him, the uncurdled ones, had no axe to grind. He wondered if that were a weakness, and whether he lacked what the world called manhood. He had never been able to find the confirmation he needed from Mara.

He went out into the courtyard. The sun had gone. Mara sat in a wrought-iron chair, its heavy ornamental black too much for her fine-boned slenderness. His first reaction was enormous relief, but it was followed by concern. He connected nervous movement with her, light deft

gestures of her hands, her quick way of expressing herself.
Now she looked utterly still, dark holes for eyes, as if she
would hurt less if she did not move. The sight started a
train of sorrow in him. So she had gone from him after all
and he would have to wait for her return.

"Cigarette, love?"

"Yes please."

He had a powerful desire to leave alone whatever had
happened and wait for it to right itself if it could, to drive
off somewhere for a couple of hours or go to his study and
get drunk. But the absurdity of expected husbandly behaviour restored his perspective. This was too big, too important to him. When you gamble for the big things, Vishal
had said, you have to risk everything. It had sounded
pompous and pretentious on the sunlit morning of the
picnic. It rang true now. And his own need was blotted out
by what he could sense of Mara's. If nothing else, he could
still be a friend.

She made no move to take the cigarette he held out to
her. He lighted it and put it between her lips.

"It's getting cold here."

"We'll go inside," she said with a frightening docility.
He watched her move with slow hesitant steps alien to
her, she who was always on the wing. Indoors he lighted
the fire and took the chair facing her in front of it.

"Unhappiness does something to one's walk, doesn't it? I
thought of that watching you walk in, as if you were not
confident about where you put your feet, and afraid the
ground was going to give way under them. I've been like
that myself."

"When?"

"Not long before I met you. I'd been involved for about
a year with a woman of rather a savage temperament. She
was married and quite a bit older than I was, and I was

prey, young and very infatuated and uncer-
It was a fatal attraction and it took me by
s not happy in it, but I had to have it. It was
ulsion. I don't think I could ever have let go on my
own. It was she who dropped me, cruelly, without any
explanation. It broke me. I thought I'd never survive it."
There was a flicker of interest across Mara's face.

"You never told me," she said.

Why was he putting himself on the anvil, he wondered,
instead of going up and getting drunk and ignoring this
whole business. But he went on.

"No. There's been a silence between us on so many matters. Not that we've planned it that way. It has just been
taken for granted as the way a couple should behave. No
intimacies except in bed. Strange, isn't it, and yet most
people accept marriage in those dried-out one-dimensional
terms and expect to live almost like strangers."

"Vishal was talking of that the other day."

"And I thought he was talking nonsense," said Jit, "but
today when I came out and saw you sitting there so blotted
out and wanted to reach you, I didn't know any other way
but his."

Because he compromised so readily she had not noticed
he never did in the ways most fastidious and subtle, those
involving his taste and judgement.

"Well, when I recovered from the shock of being abandoned, like so much garbage, I knew that there were two
kinds of people in the world, those who live by reason and
those who don't, and I knew I belonged to the first kind. So
do you. You'll never be happy in an emotional jungle
where you don't know from day to day what's going to
happen and why. If that is where you are now, then let me
help you to find your way out, my love."

Strength that was almost physical in its impact reached

out to her in his words, the kind of strength she had never thought she would need as she went her proud way alone.

She said what she had never been able to say before, "I need your help."

Chapter 17

Inder went up and down the stairs several times the next morning, making phone calls while Saroj gave the children their breakfast and sent them to school. It was when she heard him speaking to Delhi that she learned what had happened at the mill. She stood on the landing aghast.

"Inder?"

He went past her into the bedroom.

She followed, asking, "Why didn't you tell me what happened yesterday?"

He went into the bathroom, shutting the door behind him. She heard him fasten the latch.

"Inder, let me come in. Tell me how it happened. How did it burn down?"

The shower dripped, then came on full, drowning out sound. She knocked at the door urgently, impelled beyond logic to be heard, and then began to beat on it with both hands, her voice rising to a scream. She dropped to the floor, her fists pounding the wooden panels till her knuckles ached. A sharp pain low down in her abdomen brought her to her senses. She stopped crying and got awkwardly to her knees, slowly straightening to a standing position, and went to her dressing table. The shot-silk sari she had worn to yesterday's party was crumpled from a night's sleep and stained with Bunny's porridge. The waistband of her petticoat dug into her flesh. Her silk blouse strained uncomfortably against her breasts. She felt stale and her back ached from the night spent on the floor. Her face was mottled with crying, its features blurred and altered. Mechanically she picked up her hairbrush and began brushing her hair with deliberation, pressing the bristles against her scalp until it tingled, trailing them down to the very ends. She rummaged in the drawer for her nail file and carefully cleaned and shaped her nails. It was the drill she used, grasping the commonplace to find her way back to equilibrium. She had washed her face earlier in the children's bathroom but she had not been able to brush her teeth. When Inder came out of the bathroom she went in and opened the window to let the cloud of steam escape. The hard blue brilliance of the day assaulted her aching eyes, but the cool flavour of toothpaste freshened her and she stood in front of the mirror already feeling better. She would be all right soon. She pressed the backs of her hands against her flushed cheeks.

Inder was having breakfast when she came down.

"Here's an item that will interest you," he said, taking a creased newspaper clipping out of his pocket and handing it to her. "The result of your high-noon excursions with Dubey."

Saroj read it and started buttering her toast. All at once she was ravenously hungry, and remembered she had had no dinner.

him to have no further contact with you. I
im I'll not be answerable for the conse-
does."

one stopped buttering toast to look at Inder closely and
curiously, but she could not think of anything to say. She
was still at breakfast when he left and Dubey arrived.

"Inder telephoned first thing in the morning," he said.
"That's why I've come."

"I knew you'd come," said Saroj.

"I've arranged for a car to take you and the children to
Delhi, and I've phoned Gauri. She's expecting you."

"All right."

"Get up," he urged.

He followed her upstairs to her room and took in at a
glance the bed that had been slept in, the other undisturbed.

"I'll wait in the next room. Pack and get ready. And
hurry. I want to get you away in case it's difficult later.
Today's the strike."

She turned to him. "Hold me, Vishal."

He put his arms around her and held her close, feeling
the soft movements of her baby against him. Incalculable
Saroj, he thought, swollen-faced and tear-stained in yesterday's crumpled sari, but with her hair brushed to a shine,
and smelling blandly, sweetly of soap. He laid his cheek
against the top of her head and closed his eyes, inhaling the
fragrance of her. He thought he would remember that
minute when he had forgotten every other he had ever
known.

"You must dress quickly. We have to fetch the children."

"Is this running away, Vishal?"

"No my darling. It's good sense. It's for the baby."

"And afterwards?"

"Afterwards we'll see."

But she knew as she left the house with him that there was very little to see. The drama of exits and re-entrances was not for her. People like her did not leave their homes. It dawned on her with a stab of pain that she could leave now because this was not home. She had tried to build a home, grasping what material she could find, laughter, a phase of nearness, patches of understanding. But it had not been enough. There were great heartbreaking gaps through which the cold came in and the emptiness yawned. Vishal had been right. Human relationships could not be left to chance.

In the garden she stopped to collect her roses. They might not arrive in good condition but here was something she had planted and tended that had grown. She got into the car and laid them carefully across her lap, wondering how long they would keep her mounting sense of calamity at bay.

There was nothing unusual about the day of the strike. The streets looked deserted, but Chandigarh's streets had a way of looking deserted in any case. It was only if you visited the shopping sectors and found many of the shops closed that you realized it was not an ordinary day. The scene of the drama was miles away at Bhakra and only the telephone on Dubey's desk was overactive. It was eleven when an agitated voice from the works informed him: "We have been able to put only four hundred officers and chargemen inside the works." He had been ordered to put as many men inside the plant as possible immediately after the strike threat was received.

"We tried to. We started operating buses at four o'clock this morning. The strike wasn't to begin till six. But even four was too late. The strikers were blocking all the road

:hen—"

strikers?" interrupted Dubey, checking the
words.

About two thousand. More probably. They had posted
people on motor scooters in groups of fifteen, twenty, and
even a hundred. There's a strikers' administration through-
out the colony. They will not allow anyone to pass."

The speaker's voice was pitched unnaturally high.

"What are the police doing?" asked Dubey.

"They don't dare defy the strikers. They feel there
aren't enough of them to cope. Some of our officers have
been dragged out of vans and no one has been able to
enter the plant since four. What I'm afraid of is the men
inside losing their nerve. They keep saying police arrangements are failing and they aren't safe."

Dubey had a moment of sickening doubt. Then it came
over him and he was immediately certain of it, that the
only thing that was failing was the speaker's own nerve. It
was just disastrous bad luck to have a man there at this
juncture who panicked.

He spoke harshly. "There will be another police contin-
gent with you in the afternoon. Meanwhile, no one is to
give up anything."

The effect was instantaneous. "Yes sir."

"This is not a local strike. The Centre is committed to
keeping the works going. The workers are perfectly safe.
Are the food supplies in order?"

"All that is in order."

"The cleaning must be shared by everyone inside the
plant."

"How long are we to be prepared to hold out?"

"You're there. What do you think?"

"There's nothing cut and dried about that. These strikers
are out to be violent." Again the voice flagged mournfully.

"It won't be more than forty-eight hours," said Dubey very firmly.

He had no idea why he had said it, except that he was convinced of it.

"That's all right then." There was relief at the other end of the line.

In the evening the lights went on on schedule. Harpal came into Dubey's office looking youthful, almost gay.

"Have you decided what you are going to do?" Dubey asked.

"When?"

"When you retire," said Dubey.

"I'll decide that when I retire. I'm going home now, Mr. Dubey. I suggest you do the same. It's been a trying day."

It was on a special news bulletin as he was about to leave his office that Dubey heard the announcement of the Home Minister's death. He felt a peculiarly intense grief compounded of nothing personal and the need to argue himself back to steadiness. How much longer could anyone live? Old Bones had done his share and more. The funeral, the announcer said, would take place in the morning. He detailed the solemn ceremonial for the occasion. It would be considerable, the most that a nation could give a hero, for this was more than a state funeral. It would mark the end of an era known as Gandhian. In politics that had meant freedom from fear, the head held high, the indomitable will in the emaciated body of India. Gandhian politics had also meant the open decision, the open action. No stealth, no furtiveness, and therefore no shame. Every act proudly performed in the sunlight. If all of that had been worth anything, thought Dubey, it will have been disbursed over this country, down deep into our blood. Or perhaps that was where it had always been and from where Gandhi had drawn it up like water from a well to banish the thirst of defeat and despair.

He pictured the funeral procession winding through
Delhi's historic streets the next day, past ruined fortresses
to the banks of the Jumna, where the surprisingly frail
body would be committed to the flames of the funeral
pyre. He thought of the formidable police arrangements
that would be needed to prevent people from surging forward to the bier as it passed, grieving frantically, barba-
rously, uncontrollably as only Indians mourned their great.
The last rite chanted by priests, the last rituals performed
by the old man's family would be lost in the wounded
upsurge of the bereaved multitude. With that it came to
Dubey that Delhi would not be able to spare its police.

No one knew whether it was the death of the Home
Minister that swept crowds into the normally empty streets
of Chandigarh that evening. It seemed curious to Harpal
that so many people were collected at the Secretariat. His
car could not pass. Afterwards it was the hands he remembered, one or two hundred of them, thumping and beating
against his car like frenzied bats' wings. He shouted above
the noise to his driver to get a move on.

"I cannot, *janab*. The tyres have been deflated."

Cow dung plastered the windshield and was flung in a
shower against the sides of the car. The shot that rang out
shattered glass. What a fool, Harpal afterwards remembered thinking, to fire through window glass. The second
shot hit his shoulder and he slumped in his seat. He had
fainted before they got him to hospital. When he regained
consciousness he was given the news that Gyan Singh had
called off the strike as a token of respect for the death of a
patriot.

Too much had happened in one day. Dubey, back from
the hospital, took his last look at the moonlit lake. He was

leaving for Delhi two days later. There was no sound except for the footfall of a man coming up the drive towards the guest house. It was very late. In the frosty moonlight it was some time before Dubey recognized him as Inder. Heavy measured steps came up and onto the cold verandah and Inder stood, his head thrust forward in an unfamiliar posture. Dubey thought of the animal under the skin that turned vicious only when it scented danger. In youth one had believed that the brutal instincts belonged outside society, that men who behaved like criminals forfeited the esteem of others. But there were conventions that permitted crime and supported criminal behaviour within society, considered it respectable and even necessary. The man who stood before him believed himself wronged. Everyone he knew would applaud any ugliness he now chose to commit. Dubey waited in a cocoon of suspense, not quite believing in ugliness even then.

"Where is she?" said Inder.

"She's in Delhi with Gauri."

"Was this a conspiracy?"

"No. I took it upon myself to send her."

Suddenly nothing mattered but how to get beneath the fury and controlled violence of the man. It was not very important what happened to himself or to Inder, thought Dubey. What was important was that this insane lust to attack what one could not understand be checked and not blown like demented pollen from generation to generation. Let it stop now and be surrendered between them. He strained his imagination for the word, the gesture that would do it, and staggered sideways as Inder's blow caught his jaw. Before he had recovered his balance he heard Inder's footsteps retreating down the stairs. All he felt was kinship with Harpal, who lay in hospital for no reason he could understand, and with Saroj, another kind of victim, the commoner kind who paid in broad daylight, amid laughter and conversation while the sun shone.

Dubey reached Delhi before noon the day after the Home Minister's funeral and went straight to the Cabinet Secretary's office. Kachru, in a dark, close-collared suit, welcomed him with noticeable restraint, and Dubey wondered whether it was part of officialdom's correct mournful demeanour or meant specially for him. Generally a funeral was the sign of brisk if subdued activity in the corridors of the Secretariat, a vacant chair giving rise to fevered speculation as to who and what would come next. Which minister and which entourage around him?

Kachru apologized briefly. "I am sorry we had to get you here so quickly. I hope it did not inconvenience you."

Dubey said it hadn't.

"We've been so disturbed over the Punjab-Hariyana situation, and then this news here."

Dubey said nothing. He felt cheated that he had no one to report to at the end of his assignment.

"How is Harpal Singh?"

"Recovering rapidly. The bullet got his left shoulder, a flesh wound. More shock than injury. I saw him before I left. He was cheerful and determined to attend the cattle fair at Rohtak next week."

Kachru said, "The fact is, we've been concerned over the turn events took. A showdown should have been avoided at all costs. Surely some compromise could have been worked out with a little more time."

"If there had been any other solution possible we would have explored it," said Dubey.

"Still, facing the strike had its hazards. How did you decide to brush them aside?"

"The hazards were obvious. It was also obvious that a government couldn't be bullied by a strike threat if law and order is to mean anything."

"Law and order does not appear to have been maintained," said Kachru dryly.

"In essence it was. The strikers discovered the situation was not in their hands. The power supply was not interrupted. Work went on as usual. In fact, I think Gyan Singh would have called off the strike as soon as he knew he could not make a success of it. Its failure would have cost him too much in loss of face."

In defence of himself he wanted to say there was a crying need in administration to give men scope to exercise responsibility, to get on with the job, even to make mistakes. It was a need Old Bones, for all his love of compromise, had understood better than most.

"There may be something in what you say," said Kachru, "but we feel it was too grave a risk in the circumstances."

Dubey stared at him in disbelief.

"It was an action supported by the Home Minister."

The Cabinet Secretary did not contradict this. Dubey felt a prickle of annoyance. It was usual to be on the explanation side of a fence with a politician, but here he was arguing with a colleague, a freak circumstance brought about by the crosscurrents of ambition and promotion in Delhi. The Home Minister was very dead if already other shadows hovered over his chair. In the brief interval since his death the waters of officialdom had parted and closed again without a ripple, apparently unchanged, yet leaving Dubey in an environment of subtly altered loyalties.

"We are going to suggest a conference to go over the issues of Bhakra and Chandigarh," said Kachru. "Gyan Singh must be persuaded to see reason. This rift between him and Harpal is dangerous. Something must be worked out."

"The last time Gyan Singh got up from the conference table," Dubey pointed out, "it was with a separate state in his pocket."

It was not Kachru's morning for a friendly chat.

"About this attempt on Harpal Singh. It doesn't look as if the most elementary precautions were taken. The policeman who fired at him is a man with charges against him."

"I tried to get action on him," said Dubey. "It was repeatedly put aside."

Kachru looked grave.

"Now you're here I hope you won't mind my mentioning something personal."

"Not at all." Dubey prepared to catalogue the differences between profound convictions and a mockery of conventions.

"There has been some talk about your drinking, and your attitude to drink in general."

Dubey looked at his colleague dumbfounded.

"There is this matter of a liquor licence which had lapsed being renewed," said Kachru, "to a person of most doubtful reputation."

"Hansa Ram owns a restaurant. I don't know anything about his reputation and I didn't think it my business to find out. But he was entitled to a renewal of his licence. There's no prohibition in the state."

"It was a discretionary matter."

"And I used my discretion. As for myself, I drink. I don't remember being drunk, after the age of twenty-five, that is."

Kachru looked harassed. "I'm not equipped to understand all these fine distinctions. I'm a teetotaller myself. In any case, as I said, it is a personal matter. I hope you will not misunderstand."

"No," Dubey told him, "nor do I understand."

It was no time to lose his temper and he kept it down. But he was disappointed. Kachru and he and five hundred others belonged to the same ilk, products of the same rigorous training and tradition. Upon them had rested the onus of the transition from servitude to freedom, a mighty task by any standards. And today they were divided not on principle or convictions, but by nauseating hypocrisies.

He walked past the Home Minister's office, stopping in front of the heavy oak door. He had an overpowering urge to walk in, to find the old man there, and to talk to him. Death should not be so abrupt, he thought. There should be time for a moment's friendliness.

It was bleak and wintry in the yard. He went back to his old office, dialled Gauri's number, and asked for Saroj.

MORE ABOUT PENGUINS

For further information about books available from Penguins in India write to Penguin Books (India) Ltd, B4/246, Safdarjung Enclave, New Delhi 110 029.

In the UK: For a complete list of books available from Penguins in the United Kingdom write to Dept. EP, Penguin Books Ltd, Harmondsworth, Middlesex UB7 0DA.

In the U.S.A.: For a complete list of books available from Penguins in the United States write to Dept. DG, Penguin Books, 299 Murray Hill Parkway, East Rutherford, New Jersey 07073.

In Canada: For a complete list of books available from Penguins in Canada write to Penguin Books Canada Ltd, 2801 John Street, Markham, Ontario L3R 1B4.

In Australia: For a complete list of books available from Penguins in Australia write to the Marketing Department, Penguin Books Australia Ltd, P.O. Box 257, Ringwood, Victoria 3134.

In New Zealand: For a complete list of books available from Penguins in New Zealand write to the Marketing Department, Penguin Books (N.Z.) Ltd, Private Bag, Takapuna, Auckland 9.